C000156670

My Persian Girl

Jonathan Rush

Published in 2012 by FeedARead.com Publishing – Arts Council funded

Copyright © 2009 Jonathan Rush

The views expressed in this novel are not necessarily those of the author. Although many events described are historical fact, all of its principal characters are fictitious and any resemblance to real people is purely coincidental.

The author or authors assert their moral right under the Copyright, Designs and Patents Act, 1988, to be identified as the author or authors of this work.

All Rights reserved. No part of this publication may be reproduced, copied, stored in a retrieval system, or transmitted, in any form or by any means, without the prior written consent of the copyright holder, nor be otherwise circulated in any form of binding or cover other than that in which it is published and without a similar condition being imposed on the subsequent purchaser.

A CIP catalogue record for this title is available from the British Library.

This book is dedicated to my wife, Jenny; our children, Jackie, James and Dominic; and my mother, Leonora; and in loving memory of our parents Leslie, Maggie, and Ralph.

My thanks to Helena for help with the manuscript. And to Sharon who provided good advice and encouragement in the final lap.

Twenty-five per cent of the author's share of sales of this book will be donated to stroke relief organisations.

Glossary

Ayatollah
Ayatollah is a high ranking title given to Shia Muslim clerics, similar to the Christian title of Bishop.

Baluchis
The Baluchis live mainly in Baluchistan: the south west corner of Pakistan and across the border into Iran. About 70 percent of the total Baluch population lives in Pakistan; about 20 percent in Iran; and the remaining 10 per cent in Afghanistan. The Baluch population is estimated at nearly 9 million. Most are Sunni Muslims.

Farsi
Farsi, sometimes called Persian in English, is the Indo-European language spoken in Iran, Afghanistan, and Tajikistan.

Iran
The Islamic Republic of Iran, formerly known internationally as Persia until 1935, is located on the northern shore of the Persian Gulf. The name Iran means land of the Aryans who started to migrate onto the Iranian plateau at about 1,700 BC. Iran has a population of over seventy million. Tehran is the capital with about 12 million inhabitants.

Khomeini
Grand Ayatollah Seyyed Ruhollah Musavi Khomeini (1902-1989) was an Iranian politician, scholar and religious figure, and the political leader of the 1979 Iranian Revolution, which saw the overthrow of Mohammad Reza Pahlavi, the last Shah of Iran. Following the revolution, Khomeini became the country's Supreme Leader until his death. In his writings and preachings he provided the theological basis for his rule of Iran. He was named *Time's Man of the Year in 1979* and also one of *Time* magazine's *100 most influential people of the 20th century*. His last Will and Testament included the following advice to government cabinet ministers: "You all need the nation's support, especially that of the oppressed classes. It was by their popular support that victory could be achieved and the hands of tyrants cut off from the country and its wealth. If you become deprived of this support someday, the oppressed shall turn you out just the way (they) ousted the

oppressive monarchical system. In view of the tangible facts you should make efforts to satisfy the nation thus and earn their confidence. Avoid inhuman un-Islamic conduct."

Kurds

The Kurdish people live mainly in Kurdistan: the mountainous areas of northern Iraq, north-western Iran, north-eastern Syria and south-eastern Turkey. The Kurdish population is unknown but some estimates place it between 27 to 36 million.

MI6

MI6 is Britain's secret service which collects secret foreign intelligence in support of the British Government's policies and objectives. Its official name is the Secret Intelligence Service (SIS). According to its website (www.mi6.gov.uk), regional instability, terrorism, the proliferation of weapons of mass destruction and illegal narcotics are among its major challenges. Ironically, for a supposed secret organisation, SIS headquarters are in a distinctive building, overlooking the River Thames in London, which featured in a film about its most famous fictitious employee, James Bond.

Mohammad Mosaddeq

Mohammad Mosaddeq (1882 – 1967) was the Prime Minister of Iran from 1951 to 1953 when he was removed from power by a coup d'état. From an aristocratic background, Mosaddeq was a nationalist who opposed foreign intervention in Iran. He is famous in Iran for the nationalization of the Iranian oil industry, which had been under British control through the Anglo-Iranian Oil Company, today known as British Petroleum (BP). Mosaddeq was removed from power on August 19, 1953, in a coup d'etat, supported and funded by the British and US governments and, reputedly, orchestrated by the CIA and MI6. Mosaddeq was imprisoned for three years and subsequently put under house arrest until his death.

SAS

The Special Air Service Regiment (SAS) is a British Army special forces unit. Its motto is *Who dares, wins.* The British government does not discuss publicly the SAS or its operations. The SAS's most famous public exploit was in 1980 when opponents of the new Iranian Islamic republic held 26 people hostage at the Iranian embassy in London. After a six-day stand-off the SAS attacked and freed the hostages.

Savak
Shah Mohammed Pahlavi's security and intelligence service, Savak, was founded in 1957 and had the power to use all means necessary to hunt down dissidents. According to some, Savak was created with the help of American and Israeli advisers who modelled the service on the CIA (www.cia.gov) and Israel's Mossad (www.mossad.gov.il).

Shah
Shah was the title of Iranian monarchs, including the dynasty which unified Persia (Iran) and created a vast empire until it was overrun by Alexander the Great of Macedonia. The last Shah of Iran, Mohammad Reza Shah Pahlavi (the son of an Iranian soldier, Shah Reza Pahlavi, who had seized power) adopted the ancient title of Shah-en-Shah (King of Kings) styled his wife Shahbânu (Empress).

Shah Mohammed Pahlavi
Shah Mohammad Reza Shah Pahlavi (1919-80) was monarch of Iran from 1941-1979 and the eldest son of Shah Reza Pahlavi. During World War II, Britain and the USSR forced Shah Reza Pahlavi to abdicate and permitted Mohammad Reza to assume the throne. Shah Mohammad Reza Pahlavi was deposed in 1979 when he fled the country after the Iranian Islamic revolution, which made Grand Ayatollah Khomeini Supreme Leader. He died in exile one year after the revolution.

Sunni and Shia Muslims
The division between Shia and Sunni Muslims dates back to the death of the Prophet Muhammad and the question of who was to take over the leadership of the Muslim nation. Sunni Muslims believed that the new leader should be elected. The Shia Muslims believed that the leadership should have passed directly to his cousin/son-in-law, Ali.

IRAN

Shahnaz was her name. Mohammed Mostashari's sister, that is. Mohammed ('call me Mo,' he'd said) was intelligent, studied hard, and was near the top of our university class. We got on well. I'd seemed interested in his country, Iran, and why he'd come to study in London.

He appreciated me treating him as any of the others in our class and I helped explain some of the things about the English which can baffle foreigners: why we said 'sorry' even when the other person might be to blame for something; why our bitter beer wasn't chilled; cricket; and how we could be so rude about the Queen but still sing 'God save the Queen'. And mean it. He had money and a small Lotus sports car, which was pretty cool in the 'swinging' London of the late 60s.

If his bulging wallet and fancy car weren't enough, his long black hair, luxuriant moustache, side burns and saturnine good looks attracted the girls. Mo was 'groovy' which is why I was pleased and yes, OK, flattered by his friendship. One evening, as we trudged out from our lectures, he suggested we met later in a pub in South Kensington, before going on to party, which one of his sister's friends was giving nearby. After a couple of drinks we sauntered towards Gloucester Road, home to many students in the area's cheaper flats and bedsits.

The party was easy to find: music thudded out of an open second floor window, the fluttering old paintwork on its wooden frame glistening in the oblique rays of the evening sun as it scudded across London's rooftops. I remember how conversation was almost impossible in the sweltering, jam-packed room. Jimi Hendrix was belting out *Purple Haze* as I took in the smoked-filled room, which reeked of marijuana, cigarettes, alcohol and the inevitable joss sticks. Long-haired youths, like Mo and me, gyrated suggestively opposite mini-skirted girls who giggled as they chatted to each other, seemingly oblivious to the boys' attempts to capture their interest. In the background I could faintly hear the unmistakable sound of someone retching in the toilet. It was a normal student party, just like hundreds of others on that hot, sweaty London summer's night.

Mo looked around the room and dragged me over the quivering floorboards towards a girl who was standing in a corner chatting to some friends.

'James, this is my sister, Shahnaz,' he shouted over the din.

The girl turned slowly around and gazed at me with large, very un-English, oval brown eyes. She swirled her long, coal-black hair flirtatiously and grinned as she caught me staring.

'This is James, James Harding,' Mo had said and then fired off something in what I later learned was Farsi, the Iranian language.

She made a mock angry face at him and then turned teasingly to me: 'It's nice to meet one of Mo's student friends.'

I mumbled something back, my normal awkward response when confronted by a pretty girl.

Looking back, I can't remember much of our first attempt at a conversation over the party noise. I do recollect other boys eyeing Shahnaz up, some of them hovering close by waiting to try their luck. Before we could talk much more, I was jostled and pushed away by some newcomers who surged into the heaving maelstrom of the, by now, over-crowded party. I extricated myself and my partly-spilled drink and found some breathing space next to the window where I started talking to a couple of Americans, Stu and Pete, who stood wisely aloof from the heaving crowd.

'What are you guys doing here?'

They replied simply: 'R and R.'

I looked puzzled so they explained they were US Air Force pilots who had a couple of weeks' leave for rest and recuperation. It turned out they'd pulled some strings, hitched a plane ride to London, chatted to some people in a pub, and 'Hey Buddy, here we are!' Waving away the smoke, I noticed their faces seemed like, well, slum kids: young from a distance; old and streetwise closer up.

'So, where are you normally based?'

'Japan,' they replied, rather too nonchalantly, I thought. Responding to my inquisitive eyebrows, they added, a shade reluctantly: 'We fly B-52 bombers over Vietnam.'

Startled, I looked at them with a young man's secret admiration of men brave enough to go to war.

'Shit,' I thought to myself, these two guys, about the same age as me, had been flying bombers only a couple of days ago and now here they were in London, talking to me as if dropping bombs and dodging missiles over Hanoi were no different than hopping on the no. 12 bus. I wondered silently how they felt about fighting a war, which was vehemently opposed by most students in the western world.

Reading my thoughts, Pete, the more talkative of the two, pre-empted my next question: 'No, we don't agree with the war.'

12

That's a relief I thought: no arguments about the Vietnam War then.

Our brief conversation came abruptly to a close as Pete and Stu moved in on two girls who they had been watching out of the corner of their eyes. As they peeled away, I noticed that Stu's beer was spilling from his trembling can. I felt a sudden flash of sympathy for the young flier as I felt, for some unknown reason, a shiver of premonition that something terrible would happen to him.

Fed up with the noise and smoke, Mo and I left the party soon after with Mick Jagger jeering, *I can't get no satisfaction*. We and headed back to the pub which was now just as crowded as the party and, like London pubs often do in summer, had spilled out onto the pavement. But without the *Rolling Stones*, we could, at least, hear each other speak. I took a swig of beer and mentioned my encounter with the young American pilots.

Mo's reaction surprised me: 'You Americans and British are always interfering in other countries' politics.'

Like most engineering undergraduates I was apolitical. Politics were best left to those doing softer, less time consuming degrees, like English and History.

'I didn't know you were interested in international politics, Mo. Anyway, we British aren't involved in Vietnam, thank God,' I retorted.

Mo nodded dismissively, sipped his whisky (an expensive malt, I noticed), and then told me how 'you British' had once bribed a mob to hound an Iranian Prime Minister out of office, literally chasing the poor man over his garden wall. His 'crime'? All he'd wanted to do was wrest control of Iran's oil from the British government-owned Anglo Persian Oil Company, which later became BP.

Mo shook his head and said with a voice full of the weary, ageless cynicism of youth: 'You see James, in return for supporting our king, the Shah, the West gets the oil it wants from my country, and the Shah and his family get super rich. And the educated Iranians, people like my family - army officers, doctors, engineers, and lawyers - we get rich too.' He shrugged his shoulders: 'That's real international politics, my friend.'

Mo swallowed his drink along with, I suspect, some disgust with his compatriots. He then switched on his engaging smile: 'What the hell. Tell me, what did you think of my sister?'

I thought for a second: 'I thought she looked stunning. She looks like that Italian film star, Sophia Loren. She seemed very

13

nice too,' I added hastily, anxious to mask my impression that she was way out of my league.

As if reading my thoughts, Mo said encouragingly: 'I'm sure she liked you too.'

After a couple more malts, he told me 'confidentially' that Shahnaz was behaving very badly. Their father, a well-to-do property developer in Tehran, was sending her money every month to pay for her college fees on top of her living allowance. Instead of studying English at the college, Shahnaz was blowing the lot on having a good time, picking up poor English on the way. Mo had to pretend that he didn't know what was going on, otherwise his father would be furious and quite likely to punish his children severely.

I was, I had to admit, surprised that a girl from a Muslim country was allowed by her family to live by herself in 'swinging' London.

'Yes, it is unusual,' agreed Mo. 'But my father wants all his children, including his daughter, to be westernised. He would be furious if he knew what Shahnaz was really up to.'

Yes, even from what I had already seen, I could imagine Shahnaz could be a handful.

Chapter 2

A week or two later, hurrying along a drizzly Knightsbridge, late for a lecture, my mind wrestling with fluid mechanics and, not looking where I was going, I barged into a young woman coming out of the Harvey Nichols department store.

Slipping in her long, high-heeled boots, she lurched and nearly fell as she lost grip of her shopping bag, which went sliding across the greasy pavement and almost into the path of a passing double-decker bus. 'Oh hell!' I muttered under my breath as I quickly bent down to help her pick up her bag.

Standing up, the woman's unnecessary, but fashionably large, rainbow-striped sunglasses slid to the bottom of her brown nose revealing flashing angry, enormous eyes. I recognised her immediately.

'I'm er, sorry, er. Shahnaz,' I stammered, blushing at the same time.

Her expression turned from annoyance into puzzled recognition. And yes, there was now definitely a hint of a grin as she said after a moment's pause: 'Ah, of course, my brother's friend. James isn't it?'

I stood in front of her shy and tongue-tied. I gushed nervously: 'I was late for a lecture, you see. Um, I'm sorry. Er..., I wasn't looking where I was going. Bloody hell, you must think I'm a total idiot,' I finished lamely.

Now there was definitely a smile of amusement playing across her face. What should I do? Apologise again and walk on? Come on, James, I urged myself, you don't get the chance to chat up pretty girls that often - get in there!

'Would you like a coffee?' I almost shouted desperately, panic overcoming shyness. Putting her arm firmly through mine, she very much in control, Shahnaz said nothing, just nodded thoughtfully, and led me back into Harvey Nics in the direction of the lift towards the coffee shop.

I was too embarrassed to say that I had in mind somewhere a little cheaper than one of London's most expensive, *chic* department stores.

Over coffee we chatted, she in faltering but charming English, about London, my student life, what places were 'in', and some of the famous people she'd seen around the place. Mo cropped up, seemingly incidentally, towards the end of our conversation.

15

She was interested when I told her that Mo was a top student and popular with the girls. 'He will be a very good engineer,' I said.

Shahnaz looked at me and retorted scornfully: 'He will do what our father wants. He will be trained to manage the family company. His degree will have little to do with it.'

'What about you? Do you always do what your dad tells you?' I flashed back, resenting her condescending tone towards Mo.

'I have my own life, nobody tells me what to do,' she replied, almost hissing. Narrowing her eyes, she interrogated me suspiciously, 'What has Mo told you?'

'Oh, not much,' I lied hastily. 'Look, I've got to run. I've missed one lecture already. And I don't want to be late for another.' Grabbing my things, I plucked up courage and asked her if she fancied a drink one evening. Amazingly she said yes. I hovered anxiously while she scribbled her number down on one of my notepads.

'I'll call you,' I shouted, already halfway through the door before I ran, my heart pounding with exertion, all the way to my university college near the Albert Hall.

Chapter 3

Over the next month I saw a lot of Shahnaz. To me she seemed an exotic, foreign creature who had graciously consented to be seen in public with me, a drab penniless English student. I knew some girls thought I was fairly good looking. But I reckoned I was nothing really special to look at, apart from, maybe, my blonde hair.

I quickly became infatuated with Shahnaz and everything about her Asian appearance: the black thick hair; large doe-like eyes; full lips; and her soft, brown skin. Yes, I knew all this sounded, even to me, like one big cliché. But, so what, that's how I would actually describe her to my friends who had not met her.

At first my puppy-like adoration amused her and then, gradually, I sensed, she started to become genuinely fond of me and our relationship became more balanced and less one-sided. In turn, my immature infatuation evolved, almost without me noticing, into a deeper more adult feeling, which gradually became more intense as it accumulated inside me.

One evening, as we were gossiping about this and that, I looked at her and blurted out, almost as much to my, as her surprise: 'I love you Shahnaz.'

At first I thought she had misheard me, but she turned and looked at me straight in the eyes and said calmly: 'James, I believe you. That's why it's the most wonderful thing anyone has said to me.'

She leaned over the pub's wooden table and kissed me softly on the lips and slowly stroked my hair away from my eyes.

She now began to invite me back after dates into her flat, which she shared with another couple of girls. Thinking back, I barely noticed them.

Our kissing gradually turned into more intimate groping and fumbling on my part, but we never went the 'whole way'. Shahnaz always stopped us before we went that far.

Although I was only dimly aware of it at the time, despite being Westernised, whatever that really meant, Shahnaz was keenly aware of the huge importance placed on virginity by her Islamic culture. She was also terrified that if she gave into my (and her) wishes she would let something slip and be found out when she returned home.

Otherwise, we did what young lovers do in London: We walked in Hyde Park; rowed on the Serpentine; visited art

17

galleries; drank in pubs; went to West End plays; and watched films. She usually paid for both of us. Her favourite film was *Casablanca*, that lovers' perennial, especially for those new to the English language.

She insisted we saw it at least three times and loved repeating those famous lines, 'Play it again, Sam,' and every time we had a drink in the pub she'd raise her glass and giggle: 'Here's looking at you, kid.' In truth we were a bit like Bogart and Bergman: perhaps we somehow sensed our relationship would be star-crossed too.

She began to tell me about her country, some of its history, and culture. She explained that Iranians were not, as I had mistakenly assumed, Arabs, and the word Iranian was, in fact, derived from the word Aryan. We went to a couple of Iranian art shows and I learnt that Iran's civilization had flowered under their monarch, Shah Abbas, at roughly the same time as England's had during the golden age of Elizabeth I.

Shahnaz's English improved rapidly and soon I hardly needed to correct her. During this time I never mentioned to Mo that I was going out with his sister. At first it didn't seem necessary and then somehow a sixth sense made me reluctant to tell him something, which might threaten our friendship.

Anyway, I told myself, he was busy seeing a couple of girls at the same time. Two-timing was part of the playboy image he liked to cultivate.

One night, coming out of the beer garden of one of our favourite pubs, the *Windsor Castle* in Holland Park, we were kissing each other goodnight, our arms wrapped tightly around each other, when someone shouted, 'Shahnaz', with real anger in his voice.

Shahnaz, shocked, pushed me away to be confronted by a furious Mo who slapped her hard, so hard that his palm was imprinted vividly on her cheek.

'What the fuck are you doing?' I screamed, outraged as I lashed out at him.

Dodging my punches, he started to shout at Shahnaz in their own language while we started to grapple. We lurched and toppled like a couple of drunks into the gutter. Bending down, Shahnaz grabbed my arm and begged: 'James, James stop it.'

Mo and I stood up snarling and lashing out at each other. We paused glaring at each other, looking ridiculous with mud and soggy leaves stuck to our hair and clothes.

Mo shouted again at Shahnaz and she turned to me pleading, 'James, I'm sorry. I must go.'

Pulling me quickly close to her she made as if to kiss my cheek but instead whispered, softly into my ear, 'I love you too.' I put my fists down as Mo angrily jerked her away. He already had a cab waiting and roughly bundled Shahnaz into the back.

The last I saw of Shahnaz was her wild-eyed, tearful face receding away, framed like a portrait by the cab's oval rear window.

The black car drove off into the late dusk of that summer's evening; its rear indicator lights blinked a couple of times - and then it disappeared suddenly around a corner.

The next day I called round anxiously at her flat to be told that Shahnaz had rushed back the previous night and said she was leaving immediately. She'd paid all her rent and bills in advance, packed and left.

Those possessions she couldn't carry would be collected later by a friend of hers called Lila. Her flatmates were mystified and looked accusingly at me as if I was to blame. I suppose I was in some way, I had to admit ruefully to myself.

It was almost the start of the summer vacation and Mo had also disappeared. Shortly before the start of the next autumn term, an innocuous, well-creased envelope arrived for me with a London postmark.

Opening it unhurriedly, I frowned as I read its single sheet uncomprehendingly, at first: 'James, I am so sorry. I had to come back to Tehran. I am getting married soon.' Now understanding, I looked wildly down to the bottom of the letter where it was incongruously signed off: 'Here's looking at you kid, Shahnaz.' No explanation, love or best wishes. I heard no more.

Mo came back after the summer to start the next academic year. One evening in the students' bar he casually told me that Shahnaz had got engaged.

He clearly didn't know Shahnaz had written to me. 'James, you have to understand, there was a family crisis and we had to go home in a hurry. After that Shahnaz met someone. I hope you understand.'

I pretended I didn't already know and nodded silently, but inside I still felt as if I had been kicked in the stomach.

Mo and I were civil to each other after that but our friendship cooled. We spoke in lectures and the library but our paths did not cross socially. Two years later we graduated and went our separate ways.

I persuaded myself that I had got over Shahnaz but every now and then, when I was alone, I would recall those dark, big eyes with a twinge of pain and repeat softly under my breath, 'Here's looking at you kid.'

Mo pulled Shahnaz roughly away from the cab window through which she was staring at James as he was left behind on the pavement outside the *Windsor Castle*.

'Stop crying and listen, you stupid little fool. You're lucky that father wasn't visiting London and saw what you are getting up to. Something terrible has happened to Uncle Faris. We have to go home, now!'

The news shocked Shahnaz enough to stop her sobbing. Their father's brother, Faris, who was unmarried and had no children, was a second father to them.

'What's happened, Mo? Is Uncle Faris ill? Why do we have to come back to Tehran so quickly?'

To all of Shahnaz's questions Mo could only shake his head. 'No, no, I don't know. I only know it's something to do with the police.'

Shahnaz had told her bewildered flatmates she had to leave in a hurry and paid them more than enough money to cover her rent and share of expenses. She would get someone to collect the rest of her things. Mo had kept the taxi waiting and they hurried to Heathrow where he had managed to book a couple of last minute seats on Iranair.

They were met at Tehran airport in the dark by Aled who had served their family since he was a boy, just like his father, and his father before him. Despite their frantic questioning, Aled was unable to shed light on what had happened to Uncle Faris. The servant drove them off in the direction of North Tehran, towards the family's old-fashioned, sprawling villa with its ornamental rose garden, fountain and cherry orchard enclosed behind a high brown, mud brick wall.

As the car drew up the front door was flung open, and light flooded out onto the drive, illuminating their mother as she rushed out arms flapping in despair and wailing: 'Oh Mohammed. Oh Shahnaz. Thank Allah you are here.'

Gently supporting their mother, Mo and Shahnaz led her back into their home and sat down beside her.

'Mother, what is it? Why is Uncle Faris in jail?'

Between the sobs and entreaties to Allah from their distraught mother, her mystified children began to piece together what had happened.

21

About a week ago their Uncle Faris had apparently been handed a tape after prayers at his mosque, well known for the fiery anti-Shah speeches by its mullah.

'You know that your father had pleaded with him not to go to that mosque any more. But he refused. He said that it was his right to worship in whatever mosque he chose.'

The tape was a recording of speeches by the dissident mullah, Khomeini, who had been forcibly banished by the Shah into exile in Syria and was a focus of much of the Islamic opposition to the government.

'What did the tape say?' asked Mo apprehensively.

'All I know is that your father said Khomeini had called for the people to rise up and kill the Shah. And the same evening after he had been to the mosque, Uncle Faris was arrested by Savak!' She burst into tears again: 'Your father insisted you two return immediately to look after the family and the business in case he gets arrested as well while trying to get Faris released.'

Shahnaz, who knew little of her country's politics, had barely heard of the Shah's notorious secret police. But Mo had heard a lot more than Shahnaz about Savak, which rumour said the CIA and Israel's Mossad had set up for the Shah.

Mo knew they had unlimited powers of arrest and detention. He had also been warned by his father that Savak kept a close eye on Iranian students abroad so he should avoid any anti-Shah circles. He'd heard whispered rumours of people who had disappeared after being shoved out of helicopters by Savak, high above the salt lakes to the south of Tehran. And the electric shock torture they used in Tehran's Envin prison. And the systematic and repeated rape of women prisoners.

Mo shivered in fear as he put his arm around his mother. It was entirely possible that his father might get arrested as well if Savak suspected a conspiracy.

'Your father has gone to see Mr Yousef Zaberani,' she continued. 'You children won't remember him. He was a business partner of your father's, years ago when you were little and your father was still working only in the bazaar.' Mo and Shahnaz looked blank. 'He has a son called Raman. He used to play with you, Mohammed. He's a young officer in the Shah's Imperial Guard now and might be able to help,' she explained.

Mo vaguely remembered Raman, who was a few years younger than him. What was it about him? Ah, yes, once he'd caught Raman slyly stealing some of his sweets one day and had punched

22

him. He had been surprised how quickly Raman had hit back; and how strong the younger boy was.

Chapter 5

Under different circumstances Shahnaz and Mo's father, Adar Mostashari, would have enjoyed his evening visit to Yousef Zaberani's shop and office deep in the middle of Tehran's main bazaar. It was several years since he had been back there and the vivid memories of when Faris and he, as boys, had helped their father came flooding back as he walked along the pungent-smelling, dimly-lit narrow alleyways separating the stalls selling everything from jewellery to spices.

Although Yousef Zaberani had been effusive with his greetings, Shahnaz's father had detected faint, but unmistakeable, undertones of jealously in his voice.

'Mr Mostashari, what an honour. And after such a long time!' Yousef Zaberani clicked his fingers at a tea-boy and ordered tea immediately for his guest.

Several years ago Yousef had been a partner in some business deals with the two Mostashari brothers, when they had taken over the bazaar business from their father, but had declined their offer to take part in their first property venture, as Tehran started to boom in the 60s. A decision which he subsequently bitterly regretted as he observed the two brother's property business go from strength to strength and generate wealth that he could only dream of in the bazaar.

Their conversation started politely as each asked the other about their families. What, little Mohammed is almost an engineer? And Shahnaz is learning English in London? Still, Allah willing, he also had great hopes for his only son Raman - you remember him Mr Mostashari? - who, although only an army lieutenant in the special forces, had been attached recently to the Shah's Imperial Guard, a great honour for one so young.

Adar remembered Raman uneasily. The boy had been light-fingered but difficult to catch in the act of thieving. Being big for his age he had been a bully too. Still, boys will be boys and he'd probably grown up into a decent enough person. He must be tough to be in the special forces, Adar thought. Yes, Adar had also heard Raman was now part of the army responsible for the Shah's safety. Which was precisely why Adar had come to ask for Yousef Zaberani's help.

Yousef Zaberani had read about the brothers' property deals in the newspapers and had been very impressed and envious. He'd also heard that some of the Shah's extended family had even been

24

entertained at the Mostasharis' country villa. What a glittering occasion that must have been. He too, thanks be to Allah, had enjoyed some modest success but nothing like the two Mostashari brothers!

Of course he had fond memories of Faris and, like him, was a good Muslim. It wasn't Faris's fault that the tape contained anti-Shah material. How was he to know? Of course he and Raman would be glad to help. Yes, he would speak to Raman as soon as possible.

Chapter 6

During the next week Shahnaz and Mo overheard several whispered telephone conversations between their father and Yousef Zaberani. Adar Mostashari disappeared from the family home at odd hours for long periods of time, without explanation, usually returning late at night, his face exhausted with strain.

One evening he returned with Yousef Zaberani and, with a beaming smile on his face, called all the family and servants together.

'Thanks be to Allah, I have good news. Faris will be released next week! We owe Mr Yousef Zaberani, and particularly his son Raman, a great debt. Without their help I would never have got Faris out of jail.'

Clasping both his hands firmly around one of Yousef Zaberani's, Adar Mostashari shook hands formally. He was followed by his wife, Mo and Shahnaz, all beaming in gratitude.

'Thank you, Mr Zaberani, thank you. How will we ever be able to repay you?'

Yousef Zaberani bowed and murmured that it was an honour to serve his old friends, the Mostashari family.

Mo and Shahnaz bombarded their exhausted father with questions, which he gradually answered one by one. He explained that Raman Zaberani, whom he had still not seen since he was a boy, had quickly located Faris in Savak's dreaded Envin prison and managed to use what limited influence he had - he's only a lieutenant, their father said - to get a verbal assurance that Faris would not be mistreated while the charge against him was being investigated. Raman had apparently even managed to visit him briefly and confirmed he was in good health. Yes, he had been roughed up by the arresting Savak agents, but nothing serious.

Meanwhile Raman had ensured the investigating officer was presented with sworn statements by eyewitnesses, laboriously obtained by Adar, that Faris had been handed the offending tape by a stranger who was handing them out freely to worshippers as they left the mosque.

Faris, it subsequently turned out, had been interrogated intensely for several hours about the identity of the man handing out the tapes, but in the end had convinced his interrogators that he had never seen him before. Faris had signed a statement to this effect and a declaration expressing loyalty to the Shah. His passport had been confiscated for the time being and Adar had paid a large fine for Faris's possession of illegal material but he would be released next week, once the inevitable paperwork had been processed.

During all the excited questions and answers Yousef Zaberani sat next to Adar Mostashari observing him, his house and family. He approved of what he saw. Although the family was clearly wealthy, their house was not an ostentatious mansion but a traditional, large Persian villa, which had been modernised and made comfortable. He saw this as a comforting reassurance that Adar Mostashari, despite his avowed embrace of Western ways, remained underneath a traditional Persian.

He now noticed Shahnaz for the first time. What a beauty! Watching the young woman surreptitiously, Yousef Zaberani saw she had classic Persian good looks. If he didn't know otherwise, he would think she came from one of Iran's aristocratic families; one of those which had traditionally been the power behind the throne of whomever was Shah. Looking at her figure, revealed by her jeans and T-shirt, he guessed she would be a good breeder as well. She was nothing like those revoltingly thin, Western models he had seen in his wife's magazines.

Suddenly Yousef Zaberani knew what repayment he wanted. Of course, it was obvious. Adar Mostashari would surely feel obliged to consider an offer of marriage for his daughter from Raman Zaberani? Well, why not?

Events had conspired to make the previously unthinkable, entirely possible. Both families had their roots in bazaar commerce so the big difference in their current financial status was not insurmountable and now, of course, the Mostasharis were now deeply in his and Raman's debt.

And it was not as if Raman had no prospects, Yousef Zaberani thought furiously. Raman had been decorated for some secret mission he'd undertaken recently in the special forces - he wouldn't tell even his father what - and had been rewarded with secondment to the Shah's guard. The boy was ambitious and keen to take advantage of the opportunities that the Shah was creating for his loyal supporters. Yes, Raman was quite a catch for any girl.

Chapter 7

Faris Mostashari was released the following week, as promised by Raman Zaberani. Soon after, Adar Mostashari was invited by Yousef Zaberani to meet him at his office in the bazaar to discuss a personal matter - Adar presumed a business proposal which he had already decided he was honour-bound to accept.

Sitting next to Yousef Zaberani was a powerfully-built, young army officer. Adar knew instantly it must be Yousef Zaberani's son as he held out his hand, smiling and with the other hand over his heart to signify respect: 'Raman, it is truly an honour to meet you at last. I am grateful for all the help you gave me in getting my brother released. I have already told your father that my family is greatly in your debt. Anything you ask for will be yours.'

Raman accepted Adar's praise modestly and replied that he had merely made a few phone calls. Despite his misgivings about Raman as a boy, Adar couldn't help but be impressed now by Raman's demeanour. He observed that Raman had grown into a handsome and athletic young man with a determined air about him.

Prompted by his father, Raman had told Adar about his army career so far. He'd been trained by the British SAS in England and later in Oman in the desert. He was confident that he would be promoted soon and become one of the youngest captains in the army.

'I'm lucky. I am doing a job which I love. I seem to be well regarded by my commanding officers. After I carried out a secret mission recently, the Shah himself presented me with a medal,' the young man said with fierce pride.

'And now he has a secure military career it is time for him to be thinking about a wife and children,' Yousef Zaberani added, looking straight at Adar Mostashari.

Ah, ah, now he knew why Raman was here, thought Adar softly to himself, concealing his shock. Shahnaz! Years of hard-nosed business bargaining helped Adar keep his face expressionless. He braced himself for what he knew was coming.

'Mr Mostashari, I have a son, as you can see, who is of marriageable age. I have already had several expressions of interest from fathers of eligible daughters, but none has pleased me thus far. And then I saw your daughter, Shahnaz, and it was if Allah himself, peace be upon him, had brought your beautiful daughter to my attention.

I would like, honoured sir, to propose a union in marriage between my son, Raman, and your daughter, Shahnaz,' announced Yousef Zaberani.

To gain time and to allow himself to think, Adar looked hard and silently down at the intricate swirling design of the immaculate silk Persian carpet at his feet. The pattern seemed to reflect life: just as you thought you could discern some symmetrical order, the eye was teased away by some subtle and unexpected tessellation.

Adar had always wished that his beloved Shahnaz would choose her own husband. He had allowed her to go to London because he had wanted her to absorb some Western female independence and learn good English. He had also hoped this would help her marry a son of one of his wealthy, westernised business acquaintances. Someone, in fact like her brother, Mohammed.

Shahnaz had also been allowed to believe that she would be able to choose her husband and not have a traditional, arranged marriage. So if he encouraged Raman, Shahnaz would be gravely wounded and might never forgive him.

But how could he reject Raman's suit and retain his family's honour? The boy was definitely eligible and perhaps this was Shahnaz's *kismet?* After all, his marriage to Shahnaz's mother had been arranged and was successful, unlike many western marriages. Nonetheless, Shahnaz will be crushed by the disappointment, he thought. But surely even the highly-spirited Shahnaz would understand eventually that her family's honour was at stake?

Adar Mostashari took a deep breath and looked up from the carpet. 'Raman, what do you know about my daughter?'

'I only know what my father has said: that she is beautiful, educated and from a good family. I trust his judgement that she would make me a good wife.'

A polite and dutiful son's response, thought Adar; one, which left him no room for manoeuvre. Custom meant he could not prolong his response any longer.

Adar looked at Yousef Zaberani: 'I am sure any father would be proud to have Raman, as a son-in law,' he said carefully, avoiding absolute commitment. Yousef noted the absence of a firm promise but, crafty bazaar bargainer that he was, dismissed it as merely Adar's opening gambit in the forthcoming dowry negotiations. He beamed with delight at the prospect of Raman and Shahnaz starting a prosperous Zaberani dynasty.

29

'May I call upon you, sir, to discuss my son's offer of marriage?' said Yousef again formally.

'I would be honoured, sir. Please come this Friday evening after prayers,' replied Adar in a rigorously polite voice.

Chapter 8

When Adar arrived home, instead of going into the house, he headed glum-faced to his usual sanctuary when he had an unpleasant problem which needed mulling over: a well-worn, wooden bench in a sheltered corner of the rose garden. Aled appeared silently at his side with some steaming tea and a bowl of freshly picked cherries on a silver platter, which Adar wearily accepted.

'Aled, we will be entertaining Mr Zaberani this Friday evening after prayers,' he sighed. 'I want no expense spared on food or drink. All the family, except Shahnaz, will be present. Please discuss the arrangements with Mrs Mostashari. And please tell Shahnaz to come to me immediately.'

'As you wish, sir,' Aled bowed and moved off, expertly balancing the empty silver platter on the fingertips of one hand, his face expressionless but his mind churning, wondering what could be bothering his master. Whatever the problem was, it involved Shahnaz.

Aled left his master sitting alone in silence, chewing cherries and throwing pips half-heartedly across the empty fountain and into the lifeless rose beds. Despite the cool air, Adar wiped his brow and sat dejectedly. His balding, middle-aged head bowed forward and his shoulders sagged as he waited unhappily for his daughter to appear.

Shahnaz was chatting happily to her mother when the old servant found her.

'Yes, Aled?'

'Your father would appreciate your presence as soon as possible, miss,' he said.

Shahnaz looked sharply at him. Something was wrong. Aled refused to make eye contact.

'Where is he?'

'He is drinking tea in the rose garden, miss.'

Shahnaz hurried off grabbing a coat as she went. Surely Uncle Faris couldn't be in trouble again?

Adar watched his daughter as she walked briskly towards him along the garden path, coat over her shoulders, the evening sun's iridescent lateral rays glancing on and off her anxious shoulders. As she drew nearer and her long shadow enveloped him, her features became clearer. He thought, with a father's fierce pride, that she had never looked so beautiful.

He stood up uneasily to greet her, took both her hands, and tenderly guided her down so that she would be sitting next to him. He realised with anguish that soon she would probably no longer be only his daughter, but also another man's wife.

'What is it, Baba?' asked Shahnaz, using the Farsi word for Daddy.

He found he couldn't reply immediately. He swallowed and faltered at first: 'Shahnaz, what I have to tell you is very difficult for me. It will also be hard for you. But I hope you will be an obedient daughter and do your duty to protect your family's honour.'

Shahnaz remained silent, her anxiety changing to fear and puzzlement, as she fingered her necklace with a shaking hand.

'Shahnaz, Mr Zaberani has proposed a marriage between you and his son, Raman.' His words cut through the twilight, leaving Shahnaz wide-eyed in shock.

Ignoring her expression, he continued swiftly but firmly: 'I have already told him I would seriously consider this marriage.'

'No, this can't be true! It's a nightmare. Please Allah, let me wake up,' Shahnaz shrieked silently to herself. In desperation her fingers clenched so tightly that that her nails almost cut into her palms.

'But Baba, you always said that I would not have an arranged marriage. That I would not be forced to marry someone I didn't like.'

'Yes, I know my dear, but this matter of Uncle Faris has changed everything.'

'But how?' whispered Shahnaz, her eyes staring in disbelief at her father.

'The debt of honour we owe Mr Zaberani means that unless there is good reason, I cannot refuse his son. And nor can you, if you are truly my daughter.'

Shahnaz wrapped her arms tightly around her waist and started to cry. Her tears were not those of a disappointed girl, rather the keening of a young woman who has lost part of her soul.

'Oh Baba, Baba, how could you?' she tried to say, but no sound came out of her gaping mouth.

Adar gently put a hand on his daughter's shoulder: 'Shahnaz, Shahnaz, listen.' And then again more desperately he shook her: 'Listen! I have asked Mr Zaberani to dinner this Friday. I will make an arrangement then for you to meet Raman. If, after you have met him, you really feel that the marriage would be impossible, then I will prevent the matter progressing further. But I have to tell you, in all honesty, that many girls would find Raman an attractive husband. I have met him and already said that any father would be honoured to have him as a son-in-law.'

Adar saw that Shahnaz was on the brink of hysteria and that she would be best left alone. He turned miserably away, his shoes cracking on cherry stones. In the silence, which now draped the dark and suddenly cold garden, Shahnaz sat rocking backwards and forwards on the bench, the sun's last horizontal rays glinting off the tears on her cheeks.

Just before he reached the house, Adar thought he heard Shahnaz whisper something in English. It sounded like: 'Oh James.'

Adar paused for a second, looked back at Shahnaz but then shook his head as he realised he must have been mistaken. He entered the house, head bowed in sadness, the door creaking softly behind him.

Shahnaz sat slumped on the bench after her father had gone. Gradually her sobbing petered out. She raised her head and looked around the garden, dimly lit by distant light from the house. She remembered the days of her childhood playing on a swing, long since gone, pushed by her brother, Mo. Shahnaz had sat on the self-same bench, swinging her legs, listening to her mother read her stories. And, just in front of where she was sitting, she had played hide and seek with Baba who, only partly concealed by a cherry tree, had pretended to be invisible. Shahnaz, going along with the game, would shriek in mock triumph when she found her father, wrap her arms around his legs, and they would tumble to the ground together in a giggling heap.

Later on, the garden became for Shahnaz a place where, just like her father, she could retreat in order to think without distraction. It was here, as a young teenager, that she had first begun to think about her future life. Like her brother, she went to the International School where she began to learn English and became aware of another world outside Iran. It was at the International School that her brother's foreign friends started to shorten his name from Mohammed to Mo.

Shahnaz was taught about Islam, how it had flowered in Iran and the Middle East, and spread as far as Europe. But Europe had resisted and had grown strong while Islam's influence receded. Shahnaz had talked to her mother about the young English teachers at her school. About their immodest dress and lack of religion. And how unreliant on husbands and brothers they seemed in comparison with her mother's friends, whose restrained behaviour seemed prescribed by the Islamic bible, the Koran. Her mother had countered that the first wife of the great prophet, Mohammed, peace be upon him, had been so emancipated that it was she who had proposed marriage to the prophet. So there was nothing in the Koran holding women back. 'Only men,' Shahnaz's mother had added wryly.

Shahnaz had seen how life was changing quickly in Tehran. New prosperity was everywhere along with traffic jams, smog and crowded shops. She realised her family had become rich. The run-down family home was extended, modernised, and furnished with silk Persian carpets and furniture imported from Europe. Their battered old Buick became a gleaming Mercedes.

Her father had explained to Shahnaz that Iran's monarch and sole ruler, the Shah, looked to America and Britain as examples of the modern country Iran was to become. And that meant educated women would be needed in Iran to be teachers, doctors and engineers. Which will I become? thought Shahnaz. And her father had also told Shahnaz that modern Iranian women would not be pushed into arranged marriages against their will.

When Shahnaz was eighteen, she flew to London with her parents to visit her brother who, by now, was studying for an engineering degree. She loved everything about the city: clothes shops, daring fashions, restaurants, hairdressers, parks, and cinemas, the lot. One evening Mo smuggled her out of the expensive hotel, where the family was staying, into a building with a large painted sign, swinging in the wet wind, over its main door: *The Red Lion*. Once inside, Shahnaz had wrinkled her nose at a strange smell. This is a pub, explained her brother. You can smell English beer. Terrible stuff, Mo said. Shahnaz gasped as her brother ordered a glass of whisky. 'You won't tell, Baba,' winked Mo, conspiratorially, while he handed his sister a lemonade. Shahnaz surprised herself by agreeing only if Mo would let her try his whisky. She took a sip and choked as the alcohol burned her throat. Then she smiled as she felt a warm sensation spreading around her body.

'You know Baba wants you to come to London for about a year and improve your English before going to Tehran University?' her brother had said suddenly. Shahnaz had gasped while Mo had laughed at her astonished face. 'He wants me to look after you. I'll be in charge of you here.'

That's what you think, Shahnaz said to herself, determined that she would not let her brother push her around.

Shahnaz shivered as she felt the cold night air seeping through her coat, bringing her back to the present. She looked up at the dark sky and its brilliant stars and thought once more of James. Was he looking at the same stars somewhere in London, she wondered? She had known James for such a short time that she only had sketchy idea of his background.

Shahnaz remembered James's father was a government scientist and his mother a teacher. The family home was in a town called Sevenoaks in Kent, a district the English called a county. He had one sister who was a couple of years older than him. James had called his family middle class. Prosperous, but not wealthy like yours, he'd said. James had been 'quite clever' at school and had got into a top state school - a grammar school, he'd called it. He'd whistled in surprise when Shahnaz had told him how expensive Tehran's International school was.

Of course James had had girlfriends but nothing serious, he'd assured her. By contrast, Shahnaz's experience of boys had been limited to stilted conversations at the weddings and birthday parties of Tehran's wealthy elite. In her mid-teens Shahnaz became aware that she was attractive to the opposite sex: she began to get sideways glances from married, middle-aged men and open admiring stares from their sons. But always her mother or a female relative hovered in the background.

Shahnaz dwelt on the moment James had said he loved her. And when Shahnaz, realised she loved him too, she had mused happily about the prospect of marrying James. She'd frowned to herself, thinking that perhaps his family would object to their son marrying an Asian? And she was sure her family would object to a marriage to a European, a non-Muslim. Even so, she'd heard before of Iranian women marrying foreigners. So, why not her?

But Shahnaz knew she would not now be able to look her parents' in the eye and see their wounded pride and shame, if she were to reject the proposed marriage to Raman. The young officer couldn't be that bad, she reasoned. After all, Baba had said many young women would be happy to swap places with Shahnaz and marry an attractive young man with a bright future.

'Oh James, I'm so sorry,' whispered Shahnaz sadly.

Chapter 9

'Ach James, you can take the Jew out of Germany but you can't take Germany out of the Jew,' said Helmut, pointing out of the aeroplane's window down in the vague direction of Israel, as he took another swig of his umpteenth beer and belched softly.

Helmut was a middle-aged, pot-bellied German, sitting next to me on a KLM flight to Iran's capital, Tehran. It was the summer of 1978 and I was on my way to a new job in Iran.

I'd been working for a Dutch company in The Hague for about five years when I saw, by chance, an advertisement for a well-paid job in Tehran. Although I liked Holland, I knew it was time to leave when I began to start dreaming in Dutch - more of a throat disease than a language.

When I read the ad I wondered, of course, what had become of Shahnaz. It was about ten years since I'd last seen her and I'd had several girlfriends in the meantime. By chance my latest relationship had just fizzled out. To be honest, I suppose my memories of Shahnaz helped persuade me to apply. The allure of seeing her again was still there, albeit dormant.

At about the same time as Helmut made his unusual pronouncement on racial genes, we were flying over the Lebanon, just north of Israel. Which is why our alcohol-fuelled conversation had turned to the question of Israel and the Arabs, a difficult enough subject when sober and probably pointless after even a couple of drinks. But what the hell, it was a long flight, and Helmut had my attention.

'That's as stupid as me saying you can't take Britain out of the Jew,' I protested. 'Anyway, I think there's a big difference between the Jews in Britain and in Germany.'

'And what is that?' asked Helmut.

'You murdered them and we married them,' I said tartly, thinking of my family.

'Ach, very good,' chuckled Helmut.

'It wasn't meant to be funny. Anyway, since you Germans killed most of them in your country, how can you say Israelis are German?'

'Ach *mensch*,' came his riposte, 'I mean German in the widest sense. Before the world wars, Germany was the top culture in Europe: music, art and theatre. Look what the Jews spoke throughout Germany, Poland, and Hungary. Yiddish that's what. And what is Yiddish?'

The question was clearly rhetorical: a callow young fellow in his early 30s, like me, was clearly not allowed to answer.

'A bastardised form of platt-Deutsch - low German - that's what. James, you think what I say is ridiculous,' Helmut said looking at my incredulous face, 'but just look how efficient their army and air force are. How ruthless they are in seizing land they believe they have a God-given right to. They want Lebensraum-space to live! Now, who do they remind you of?'

I refused to give Helmut the satisfaction of my answer. Of course I knew what he was getting at: by some obscene, tragic irony, Helmut reasoned the Israelis had come to resemble the very people whose 'final solution' had given impetus to the birth of Israel.

Helmut sighed with *schadenfreude* writ large on his face: 'Of course it will end in disaster.' He chuckled again and raised his glass: 'Here's to Israel. True Germans and they can't deny it! Prost!'

After an embarrassed pause, I turned and looked nervously around in my aisle seat but, fortunately, none of the other passengers seemed to have overheard or were interested in our conversation.

The plane was full of sleek-looking Iranians, some with families returning home, and expatriates, people like me: engineers, teachers, builders, technicians in short a microcosm of what I expected to find in Tehran.

Everyone was busy drinking, eating, chatting, dozing and reading; doing whatever people do on long flights. Nobody near us returned my nervous glance.

I turned to Helmut who was wiping beer drops from his lips and double chin, the warm sunlight refracting through the window and glinting off his sweaty forehead: 'I think you're nuts. Israel is determined that Jews will never again be trampled on. That's why they are so tough on the Palestinians. It's a reaction to the way you Germans treated them, not because they are Germans!'

I went on rather pompously: 'And the rest of Europe turns a blind eye. We are prepared to sacrifice the Palestinians on our altar of collective guilt about the Jews.'

'Altar of collective guilt! What *scheise* you talk,' exploded Helmut with all the ingrained self-conviction of those who will brook no argument. 'Where do you pick up such rubbish my friend? We can't stop Israel because the Jews control the two most important things in America.'

'And what are they?' I prompted, taking an apprehensive gulp from my beer to keep him company.

'Wall Street and Hollywood,' he said patiently, almost as if speaking to a child. 'They control the money which means they have the politicians in their hands. And they keep the masses happy with the film fantasy world.'

'Were you a Nazi, Helmut?' I asked, dreading, but knowing already, what his reply would be.

'Of course I was. And why not? They picked my country up from the gutter and made us feel proud to be German again. And I was ambitious. I thought I could get to the top by joining the Party. But of course we all realised eventually Hitler was mad. You would have been a Nazi too, James, if we had succeeded in crossing that little canal between France and England.'

Thank God you didn't, I thought. I could see it was fruitless arguing with Helmut about Israel. Besides, it seemed to me, he had a point: many successful American businessmen and film directors did seem to be Jewish. But so what? A conspiracy? Anti-Semitic rubbish, I thought to myself. I decided digression was in order.

'So how do you know this part of the world so well, Helmut?' I asked.

He paused and replied softly: 'I was a Luftwaffe fighter pilot. My job was to kill your boys in the RAF.' I saw real pain in his eyes as he grimaced out of the cabin window towards the brown distance where there should have been a horizon. Even in our air-conditioned comfort one could sense the crackling heat and swirling dust 35,000 feet below us, rising up and obliterating our view.

'It was hell. It was just as bad for the RAF in the heat and the sand as it was for us. Flying patrols, attacking tanks, dodging enemy planes, engine failures, and nearly every day losing another friend. You look out of the window and see mountains and desert. I see a graveyard. Everyday I thank God I am alive and can enjoy a cold beer.'

He sat for a few moments, his head bowed and his eyes half-closed, as if his memories were too sad to face. I felt sorry for this small, fat man despite his views. Right or wrong, he seemed to have fought bravely for his country and now didn't care what people thought of him, or his opinions.

'So why do you work in the Middle East if it has so many bad memories for you?' I interrupted.

'Money, you fool! And the women!' Helmut shouted, spraying beer and spittle onto the upright seat in front of him, reinvigorated by the prospect of clearly two of his three favourite things (beer was clearly the third).

This time I was conscious of seats creaking and moving as other passengers nearby surreptitiously leaned towards us to catch our conversation. I shifted anxiously, conscious of my palms becoming clammy: perhaps the Arab-Israel question was a safer topic after all?

'Women! Yes, the women. Are you married? No matter if you are,' Helmut bulldozed on. 'Believe me, James, the whores in New Tehran are the best I have ever seen, much better than in Hamburg's Rieferbahn. And they are desperate for money - they will do anything! I would be very happy to show you around,' he added generously.

Bizarrely he hummed a few lines of *There's Nothing Like a Dame* from *South Pacific* and then took a quick drink from his freshly-filled glass.

Chuckling again he looked at my face: 'I disgust you I can see. Well, welcome to reality, my boy. I am a fat, 60-year-old man. No wife, no family. How am I going to get a woman?'

Glancing at my left hand he said: 'I can see you are not married, No?' I nodded. 'Well why not come with me and sample some of the delights of New Tehran?' he pressed.

'No thanks,' I stammered, red-faced in embarrassment, as only an Englishman can be caught talking about sex in public, desperately keeping my voice as low as possible.

Despite my attempt, I noticed with dismay an Iranian, darkly handsome in a crisp, cream silk shirt and expensive grey tie, swivel slowly around in his first-class seat and look disdainfully down the aisle towards Helmut and me in economy class. Our eyes crossed for a second and I saw wariness and, yes, cruelty too in his gaze, before he hooded his dark menacing eyes.

Helmut shrugged, obviously expecting my rejection. 'Have you ever met any Iranian women before?' he asked.

'No,' I replied quickly, too quickly, as a voice inside my head screamed 'Liar'.

I looked down at my feet to hide my guilty expression. Helmut glanced at me dubiously. I muttered something about being tired, leant back and closed my eyes.

Our plane sped eastwards, piercing the darkness like a shooting star, reflecting the moonlight from a bright rising crescent, as the stars in the west dwindled behind us.

Chapter 10

I don't know quite what I had been expecting, Xanadu perhaps, but my first view of Tehran was disappointing. The previous half an hour or so my hopes had risen when we flew over white mountains, their snow-clad peaks glinting brightly in the moonlight, signposting the way to a mysterious, oriental city.

As we began our descent, just after dawn, I looked out of the window again, ignoring Helmut's boozy breath, but could only see a dirty brown haze covering the entire city. Yes, I'd read about Tehran's smog problem before but this looked worse than I had expected.

Meanwhile Helmut had scribbled his telephone number on a scrap of paper, which I pocketed, while giving him a half-hearted assurance that I would call him when I could. Fat chance, I thought as we landed with a bump and taxied towards the airport terminal.

There was bedlam in the terminal hall where passengers from two or three flights had arrived at about the same time. People pushed and scrambled for trolleys and fended off porters, who were aggressively touting for work, while we all tried to grab our luggage from the carousels, which stopped and started at random.

Although a sunny winter's morning, it was cold; freezing in fact. The baggage reclaim hall was unheated and I could see my and the other passengers' breaths as we pushed and shoved each other out of the way towards the customs desks.

I shivered standing in the undulating queue and regretted not putting some warmer clothes in my hand luggage - I just hadn't expected Tehran to be that cold.

As I pushed my trolley through customs and passport control, I noticed a couple of sinister, broad-shouldered men watching every passenger, including me, as I pushed my battered trolley by. With their dark glasses and bulky jackets they could have stepped out of a Hollywood gangster movie. I saw them involuntary stiffen as they recognized the expensively-dressed Iranian who had stared hostilely at me and Helmut on the plane. I noticed too that he was immediately waved through the formalities. A big shot, I guessed.

Once through customs, I was greeted by my colleague, Steve Jones, who I was going to replace.

'Good flight?' Steve asked politely.

'Yes, thanks. God, it's cold here,' I replied, my teeth chattering.

We stepped outside the terminal and Steve said, 'Tehran is a capital of extremes, James. Bloody cold in winter and stinking hot in summer. You'll notice some other extremes too,' he added softly, almost to himself.

Steve helped me with my luggage into a smart, shiny BMW driven by a swarthy, partly-shaven chauffeur.

We accelerated smartly away from the terminal, the driver's prayer beads, hanging from the rear vision mirror, swaying back and forth. I noticed, too, a box of tissues sitting on what looked oddly like a Persian carpet, fixed to top of the front dashboard.

'I thought I'd get a cab so we could have a chat while you see Tehran for the first time,' Steve explained.

Steve was nearly ten years older than me. Despite his slim figure and tanned face, with his grey-flecked beard he looked more than his late thirties. Back in England, a couple of colleagues had warned me that he was a bit of a loner. I've never been a one for office gossip so hadn't bothered to ask why.

Driving around an enormous and spectacular floodlit arch, we sped off towards the city centre. The traffic became heavy and noisy, but still flowing freely.

But after about thirty minutes speeding along a dual carriageway, we suddenly ground to a halt, caught up in a dense traffic jam. Our air-conditioning prevented us from choking on the brown exhaust fumes which, even in the freezing, morning gloom, I could see shimmering in the car headlights.

After ten minutes of going nowhere and our driver grumbling under his breath, he turned around and said to Steve impatiently, 'OK, if I go other side?'

Chris nodded and turned to me smiling, 'Hang on to your seat, James.'

With that the driver yanked his wheel round and bumped the BMW over the frozen central reservation to face the oncoming traffic on the other side.

'Christ, what the hell's he doing, Steve?'

'Driving the wrong way on a dual carriageway,' Steve said, matter-of-factly, grinning as he gently stroked his beard into a point.

For twenty knuckle-clenching minutes we drove along the highway against heavy traffic. Horns hooted, headlights flashed, and drivers wound down their windows and swore at us, as our driver steered his BMW, cutting the oncoming stream into two.

Finally he turned off and drove into the calm of tree-lined suburban streets and respectable-looking houses and apartments. We eventually parked outside a white marble-faced three-storey block of flats.

White-faced and shaking I looked at Steve. 'Welcome to Tehran,' he said, chuckling and still stroking that damn beard.

Chapter 11

Shahnaz heard Raman come in long after midnight. She tossed uneasily as he got into bed, smelling of the expensive Italian cologne he liked so much. He must have washed, she thought to herself.

'I had to report urgently to the general before coming home,' he whispered.

Shahnaz barely heard him as she drifted back to sleep, her long hair splayed over the pillow.

It was some time before Raman, his head spinning, fell asleep. He stared at the ceiling, his cold eyes triumphant at the general's warm words of congratulation, following his successful mission.

Shahnaz woke the next morning and dressed quietly without disturbing him. She glanced at his hard, athletic body with distaste, wondering how many other women he'd slept with whilst in London and Paris. Quietly opening the bedroom door, she tiptoed along to their six-year old twins' bedroom. Fayed and Tourak were already awake and the nanny was dressing them.

Raman was still asleep upstairs as Shahnaz helped the twins, one by one into the warm, black Mercedes, already purring outside the front door. She joined them in the back seat and closed the door, the car's dark-tinted windows sealing them from any inquisitive eyes in the cold, outside world. The driver, who didn't need to be told, pressed the electric front gate button and the car purred smoothly down the white marble-chipped drive, bordered by straight-edged lawns, through the gates and into the heavy north Tehran traffic. After about twenty minutes the car drew up in front of the city's International School.

'Wait here. I shall be longer than usual,' Shahnaz sharply instructed the driver, Bahram. He nodded politely. He'd learned long ago to ignore Shahnaz's obvious resentment at his appointment as the family's chauffeur.

Shahnaz took her twins into their classrooms with its walls brightly displaying the children's project work, all of it in English.

'Where is Miss Martin?' she asked the Iranian teaching assistant, instantly regretting her forceful tone.

'She's just, just coming, Madam. I saw her arriving in a taxi a few minutes ago. I er...' Before the assistant could nervously finish her sentence, Jilly Martin bounced into her classroom, newly made up and a bit flustered, Shahnaz thought.

'Good morning, Mrs Zaberani. How can I help you?'

44

'Hello Miss Martin. I just wanted to tell you that Fayed has a dentist's appointment after lunch. Would you mind if I picked him up early?'

'Of course,' Jilly smiled, relieved that's all it was. Jilly liked the twins who were bright and had the full support of their mother. She did find it odd, however, that she had never seen the father at any of the parents' evenings.

Jilly Martin was a fresh-faced young Englishwoman of about twenty-six. She'd been working at the International School for about a year, glad to have escaped the low pay and dispiriting conditions at her previous primary school in East London.

At her interview she'd laughed inwardly when she'd been asked if she had experience of teaching foreign children. More than half her class had been immigrants, most of whom couldn't speak English. New from teacher's training college, her idealism had gradually waned as she became frustrated by her class' slow progress. Why weren't there additional resources to have separate English language classes? She'd asked her head teacher who had smiled sympathetically at Jilly's naivety.

Jilly had felt guilty at abandoning her class. It wasn't the kids' fault, many of them were bright and shone once they had grasped enough English. But within six months at the International School, she'd already saved enough to put down a deposit on a flat not far from her parents' London home.

Jilly had been delayed this morning because she'd been out late with a boyfriend telling him that they should break up. He'd been disappointed and had spent half the night trying to persuade her that they should stick together. As a result she was late and out of her normal routine.

Her Iranian headmistress had previously warned Jilly that Mrs Zaberani's husband was someone powerful in the Shah's government, so she should treat the Iranian mother with more than usual care.

Shahnaz had noticed Jilly's hastily applied make-up and half guessed the reason was to do with a boyfriend. Oh how Shahnaz bitterly envied Jilly's freedom to choose to do what she wanted, even if she made mistakes.

Back in the car, Shahnaz's mind reeled back to a time when she too had been free and single. It was about ten years ago in London. It felt like a lifetime.

'I wonder what happened to James?' she half-muttered to herself, ignoring the Bahram's inquisitive glance in his rear vision mirror. Shahnaz's expression softened as she remembered James's declared love for her and how she had finally been forced to acknowledge her own feelings at their fraught parting. She had almost forgotten what it was like to be held with real passion by a man in his arms. Oh well, he's probably married with children now, like me, she thought.

Her head bowed in her hand, she wondered what she would feel if she met James tomorrow. And what would he feel, she asked herself.

The question hung unanswered in the air as the saloon glided silently back through the ornate gates of the imposing house and came to a gentle stop outside its solid wood double front doors.

Ali, the servant, opened the door at precisely the right moment for Shahnaz to step uninterrupted into the sumptuous entrance hall decorated with silk Persian carpets, gilded chairs, mirrors, wall hangings and flowers. Shahnaz walked through the hall and headed for the conservatory where she normally had breakfast.

Chapter 12

Upstairs Raman heard Shahnaz return while he was still dressing. He loved the expensive feel of silk and was in no hurry to finish doing up his tie around the collar of his clean, cream shirt before putting on a lightweight, dark blue suit. He bought his shirts and ties in London but preferred Italian suits and shoes. The hotter Italian climate was probably the reason why they were better than the British at some things, he thought. He patted on some of his Italian cologne and slicked back his thick black hair, before joining Shahnaz in the conservatory.

Raman was still too keyed up to eat much breakfast. He nibbled some bread and sipped his hot, sweet tea, served by Ali, straight from a bubbling silver samovar.

'Was your flight all right?' asked Shahnaz mechanically.

'Yes, apart from a fat, disgusting European drunk sitting too close to first-class.'

'How was London?'

'It went very well. I had to report to the general as soon as I arrived back. I'm sorry to have disturbed you when I got home.'

Yes, the long meetings over two days in London had gone very well. For the first time Raman had been given the responsibility to lead the team from Iran's secret police, Savak, at its regular meeting with its opposite numbers from the West: the CIA, MI6, Israel's Mossad, and the French DST. The Westerners had been impressed by the raw intelligence and detailed analysis he gave them on Iranian, Arab and Kurdish dissidents in Syria, Turkey and Iraq. In return he'd got high-grade reports on the most active of the Shah's opponents who had fled to London, Paris, New York and San Francisco. A very good deal, thought Raman.

In separate meetings, the Israelis had given him a dossier on one of the Shah's most dangerous enemies, who was living outside Paris, containing a breakdown on his activities, including links with the PLO and other terrorist organisations. Mossad was convinced a plot to assassinate the Shah was at an advanced stage. Raman subsequently got tacit confirmation from the French that they would turn a blind eye if the man were to disappear, in return for a successful outcome to some negotiations on oil concessions.

When the general had heard Raman's report, he had clenched his fists and hissed through his teeth, 'Well, we have no choice then. We will have to kill him. But it must look like an accident.

We don't want to embarrass the French too much,' he winked at Raman.

'I want a plan on my desk by the end of this week. Well done Raman, the Shah-en-Shah (king of kings) does not need to know the details, but he will be very pleased,' the general beamed, nodding his head in approval.

Raman had been delighted: responsibility for the assassination of one of the Shah's most wanted opponents in Europe was the highest possible recognition of his worth to Savak. Already the army's youngest colonel, he could expect further promotion if the Paris operation went smoothly. And it would; no, it must, he said fiercely to himself.

Shahnaz shivered as she caught the look of cruel determination on Raman's face.

'Aren't you feeling well?' she inquired.

'No, I'm fine. I have a lot of important things to organise this week, so I will be home late most nights,' he replied, while his face quickly masked his emotion. Raman kissed her and left abruptly. Shahnaz nodded goodbye and drank her coffee.

'So what's new? I hardly see you these days. Which is good because I detest you,' Shahnaz said silently to herself, conscious that she might sound like a little girl, and ashamed that she did not have the courage to say it to Raman's face. But he knew it anyway.

Shahnaz looked up as she heard the Mercedes start up and swish down the drive past the conservatory. She jumped as a tyre spat a marble chip at one of its glass panes and caught a glimpse of Raman and his driver looking straight ahead. Neither turned to acknowledge her. It was as if she didn't exist.

Chapter 13

The bright sunlight flooded into my bedroom waking me up bleary-eyed. I'd slept badly following the taxi ride back from the airport. Driving on the wrong side of a dual carriageway had clearly disturbed me.

Looking around I saw the flat was sparsely but adequately furnished. It was obviously well heated because the tiled floor was not cold on my feet as I padded towards the toilet.

On the way I glanced out of the window and then stopped to take in a view of snow-capped mountains against a vivid blue sky. In the distance was a tall peak dominating the surrounding range.

'That's Mount Damavand. Beautiful isn't it?' said Steve who had appeared behind me. 'There's some of the best skiing in the world not far from here,' he added.

Steve explained that Tehran was built on a slope running from the foothills in the north down to the dirty plain of New Tehran. I grimaced inwardly as I recalled Helmut's words about the latter's attractions. As a rule, the further north and higher up the slope, the cooler it was in summer, and therefore more expensive the houses.

Open drains, called jubes, ran either side of the main roads running from the wealthy north to the poor south, taking rain and rubbish down the hill.

'So the rich live in mansions on top of the hill and the poor live in slums at the bottom?' I asked.

'You've got it in one. There are still some old places in the south which are worth a visit like the bazaar, the old British Embassy, and the British Club.'

'What's the British Club like?'

'It's OK if you like squash, boozing in the bar with colonial types, and watching English films,' replied Steve scornfully. 'Personally I prefer walking in the hills and skiing.'

Can't you do both? I thought as I realised Steve was living up to his reputation as a loner. I was a reasonable squash player and had brought my kit along, more in hope than expectation. I decided that I would check out the British Club, despite Steve's lack of enthusiasm.

Later on that day Steve hired another car to show me around Tehran, fortunately not with the same driver who had picked me up at the airport. Steve rarely drove in Tehran: 'It's too dangerous and if you have an accident there are always insurance problems.'

I could already empathise with his point of view but I had noticed other Europeans driving around in the traffic, apparently unconcerned.

Looking out of the cars windows, I saw the houses in the north confirmed Steve's words: they were owned by rich, and I mean, really rich people. White marble palaces with tinted windows enclosed by gilded frames were flanked by pristine Mercedes and Roll Royces and manicured, sweeping lawns.

There was every pastiche architectural style from Grecian temple to English Tudor, culminating in a heavily-guarded building whose ornate appearance, glimpsed through the heavy metal entrance gates, could only be described as Islam meets Liberace. I didn't need to be told by Steve that this was the Shah's palace.

Driving south, about halfway down the hill where we lived, the houses and apartments became more modest. But as the slope became flatter in the far south of the city, past the bazaar, the housing became ramshackle and deteriorated into the mud walls and flimsy roofs of New Tehran's slums. Steve asked our driver to pull in and parked so I could absorb the atmosphere. I wound my window down and involuntarily wrinkled my nose as I was hit by a strong and pervasive stench of rotten meat, sewage, and human sweat.

'All the rubbish in the jubes ends up here,' said Steve needlessly.

The scene around us was, to English eyes at least, Dickensian. Kids in filthy clothes ran shouting down narrow alleyways, street butchers sold lamb cut fresh from carcasses hanging from bloodstained lamp posts, and others noisily hawked their wares of cool drinks and pistachios. Through the din, Toyota pick up trucks hooted and forced their way through the crowd.

In contrast to the North, where nearly all the girls could have been from London or Paris, the women here wore strict Islamic dress: a shapeless black shawl from head to ankle, which Steve called a *chador*.

Seeing we Europeans staring at them from our car, the women drew their *chadors* tighter, some by tugging it through clenched teeth, to veil their faces completely, as if they feared contamination. And all around us was the hubbub of millions of people, desperately trying to scratch a living.

'Seen enough?' asked Steve.

I nodded, feeling guilty about our air-conditioned limousine and the relative luxury of our company flat. How do people survive, let alone live in a place like this? I wondered.

'Come on, I'm taking you for a meal tonight,' said Steve, as he ordered the driver to drive off. I closed my window up tight.

Chapter 14

A ridiculous fez-wearing doorman opened our cab's door, bowed and escorted us down thick-carpeted steps into a restaurant called the *Khancella*, literally the King's cellar. We were ushered by genuflecting waiters, their crisply-starched white shirts crackling, as they bent to pull out and help us into garishly gilded chairs.

I looked around at the other people in the restaurant. Most were smartly-dressed Iranians. The women blew cigarette smoke sideways out of scarlet lips and their heavy gold jewellery, around their necks and wrists, swung and jingled as they flicked lustrous black hair to and fro across bare shoulders – now I couldn't help but recall Shahnaz. There were other Europeans too, sprinkled around the room enjoying themselves chatting, smoking and laughing.

After a few drinks Steve started to brief me about the new port of Chahbahar, the project that I would be helping plan. Chahbahar was strategically important because it was outside the Straits of Hormuz, the narrow entrance to the Persian Gulf, which separated Iran from the United Arab Emirates. Steve explained relations between the two countries were strained by disputes over various small islands in the gulf and claims to oil rights.

But our planning had run into a problem. The port needed a breakwater. And for the breakwater we needed hard rock. But the geologists Steve had employed had found nothing.

'We've got to find a quarry as soon as possible. No rock, no port, no money for us. It's as simple as that,' said Steve seriously.

'Sounds like we're between a rock and a hard place,' I replied cheerily.

Steve frowned and ignored my feeble attempt at a joke.

'I guess we need to get down there quickly?' I asked earnestly, trying to reflect the look on Steve's face.

He nodded: 'The journey takes a couple of hours in an Iranian Air Force plane. Unfortunately they're booked up for the next couple of weeks so it's a two-day journey, I'm afraid. We'll have to fly first to Zahedan, near the Afghan border, and then catch a bus.'

'Sounds fun to me,' I shrugged nonchalantly.

'Could be,' said Steve, unconvincingly.

We ate a spicy main course and drank a couple of bottles of local wine. I was surprised by how good they tasted. I'd become a serious wine enthusiast over the last few years and had been on a couple of wine-tasting courses. I now fancied myself as a good judge, sometimes dreaming of making my own wine one day.

'Well, some say the Iranian city of Shiraz was where wine making originally started,' said Steve, noticing my appreciation.

Over coffee and a sticky baklava dessert, Steve lit a cigarette, coughed nervously, and looked around to see if anyone could overhear us. 'James, I've got something very important to tell you. Something that Tim (our mutual boss in London) has asked me to say to you. It's strictly confidential, OK?'

I leant forward, helping to shield our conversation.

Steve cleared his throat, 'You know our contract here is in partnership with a local Iranian firm?' I nodded and Steve continued. 'Well, after we had won the contract, our partners told us that fifteen percent of our fees had to be paid into the private bank account of someone senior working for the client, Iran's Ports and Shipping Organization.'

Now it was my turn to cough nervously as I wrestled with what Steve had just told me. In essence we were paying a bribe.

'Look James, Tim says if you are uncomfortable with all this, you can just walk away. You can leave Tehran now and we'll assign you to a job somewhere else,' said Steve eyeing me intensely.

'Did we know that we would have to pay this, er, commission when we put our bid in?'

'No, definitely not. We were told it was take it or leave it after we had been unofficially informed that we had won the contract,' whispered Steve awkwardly, avoiding my eyes.

Bloody hell, I'm being asked to be an accomplice to a sleazy kick-back, I thought. On the other hand, we were a young, new organisation and this prestigious contract had been won against bigger and better-known competition. If we lost it, our small company would probably fold.

'Why didn't Tim tell me in London what was going on?'

'It's strictly off limits in London. Only a couple of people are in the know. And that's the way it has to stay,' said Steve quietly.

And Tim could hardly have written into my employment conditions, 'Must pay bribe to client', I thought grimly to myself.

'Will you stay?' Steve asked.

Yes, of course I would. I already knew that was the way business was often conducted in the Middle East.

'Good,' said Steve in a relieved voice. He paused and then thought ahead for a few moments: 'I've run out of clean clothes. I've got to pick up some from my dry cleaner first thing tomorrow, but we'll still have time to catch the daily flight to Zahedan.'

Suddenly the meal had left a foul taste in my mouth. Steve paid the bill. On the way out the doorman smiled obsequiously, as if he were party to our guilty secret, when Steve handed him a tip for hailing a cab. We were driven back to the flat in silence.

I took a long time to fall into an uneasy sleep turning over in my mind what Steve had told me.

'Come on, James. I want you to meet Navid,' Steve said, shaking my shoulder, drawing the curtains with a hearty swoosh. I looked blank.

'My laundry man,' added Steve with a grin. 'Remember I told you last night?'

'Oh yeah. Give me a few minutes to get ready,' I yawned.

I blinked in the sunlight outside the apartment block and turned to follow Steve who strode briskly off, ignoring the busy beeping of taxis keenly soliciting fares from a couple of foreigners on foot. We turned the corner onto a wide boulevard, running up and down Tehran's hillside. After about five minutes Steve turned into a small doorway, brushing aside the plastic streamers keeping the flies out.

In front of us, sweating and unshaven, behind the counter of his shop, stood a short man. His damp, hairy chest spilled over the top of a dirty vest, which was haphazardly tucked into oil-stained shorts. The temperature must have already been over 100°F and the smell of chemicals was overpowering.

'*Salaam alykum*, Navid.'

'Good morning, Mr Steve,' replied Navid, at the same time nodding at me, determined to show off his English to a new foreigner.

'Just as important as my washing, Navid knows everything that's going on in the country. He knows all the politics. Isn't that right Navid?' grinned Steve. It was more of a statement than a question.

'Yes sir,' Navid replied with a solemn face, which contrasted oddly with Steve's cheeriness.

'So what's new?' asked Steve uneasily, obviously surprised by Navid's mood.

Without answering, Navid turned his back on us and stretched to lift Steve's clothes from a rack with a long hook. Expertly folding the clothes on the counter, he took Steve's money. Only now, wiping the sweat off his greasy forehead, did the laundryman look at us again. His face was grim. 'Big trouble, Mr Steve. Bomb in cinema kill many peoples.'

Putting on a pair of greasy glasses, Navid bent down to write out Steve's receipt. As he did so I was sure I caught a glimpse of tears welling up in his eyes. Pushing the receipt across the counter and avoiding eye contact, Navid turned away abruptly and disappeared back into the shop's dark forest of hanging clothes, leaving in his wake a ripple of plastic covers.

Steve raised his eyebrows and let out a soft whistle: 'Jesus, I've never seen him that upset before. Navid's normally very talkative. I wonder what tomorrow's paper will say. Navid is usually first with the news.'

'How come?'

'He's religious - gets the news from his mosque. Also his son is doing national service and gives him the army gossip.'

We stood for a few awkward moments. Once it was clear that Navid was not going to reappear, Steve shrugged his shoulders, scooped his clothes up, and stepped out onto the busy sidewalk.

About fifty yards further down the hill, at a kiosk serving hot drinks and food, a young man quickly swallowed his tea and stubbed his cigarette out. Adjusting his bulky leather jacket and sunglasses, he fixed his gaze on James's back and followed the two foreigners up the gentle slope.

The Savak agent's instructions were to follow James Harding for a couple of weeks. His superior officer had explained that anyone new to the apartment block, where the foreigners lived, had to be checked out. The agent didn't know why and didn't care. He was well paid to watch and listen and leave the thinking to others.

Chapter 15

'G'day, you guys had better hurry up and get some beers in. We reckon we'll drink the fucking place dry in another couple of hours,' the man in the faded T-shirt said laconically in an Australian twang.

A bunch of boozing Aussies was the last thing Steve and I had expected to find after we had flown in to Zahedan. The man behind the reception desk in the town's only hotel had merely pointed us towards the back of the hotel, when we had asked if we could buy a beer. We'd pushed through the swing doors and jumped, startled, as a cacophony of noise and cloud of cigarette smoke exploded out from the bar's dimly lit interior.

'The name's Phil, mate,' the Australian slurred, swaying on his feet as he held his hand out.

Phil was wearing a T-shirt which had once been white. Still readable though across his chest there was a bizarre slogan:

WA
A Great Place To Be
50 Million Blow Flies Can't Be Wrong!

Phil wasn't joking about drinking the bar dry. Looking around, it seemed more like a rugby club, than a scruffy hotel on the edge of an Iranian desert. A couple of men were can-canning on the bar, and about half-dozen were singing along, slurring badly, to a tape of an old Aussie folk song: *The Pub With No Beer!* Next to us, on a chipped Formica table, wobbling dangerously was an arm-wrestling match surrounded by punters eagerly placing bets. Only Skippy seemed to be missing.

Picking our way carefully over empty beer bottles and nearly tripping over a pair of feet protruding from under an upturned table, we pushed our way through the turmoil to the bar, which was covered in puddles of spilt beer and overflowing ashtrays.

An exhausted but happy barman rolled his eyes at us, as if to say, 'you crazy foreigners', and silently pushed towards us, without our asking, a couple of already-opened beers. Mouthing thanks we pushed our way back to an empty spot near Phil.

'What the hell's going on here?' we yelled.

'Listen mate, we been grounded for two days now. This fucking bull dust gets into our engines and makes it too dangerous to fly. Now we're going to drink this dump dry! Nothing else to do around here, anyway,' he grumbled into his bottle.

It turned out that Phil and his mates were geologists, pilots and mechanics with an aerial prospecting company from Western Australia.

'What are you looking for?' I screamed, my throat already hoarse.

'Nuclear bombs, mate,' Phil replied laughing, swigging from his bottle.

What he really meant, he explained, was they had a contract to criss-cross the desert in planes equipped with Geiger counters to search for uranium deposits.

'I reckon the fucking Shah wants uranium for nuclear missiles. He says it's for that atomic power station you Poms are helping the Germans build down on the coast at Bushir. But he can buy all the fucking uranium he wants from Australia. Nah, he wants his own uranium, so he can build nukes on the sly. He wants to bomb fucking Iraq, Pakistan or Israel, we all reckon.'

Without waiting for our reaction to his take on the international arms race, Phil continued, 'So, what are you guys doing here in this shithole?'

'We're catching the bus to Chahbahar tomorrow.'

'What, the local bus? Jeez, you Poms are crazy!' Phil chuckled, looking at us with disbelief through his bloodshot eyes, and shouted above the noise to the party at large. 'These two Pommy bastards are catching the bus to Chahbahar. Give'm some more beers; they'll fucking need it!'

'You can borrow my parachute, mate,' someone else laughed.

'Yeah, and take my mother-in-law too,' added Phil morosely.

Several hours and many beers later, Steve and I crawled back to our rooms above the bar.

In bed, between the coarse sheets and trying to get comfortable on the hard mattress, I looked up at the obligatory framed picture of the Shah tacked to the ancient plaster wall. This one was covered with a patina of dust, which highlighted a small crack in the glass just above his lips, making him look as if he were grinning demonically.

'You crazy sod. You're not really trying to develop nuclear weapons. Are you? And we Brits are helping you? Even we wouldn't be that dumb, would we?' I slurred.

The Shah chose not to answer me but continued to gaze regally at some point, far in the distance. Suddenly the noise from the bar below reached a crescendo of throaty, drunken laugher. The floor and walls shook and the Shah's picture tilted slowly, peeled away, somersaulted downwards, and smashed, scattering glass shards everywhere across the floor. I was too tired to care and tried to sleep, but not before my ears were deafened by one final and triumphant chorus of *The Pub With No Beer*!

I sighed fitfully as I dozed off: 'There's something not quite right with this country.'

'Cinema manager arrested' was the bold headline on the day-old English language newspaper, *Kayhan,* lying on a table in the hotel's reception, as I walked past into the dining room. Seated at my table, disconsolately toying with my breakfast of yoghurt, stale nan bread, and the inevitable sweet tea, while trying to ignore my hangover, I read the rest of the story. A horrific fifty people were believed to have been killed in a cinema fire, trapped behind locked doors.

I tried to imagine what it must have been like in the smoke and flames with the screams of panicking men, women and children as they tried to smash the doors down. And their hysterical cries for help as they realised they were doomed. The manager had broken safety regulations and was now under arrest, according to the newspaper.

Good, I thought, I hope they hang the bastard.

I folded the paper and looked accusingly at Steve who had just pulled his chair up to the table.

'Steve, there's no mention of a bomb in this cinema fire,' I said, pointing at the article.

Steve just shrugged his shoulders and smiled enigmatically: 'Who knows what happened?'

We finished picking at our breakfast, headed out of the door, and caught a decrepit, ancient American taxi to Zahedan's bus station.

Why was there no mention of a bomb in the newspaper? Either Navid, the dry cleaner, was wrong or someone was lying? I mulled over the problem as the old Dodge rattled and squeaked over the potholes.

Like our cab, the Chahbahar bus had seen better days. Peeling paintwork exposed alarming areas of rust in the wheel arches and around the radiator grill. All bumper bars had disappeared and several windows were cracked. There seemed to be something, which looked suspiciously like a couple of bullet holes near the front door. On top was an impossibly high, towering load of luggage covered partially with a plastic tarpaulin. We showed our tickets and prudently grabbed a couple of seats near the front door, in case we needed to escape quickly.

The bus was packed with people, assorted chickens clucking in cages, and one lamb jealously protected by an elderly crone on the back seat. Our driver looked like a Mexican bandit and it soon became clear that he drove like one too. We headed south, horn blaring, on the Chahbahar Road as Zahedan disappeared behind in the swirling dust, as we started to drive on for hours and hours.

The scattered vegetation alongside the patchy and potholed tarmac became even sparser. The air was still heavy with dust and, as the rising sun became stronger, the temperature rose and rose and became unbearable. But there was no relief from the fiery cauldron. Opening the windows fully only made matters worse: choking dust gusted into every crevice and made everyone cough and their eyes stream. It became darker outside and the dust thicker.

Suddenly brilliant, jagged forked lightning instantaneously lit up, for a second, the murky gloom enveloping the road and the barren countryside. For a full hour we experienced an intense electrical storm with no rain. Our driver became blinded by the irregular alternating light and dark, forcing him to swerve madly at the last minute to avoid obstructions and careen drunkenly around corners, the bus listing like a yacht in a terrible gale with the lamb bleating, chickens screeching, and passengers wailing to abandon ship.

'Steve, you took the bus on purpose to terrify me, didn't you?' I shrieked. But for once, even the normally phlegmatic Steve looked too scared to reply, his wrists clamped to the passenger rail next to the door. I vowed to myself that I would never, ever catch the Chahbahar bus again, as we shuddered onwards, pitch forked through our stroboscopic hell.

We weathered the storm and, at last, it was possible to see an indistinct horizon through the thinning dust and then increasing patches of blue above the bus skylight. We rumbled on for another hour until finally our driver, hooting like a madman, rattled past the mud houses of Chahbahar's outskirts, down its scruffy main street, and there, suddenly, sparkling in the setting sun, were the blue waters of the Gulf of Oman.

Chapter 17

'Keep your eyes skinned for any outcrops of good looking rock,' Steve shouted. By a mix of banging on the hired pick-up's cabin roof and bending down alongside the driver's window to point the way, we managed to direct our pick-up from hill to hill along the hard stony ground of the Baluchistan desert.

We were hunting for a rock quarry site for stone tough enough to be used in our harbour's breakwater.

Standing up in the back of the pick-up, we sped into the arid wasteland, shouting and laughing like a couple of excited schoolboys. Steve looked like a long-haired sheepdog sticking its nose out of a car window: his beard split and flattened to a goatee and his hair trailed in the wind. He turned and laughed at me so I guess I looked just as ridiculous.

Occasionally we spied a plume of dust like an airliner's contrail, far away in the distance, as a nomadic Baluchi drove along in the modern ship of the desert, the ubiquitous Toyota pick-up. Otherwise, we were completely alone.

Of the half a dozen outcrops we had already checked that morning, only one seemed a reasonable prospect. After chipping away with our geological hammers, we collected some samples for testing and analysis in England.

Midday arrived and our driver suggested lunch at his brother's house. Why not? We accepted politely, interested to taste the local food. We drove into an isolated hamlet of about five mud huts, a few tents, a herd of goats, and chickens pecking haphazardly at the hard ground. It was so well hidden up a wadi that you could have passed within hundred yards and not noticed anything.

In one of the larger huts, our driver invited us to squat down in front of our host, his brother, whose sparklingly-clean long white robe contrasted with the well-worn Persian carpet.

'Salaam alykum,' our driver's brother greeted us.

'Alykum salaam,' we replied politely.

'Thank you,' I said as an old woman in a brightly coloured shawl served me one of the larger goat's hooves sticking out of a pot of curry. The curry sauce was fiery, the bread fresh, and the yoghurt cooling.

Our host was chatty: 'What you do here?'

'Looking for good rock to build a harbour in Chahbahar.' He was unfazed, as if Englishmen looking for stone quarries came by his village every day. He pondered over our problem for a few seconds and then demanded, in his native language, some clarification from his brother, our driver.

He nodded and turned to us, his eyes sparkling in satisfaction and pointed: 'You must go that way for maybe thirty minutes.' He gave rapid directions to his brother who nodded in understanding.

'You engineers?' our host continued.

'Yes.'

'Me crane driver with British engineers in Bahrain,' he said proudly. 'You build harbour here, I stay help.' As if to enhance his credentials, he asked, 'How many passports you have?'

'One,' I replied, puzzled.

'Ah, ah, me three,' he said, proudly sticking three fingers in the air to reinforce the point.

'One fucking Iranian, one shitty Pakistani, and one crappy Bahraini. But me Baluchi here,' he pointed to his heart. 'Passport mean nothing. Learn fucking good English in Bahrain!'

No words were needed from us. He could see from the expression on our faces that we were impressed by his English vocabulary. Tea was served to finish the meal.

'You English like milk in tea?'

'No, no, not if it's too much bother.'

'No bother.' He shouted an order to the old crone who had been sitting quietly in the corner. She scuttled hastily away, her shawl flapping behind her. We sat quietly while our host picked his teeth with a small pointed stick. Finally the awkward silence was broken by the sound of bleating goats being herded into the village.

'Ah, milk come,' he said with the beaming smile of a proud host.

Our tea finished, we shook hands and bowed politely to our host and promised to return when we next visited the area. Yes we agreed, the curry had been 'fucking good'.

Sure enough, after exactly thirty minutes' drive in the direction he had pointed, we found the most promising hard rock of the day.

'The breakwater should start about there,' said Steve the next morning, marking the spot by skimming a pebble across the small waves. Shoes and socks in hand, Steve and I were splashing through the shallows along the beach the looking at the site of the proposed harbour.

'And the entrance to the port will follow on from the main street,' pointing to where our bus had rattled to a stop in front of the decrepit hotel where we were staying.

The tree-lined, golden beach and clear blue water of Chahbahar bay were idyllic. I felt a twinge of guilt that our enormous harbour, in the name of progress, would destroy the view forever. We turned our backs on the beach reluctantly to catch our plane.

We'd been lucky. Steve had seized a couple of cancelled seats on an Iranian Air Force plane, even though we would have to change aircraft on the way, so would have three or four hours to kill in Isfahan.

'You're lucky,' said Steve. 'You'll enjoy Isfahan.'

Chapter 18

'What went wrong?'

Steve and I were standing in the octagonal pavilion at the centre of Isfahan's two-storey, 17th century Khajou Bridge, which also acted as a weir, impounding the River Zayandeh to create a six-foot basin of irrigation water.

'What went wrong?' I repeated, looking down at the reflection of my face on the dark green pool.

'What do you mean?' asked Steve.

'Well, why did Islam stop developing? When they built this bridge here, Europe wouldn't have been able to conceive anything like this fusion of engineering and architecture. And we probably wouldn't be able to do it today. So what happened? Why did our technology go on developing and theirs didn't?'

Steve had taken me on a whistle-stop tour of the city. We'd stood on the covered veranda at the portal to Shah Abbas's palace and tried to imagine what it must have been like to watch the world's first games of polo in the great medan square below. And we'd accepted a nod and a wink from a guide to bribe him so he would take us unbelievers up a claustrophobic, never-ending spiral staircase inside a tall minaret next to the square. At the top we'd swivelled around, taking in the panorama of the city far below. We felt so close to the intricate swirls on the brilliant azure and golden tiles on the dome of the Masjed-e-Shah mosque, that our hands had itched to reach out and stroke them.

We'd gazed too into the still waters of the delicate ornamental ponds of the Sehel Sotoon Palace, the Palace of Forty Pillars, which actually only had twenty pillars, but forty, if you included the pillars' reflections.

We'd seen, appropriately for two Englishmen, the Church of St. George in the old Armenian quarter, partially shaded from the baking sun by a spindly tree. Similar to the Jews in Christendom, the Armenians had been encouraged to live there by Shah Abbas, who prized their financial management skills, just as much as their ability to make wine.

Now, gazing down at our reflections in the calm river, I asked Steve: 'Don't you feel that it's a bit like taking coals to Newcastle? These Iranians shouldn't really need us?'

'Yes it's strange. I agree with you, something must have gone wrong with their culture,' Steve shook his head. 'Perhaps it's al-Wahabi's fault? You know, the Arab puritan, who became a leading Muslim thinker in the 12th century, from what I've read, at about the same time as Islam was defeated by the Crusaders and kicked out of Spain.'

No, I hadn't heard of al-Wahabi. I listened in silence, impressed by Steve's knowledge.

'The new Islamic rulers who successfully fought back, like Saladin, blamed the previous rulers for being too soft, like the one here in Isfahan.'

'After that,' Steve went on, 'I think there was a sort of civilisational suicide as they regressed to believing the Koran had the answer to literally everything. Imagine how backward Europe would be if the Inquisition still told us what to believe. Look how they tortured Galileo. Imagine what they would have done to Darwin.'

I tried to absorb what Steve had said. My thoughts were disturbed as a pick-up van came bumping along the road. The back of the van was piled high with freshly cut chicken pieces: wings, legs and thighs. We glimpsed armies of flies crawling over the raw meat. Blood trickled down onto the road behind the truck through its open tailgate. We guessed that the meat was headed for Isfahan's tourist restaurants and hotels.

The driver spat defiantly out of the window as he saw our look of disgust, almost as if to say: 'I don't give a damn what you foreigners think.'

'I feel sorry for the people who'll have to eat that,' I said.

'Me too.'

Steve glanced at his watch: 'We mustn't miss the plane,' he said anxiously. 'We've got to get a cab now or we'll be stuck here for a week. I certainly don't want to eat that disgusting chicken.'

Before turning to follow Steve, I peered over the parapet one more time. I dropped a pebble and watched it splash into my reflection. The ripples spread out and were quickly, almost disdainfully, absorbed by the limpid, dark water.

At the air force base our Hercules transport seemed to be the only plane in operational use. As we taxied away from the terminal, the wash from its propellers flapped the engine dust covers on the rows of neatly parked fighter jets, their silver wings glinting in the bright sun.

Once we were airborne and our plane had levelled off, Steve undid his uncomfortable military safety harness. Pointing at the numerous instruction and warning signs in American English, he said, 'You know that most Iranians, even the westernised ones, resent the Americans, James.'

'Why's that?'

'Because many of them think the Shah's just their stooge. Back in the early 50s one of their prime ministers tried to nationalise their oil company but we Brits and the Yanks stopped it and put the Shah firmly in charge.'

'Ah yes. I've think I've been told that before,' I said, recollecting Shahnaz's brother, Mo, telling me the same story on a hot summer's night in London ten years ago.

'But they're not dumb. They accept that the Shah needs the Yanks for all that oil money. But they believe the bargain is too one-sided. They think that they are forced to buy too much military equipment from the Yanks in return. You saw all those rows and rows of parked fighters back there in Isfahan? And no pilots to fly them?'

I nodded.

'They're also, oh I don't know, ashamed, I guess, that they're forced to be an ally of the country that keeps Israel going,' Steve continued. 'Every time a Palestinian is killed, the radical mullahs start screaming and upset everyone. They also get the feeling that are they are somehow inferior to the Americans in their own country.'

'How come?' I asked.

'Well, I know it's a small example, but there was a lot of angry talk about the fact that Iranians were barred from joining the Tehran American Club.'

'I hear they're allowed to join the British Club though,' I said.

'Yes, probably another reason why we Brits are officially classified by the Yanks as TCNs.'

'What's that?'

'Third Country Nationals. It's a term the Yanks use for anyone foreign whose status is between American and Iranian.'

'You're kidding! You mean we English are also officially regarded by the Yanks as inferior? It sounds so, well, colonial.'

'Exactly,' said Steve dryly.

'Steve, what the hell is actually going in this country?'

'Let's have some beers back in Tehran with someone I know. I think he'll be able to tell you.'

Chapter 19

I was getting fat. I was drinking and eating too much with Steve and could feel my belly getting bigger and my trouser belt tightening. I decided to join the British Club and play some squash.

'Can I help you?' a smart Pakistani doorman in white coat and black trousers politely challenged me as I pushed open a rusty gate in a wall and entered the club's courtyard: a walled oasis of plants, creepers and shady trees surrounding an outdoor terrace.

'Yes, I'd like to find out about becoming a member.'

The doorman pointed in the direction of some open French windows leading invitingly into a cool bar where I could see a group of expats chatting and drinking under a slowly turning ceiling fan.

'The Club Secretary is over there, sir.' Steve had been right; there was a definite colonial atmosphere.

'So why are you in Tehran, James?' asked a florid-faced man in a blazer. The gold badge on his breast pocket looked too gaudy to be authentic. I recognised the type: full of self-importance because of his position of minor social power. I immediately sensed I would have to humour him to get into the club.

'I'm planning a port down in Chahbahar,' I replied a shade pompously.

'Not another bloody engineer,' sniggered one of the group, into his beer glass.

'Shut up, Bob,' said a young woman sitting on a bar stool next to him, toying with a drink. Looking at me sympathetically, she said: 'Ignore him, he's rude to everyone.'

'Why do you want to join?' asked the blazer.

'I like playing squash and I hear you've got the only courts in Tehran.'

I admitted I didn't have a proposer or seconder and the blazer looked happily pessimistic.

'I'll propose him,' said the girl impulsively, 'And Bob will second you, won't you?' It wasn't a request, more an order. Bob grunted an assent as she gave his shins a light warning tap.

'All right then, you're in,' said the blazer reluctantly, disappointed that he couldn't exercise his right of refusal.

'We do need more squash players. So Jilly, perhaps you could take James to my office and help him fill in the application form.'

'I'm James Harding, by the way,' I said as I followed her. 'Thanks for sponsoring me and getting Bob to agree.'

'It was a pleasure. It's true, we are short of squash players. The price of my sponsoring you is to give me a game,' she said, smiling.

Jilly Martin was her name. She taught at the International School and, like most Brits, had come to the Middle East to save some tax-free money. The British Club was full of them: people who liked the lifestyle and climate so much so that many didn't want to return to the UK.

Jilly was attractive with her blonde hair, tanned legs and slim figure. We played squash a couple of times and then started to go out. She had a good sense of humour and could gently tease someone without them knowing, until she gave the game away by gently giggling. I introduced her to Steve who, to my surprise, approved of her.

'See Steve, not everyone at the British Club is a boring, colonial type.'

'OK, I admit I might be wrong. Jilly's nice.'

Jilly was a fan of Steve McQueen. And so one evening we both went to see the *Thomas Crown Affair* at the British Club, showing outside on the screen in the garden. After the credits, we lounged back in our deck chairs, sighing contently in the warm evening, breathing in the scent of lilies and spectacular bougainvillea, while we languidly swirled ice cubes around in our tall glasses of gin fizz.

'Why, hello Jilly,' said a tall, laconic-sounding man in his mid-thirties, interrupting our reverie. 'Are you coming to the Queenie's birthday bash?'

'Yes thanks, I am,' Jilly replied coolly. 'Charles, would you mind if I brought James along too?' she suddenly said, plucking my shoulder. 'James this is Charles. He works in the embassy. They're having a big party next week to celebrate the Queen's Birthday.'

Charles put a hand through his fair, receding hair and regarded me through his glasses uncertainly for a moment. 'What are you doing over here, James?'

'Working on a new port down in Chahbahar. That's down in....'

'Ah yes, I know where it is,' he cut impatiently in before I could finish. 'Yes, do come. Jilly, please make sure you give

James's details to my secretary, there's a dear.' He excused himself and moved on to another group of Brits near the bar.

In answer to my raised eyebrows, Jilly said, 'Charles is OK, James. Yes, I know he sounds a bit affected. But you know these Foreign Office types?' She paused: 'We had a little fling, but we're just good friends now.'

'What does he do in the embassy?'

'Something to do with security, I think. You will come, won't you, James? It's quite a posh do and there are lots of foreign diplomats and Iranian bigwigs too. I'll need chaperoning, otherwise I'll end up being pawed by some drunk with a wife and three kids back home.'

Chapter 20

The embassy party was all very pukka: smartly dressed white-gloved Pakistani waiters served soft drinks, champagne and canapés, while the officials circulated, ensuring no one was left by themselves.

'Jilly darling, so glad you could make it,' Charles nodded at me as he grabbed her arm, 'You must meet the Thomases. They're new here and need advice about schools.' Jilly mouthed 'sorry' at me and allowed herself to be pulled into a throng of people.

I drifted off towards the French windows and, looking out, wondered idly how much water was needed to keep the grass as green as a Surrey lawn. A vaguely familiar face, in an American blue Air Force uniform, bursting at the buttons, looked in puzzled half recognition at me from a circle of people on the other side of the room. Before I could saunter over to join their conversation, someone accidentally stumbled into my back - it felt like a woman, unsteady on her high heels. I dropped my glass, fortunately nearly empty, onto the thick Persian rug. It didn't break and I knelt down to pick it up, but she beat me to it.

'I am sorry,' she said bending back up, holding my glass out. But as I reached to take it from her hand, our eyes met and froze. It was Shahnaz.

For an instant we were both too shocked to speak. Attempting to make light of the situation, I said stupidly the first thing that came to my mind: 'Here's looking at you, kid,' accompanied by what I hoped was a Bogart grin.

Shahnaz gasped and my glass dropped again. This time it missed the carpet edge and smashed on the black and white chequered tiled floor. There was a small lull in conversation around us but, in an instant, the well-trained embassy servants moved in, cleaned the mess up and gave me another drink. The hubbub of conversation resumed.

'Is everything all right, Shahnaz?' I recognised immediately the athletic-looking man, who appeared at her side. He had been the Iranian VIP in first class who had glared in disgust at me and Helmut on the plane coming out to Tehran.

'Yes thank you, there is no problem,' Shahnaz said stiffly to the man who I guessed was her husband.

She introduced us. 'Raman, this is James.'

The man looked at me. I felt his dark eyes swiftly summing me up.

70

'He is an old friend of my brother from university in London,' added Shahnaz.

I could see that Raman didn't recognise me. We exchanged brief handshakes and he moved off, keen, it seemed, to talk to someone else. Out of the corner of my eye I saw him buttonhole Charles. By now Shahnaz had recovered her composure.

'James, what are you doing here?' she asked calmly, with only the faintest tremor in her hand holding her glass of orange juice. I noticed that her fingernails were now a more subtle colour from the bright red I remembered.

Looking more closely, it was obvious, even to me, that she now looked very chic with her well-groomed hair, black silk dress, and understated jewellery, apart from some very large diamonds on her fingers. All traces of the wild party girl of the 60s had disappeared.

I assured her my presence in Tehran was nothing to do with her; it was simply because I'd been offered a good job. The population of Tehran was officially eight million, unofficially double that, so I had thought it would be unlikely we would ever meet. I couldn't tell whether she believed me or not.

I described my job and we chatted inconsequentially about my first impressions of Tehran and my visit to Isfahan. I gathered that Mo, as she had predicted, was working with her father and they were doing very well. I noticed every now and then we got a couple of inquisitive glances from other people, but I detected that they seemed more interested in Shahnaz than me.

Finally, when I couldn't keep the question bottled up any longer, I asked quietly, 'Why did you never let me know what happened to you?'

She took a deep breath and replied softly, deliberately keeping her voice low, 'I had no choice, James.'

While we were in the *Windsor Castle*, her father had apparently called Mo and ordered him and Shahnaz home, at once.

Shahnaz recounted the conversation her brother had had with her father: 'Listen Mohammed, we have a family emergency. It is a police matter so I can't speak on the phone,' her father had said. You've just about finished your term haven't you?' he had asked Mo.

'Yes, father.'

'Well then. Collect Shahnaz immediately and take the next flight home.'

Mo had tracked Shahnaz down to the pub without knowing she was with me. Shahnaz was whispering now, her face expressionless, that when Mo saw her kissing me in public, he had exploded with fury at the sight of his sister behaving what he regarded as dishonourably in public, made doubly worse because he also felt, justifiably, deceived by a friend.

'So what was the family emergency?'

'I can't tell you now, James. Maybe another time,' she finished doubtfully, looking around.

She made to move off to rejoin her husband who had beckoned her from across the room, but I grabbed her arm. Absurdly I said: 'Here's my business card. Please call me.'

She gently released my grip, shook her head, and walked off. She didn't take my card or look back.

'I see you know Mrs Zaberani, James,' remarked Jilly, appearing at my elbow, together with Charles.

'Who?'

'Mrs Zaberani, silly. I teach her boys.'

'Oh, is that her name?'

'Was that her husband? He's meant to be someone important in the government,' asked Jilly.

'Yes, I think so.'

'Do you know her husband too?' asked Charles. I sensed he was probing despite his voice's run of the mill tone.

'No, I'd never spoken to him before today. What does he do?'

When Charles replied, his face was devoid of expression: 'He's a colonel in the army.'

'Oh,' I looked surprised, 'he didn't seem like an army officer to me in his smart suit.'

'Well, you can never tell with these Iranians, dear boy,' Charles drawled. 'They're as tricky as a bag of monkeys.'

'They sure are,' said the fat American in a blue uniform with a chest full of medals, who had stared at me earlier on. He joined us, puffing on his cigar. His military name badge said P. Barbowski.

'Haven't we met before?' he asked, inspecting me closely. 'My name's Pete Barbowski, Major Barbowski.'

'I'm not sure,' I replied. There was certainly something familiar about him but I couldn't put my finger on it.

'Yeah, I've got it now,' the major said. 'London, 1968. A party. A pretty wild student party, as I recall. I was with my buddy, Stu. We were on R & R from Vietnam.'

Now I remembered. Cradled by his fat jowls, I could just discern the face of one of the two young US Air Force bomber pilots at the party where I had met Shahnaz.

'Jesus, this is turning into James's bloody reunion! Is there anyone else from your past here, James?' said Charles, mockingly.

'Not that I know of,' I laughed uncertainly.

I looked at the American: 'How's your friend? What was his name, er, Stu? I remember he seemed quite tense.'

'A missile got him over Hanoi,' he replied flatly.

I blurted: 'Oh God, I'm sorry.'

'Yeah, we were too. But it goes with the territory, I guess.'

'You're a bit of a war hero aren't you, Pete?' said Charles breaking the embarrassed silence.

'Nah, I was lucky. Now I fly a desk. I tell the Iranians what missiles they should buy from Uncle Sam. Charles helps me sometimes, don't you, buddy?' he added.

Charles merely nodded and looked distant. He was good at that, I noticed.

The party was slowly drawing to a close. Most of the non-Brits were starting to drift away. I saw Shahnaz, across the other side of the room leave with her colonel husband. She flashed a brilliant smile goodbye at the ambassador and his wife; I tried to catch her eye, but she turned quickly away.

Fuelled by free embassy drink, the party gradually degenerated into a booze-up for the expat hangers on. The ambassador and his wife had long gone before Jilly and I, much worse for wear, left. Jilly shouldn't have driven really, but it was highly unlikely the local police would stop a European, she said.

Chapter 21

'Damn, damn, damn,' Raman swore under his breath as the car left the British embassy.

The British seemed to have got wind of the fact that Savak was planning an assassination in Paris. His confidence that the French wouldn't tip the British off had been clearly misplaced. It was clear from what that interfering British MI6 officer, Charles, had said at the embassy party that they were not in favour of any Savak assassinations in France.

'The French might have given you their blessing, Raman, but any risky operation in Paris could affect our own activities elsewhere. And our cousins,' meaning the CIA, 'would be similarly upset,' Charles had warned.

Raman would have to move swiftly now before the CIA heard about his operation too and tried to put a stop to it.

'Bahram, drop me off at the office and then take Mrs Zaberani home,' he ordered. 'I will be gone about a week,' he said to Shahnaz. 'Something urgent has come up.'

Once in his office, Raman immediately called Paris. The call was terse and brief: 'Expect me later today. Operation Darius starts now.'

'Yes, colonel.'

Left alone in the car's back seat, Shahnaz was still in shock. The last person she had expected to see at the Embassy party was James. Seeing him again brought the comparison between James' affection and Raman's cold indifference into such stark, disturbing contrast that she began to sob the controlled, but nonetheless heart-wrenching, tears of a woman and mother trapped in a miserable marriage.

Looking back, she remembered when she had first met Raman at the stilted, formal meeting arranged by her parents at her family's home. She felt ashamed now to admit to herself that she had been pleasantly surprised to feel physically attracted to Raman. He had also seemed considerate and keen to impress her parents as he sat opposite her around the large dinner table. Her mother had been delighted: 'Such a handsome, well-mannered young man, Shahnaz. And with a great future in the army. You could do far worse, my dear.'

So Shahnaz had put any doubts she had to one side and married Raman. At first all went well. Shahnaz busied herself, with the help of her mother, creating a comfortable home in the large house, which had been part of her dowry.

Raman had been pleased that she was still a virgin but the sex was disappointing from the start. His foreplay was perfunctory and mechanical, lacking in any emotion. Afterwards, Shahnaz would often lie with her arms around a pillow staring at the ceiling imagining what it would be like if James rather than Raman were next to her.

True, Raman was delighted when she announced she was pregnant: 'The first of many Shahnaz,' he'd said meaningfully. He'd left her alone until a month or so after the birth of the twins.

One night when he came back late again from work she, half-asleep, had resisted his request for sex. He'd shouted at her telling her to obey as a good wife should. She'd slapped him as he started to force her but, to her horror, she saw this made him even more excited. He hit her hard and his strength was overpowering.

'You bitch, I'll show you who's the master here!' he'd shouted in grinning triumph as he plunged painfully into her again and again, one powerful hand around her throat, the other forcing her knees apart. After that, she would lie back supinely, or bend over on her hands and knees submissively, depending on his orders, when he demanded sex. She realised in self-disgust that she had become merely a receptacle for his semen. As a way of retaliating, she covertly took contraceptive pills, knowing he wanted more children.

Fortunately, Raman began to work even longer and more irregular hours and his time for her and the family dwindled. He'd also become bored with the acquiescent, easy sex and soon his demands became less and less frequent, and finally petered out altogether. She realised he was getting sex from other women. She didn't care.

Chapter 22

Savak's Lockheed executive jet landed at Paris about six hours after leaving Tehran. Its sole passenger was Raman. Wrapped up heavily against the winter cold, he walked unheeded through the diplomatic channel and into a waiting dark limousine carrying CD plates.

The Operation Darius team was small - only four Savak operatives who posed as embassy drivers and security guards. They'd been shadowing the exiled opponent of the Shah - code named Darius - for about two months now. Darius was clever. He varied his routine and route everyday as he came and left his flat in one of Paris outer suburbs. But at least once a week, sometimes twice, he visited the office of a small dissident group in the centre of Paris, which organised protest demonstrations against the Shah and published newsletters for supporters in Europe and the USA.

Raman had decided the best opportunity would be when Darius visited the group's office and used the Metro, Paris's underground railway system. The method he'd originally selected was a virtually untraceable poison pellet on the end of an umbrella. He knew the Bulgarian government had successfully used this method to murder a BBC journalist in London, who had made regular and embarrassing broadcasts, unacceptable to the regime. The assassin had simply melted away into the busy crowd of commuters and the unfortunate victim had barely noticed the prick of the umbrella.

The main drawback though for Raman with this method was the amount of money the Bulgarians wanted, and the certainty that they'd tell their real bosses, the KGB. Savak did not want too many foreign agencies to know the details of one of their operations. Anyway, there was now not enough time to procure and train with the poison pellet. The urgency meant that Raman's fall-back plan, primitive and risky though it was, would have to be implemented.

Waiting at his hotel, Raman had got the call at about 7.30 am two days later.

'Darius is on the move. He's heading for the centre. The other two are shadowing him.'

Raman changed into the clothes of a conventional, dull businessman. Grey suit, short overcoat, black shoes with a firm rubber grip, and finally a pair of glasses with plain lenses. He was in no hurry. Whichever route the target decided on today, he knew the destination. Raman caught the Metro to the Paris smart 16th arrondissement and walked into a café where he ordered a coffee and croissant. He settled down to glance at *Le Monde* and read *Time* magazine.

Sure enough, about twenty minutes later Darius came walking briskly along the narrow street, stopped, looked around to see if he'd been followed, and disappeared into the office building opposite the café.

Pathetic fool, thought Raman. As if you'd spot my people following you. All of his men had been well trained in surveillance techniques by the British, he recalled with some irony. Shortly after, his assistant who was also dressed unremarkably joined Raman.

'The other two are in the café at the end of the street,' he told Raman.

Raman nodded. From his team's reports, he knew that they had time to kill. Provided they bought regular cups of coffee and croissants, he knew the café owner wouldn't mind them staying and reading their magazines. The only risk was the unlikely occurrence of someone from the dissident group popping into the café and becoming suspicious of the two men who would look Iranian to sharp, familiar eyes.

After an hour or so, Raman's assistant suddenly stiffened and stubbed out his cigarette. Darius had left the office building and was walking towards the Metro station. Picking up his *Le Monde*, Raman allowed his assistant about a minute before he too got up and sauntered out of the café. Darius had already disappeared around the corner but Raman had no difficulty in spotting the other three members of the team scattered ahead along the busy pavements.

Darius disappeared down into the Metro. Raman and his assistant followed shortly descending steadily, but not hurriedly, down the brightly scuffed metal-capped steps and into the busy Metro station concourse.

Darius moved onto the platform densely packed, fortuitously, observed Raman, with a large group of excitedly gossiping American tourists, fresh from visiting the Arc de Triomphe. Raman's team began to shuffle through the unsuspecting throng closer to Darius while Raman walked to the edge of the platform where he looked down the dark straight tunnel.

After a minute, he could just see the headlights of an approaching train. He folded his *Le Monde* and stuck it under his shoulder, the signal that the operation was 'go'.

His team, who had timed it to perfection during rehearsals, knew it had just two minutes before the train arrived. Moving slowly, Raman began to approach Darius and deliberately stared at him. Unnerved by the stranger's steady gaze, Darius involuntarily moved backwards, closer to the edge of the platform.

Excellent, thought Raman, just like herding a goat to slaughter, as he continued to move towards Darius who stepped backwards even further towards the edge. The rumble of the approaching train became louder by the second and Darius suddenly became aware of his danger. He tried to move away from the edge but was blocked by Raman's assistant, who had bent down, pretending to pick up his dropped newspaper.

Panicking now, Darius opened his mouth to shout for help, but his voice was drowned by an outraged shout, in English, of: 'Stop him, he's stolen my bag.'

The throng of American tourists was transfixed by the sight of a supposed thief, escaping with a briefcase, being chased through their group by his victim who clumsily pushed and shoved them out of his way and finally tripped over one of them onto the platform. All tourist eyes were drawn towards the spectacle and hands were outstretched to help the poor man, prostrate and groaning on the ground.

A split second later, the train's brakes started to squeal loudly as it came out of the tunnel. Raman's assistant stood swiftly and clamped Darius's arms in a tight grip. Raman moved quickly forward and pushed Darius, using all the strength of his well-toned muscles, off the platform.

Darius flew backwards, his suddenly released arms splaying outwards, and landed with a thud on the railway sleepers between the rails. His last anguished, defiant Muslim cry of *'Allah o akbar'* - God is great - was snuffed out instantly as he disappeared, unnoticed by anyone nearby, under the train.

Another second past while the tourists helped the thief's victim to his feet. Suddenly a woman screamed in revulsion as she pointed at a bloody dismembered torso lying on the track between the train's wheels and the foot of the platform.

Raman and his assistant were already several feet away by now as they moved sideways through the throng of upset tourists. Someone began to vomit. There was bedlam as innocent mouths gaped open and eyes widened in disbelief, as they looked at what remained of a human being who had been sliced and diced within a few feet of them.

Talking later to the police, none of the tourists had seen the man fall and nobody knew what had happened to the other man whose bag had been stolen. Yes, a couple thought they had glimpsed out of the corner of their eyes two businessmen standing close to the man who had fallen.

Could they describe them? No, they were ordinary businessmen, just like thousands of others. The police soon gave up and shrugged their shoulders as the man's remains were bagged up and taken away for forensic examination. The Metro station reopened within a couple of hours.

Suicides were not unknown on the Metro and there were established procedures to deal quickly with the situation. All that remained afterwards to mark the spot of someone's death was a well-trodden, discarded copy of *Le Monde*, which was soon blown along the platform by the next train.

It was so easy, thought an exultant Raman as his team exited the station, split up, and made their planned separate ways without looking at each other.

Within an hour, Raman was back on board Savak's Learjet. He could not wait to report in triumph to the general back in Tehran.

Chapter 23

It was about five years after they got married, that Shahnaz found out Raman worked for Savak.

Raman had come home drunk late one night, as usual. Reeking of booze, cigars and cheap perfume, he slumped into his favourite armchair and ordered coffee brusquely from Ali. He looked across aggressively at Shahnaz who was watching TV.

'My dear,' he slurred sarcastically, 'I have been celebrating. I have been promoted. I am now the army's youngest colonel! And I have been transferred permanently to state security.'

Shahnaz remained silent.

'Aren't you going to say something, you stupid cow?' Raman suddenly shouted, his bloodshot eyes narrowing to slits and his fists clenching.

Always at the back of Shahnaz's mind was the suppressed terror that he might try to rape her again, so she turned calmly to look at him, eyes downcast, and said meekly: 'Congratulations, Raman. I am sure the boys will be very pleased, I shall tell them first thing tomorrow morning.' She knew from experience that if she mentioned the boys it usually diverted his attention away from her, particularly when drunk.

Ali shuffled into the room with the coffee. Raman eagerly gulped it down unaware of the brown drops trickling down his stubbled chin and onto his lipstick-smeared collar.

As she had hoped and expected, he now looked at Shahnaz and asked in a more reasonable tone: 'How are my boys?'

'They are doing well, Raman. Their class teacher, an English girl called Jilly Martin, is very pleased with them. They already speak good English. I wish you would come to the parents' evenings some time and see some of their work. You'd be very proud of them.'

'Well, maybe I will come,' Raman said.

But Shahnaz knew he wouldn't. More and more she noticed Raman was reluctant to attend social or public gatherings. The only exception was events organised by the army or government, when he insisted Shahnaz accompany him and wear her finest clothes. Occasionally he brought a colleague home for a drink, or meeting late at night, but Shahnaz was usually not introduced and the visitor would quietly slip out the front door without disturbing anyone, even the servants.

It was not long after Raman became a colonel that Shahnaz's friends began to drop her. There was nothing obvious at first that she could put her finger on, but she gradually became aware of a cooling off in their manner towards her.

She noticed that if she arranged to meet a group of them, there were often sidelong glances in her direction, as if they had been surreptitiously gossiping about her. Once she picked up a half-whispered question: 'Does she know?'

Puzzled, Shahnaz asked herself: 'Do I know what?' She had thought at first that perhaps someone had discovered that Raman was having an affair. But the snatched looks and averted glances she detected were definitely not those of women excitedly half whispering behind their hands about fragile marriages and husbands' peccadilloes.

She was further perplexed when a year later the twins were not invited for the first time to a friend's birthday party. Shahnaz knew the mother well; they went back a long way to when they had played together as little girls. Hurt and confused, Shahnaz called her old friend.

After obtaining a promise from Shahnaz that she wouldn't repeat what she heard, her old friend confessed that she was too scared to be seen with her.

'My husband has told me not to see you any more. I'm so sorry, Shahnaz.'

'But, but why not?' Shahnaz asked her.

'Do you really not know?'

'No, no, I, I.. don't,' stammered Shahnaz miserably.

Her friend whispered something so faintly in a voice full of fear that Shahnaz couldn't hear what she'd said and asked her to repeat it.

'Shahnaz, Raman works for Savak.'

Shahnaz had been stunned and unable to carry on the conversation. She had robotically thanked her friend, said goodbye and replaced the receiver. Unsteadily she had walked to the lounge and slumped down into a chair overlooking the garden, her thoughts swirling around.

Shahnaz was no longer the naive young woman she'd been when she returned from London. She knew that Savak was virtually a law unto itself in Iran and regularly detained and arrested people on the faintest of suspicions, just as they had with Uncle Faris.

She too had heard the rumours of torture and killings. She could understand now only too well why her friends were reluctant to be seen in public with her any more. With growing horror, she also began to suspect that, perhaps, Raman enjoyed his job because he got pleasure from hurting people.

Should she confront Raman and ask him direct if he worked for Savak? She quickly dismissed the idea. Raman would only laugh at her concerns and might even start to limit her freedom to come and go, if he thought there was a risk she might disapprove of his job in public.

Chapter 24

Shahnaz's father had found out about Raman's role in Savak almost by accident. Adar had been pleasantly surprised, but also a little suspicious, when the family company had unexpectedly won a couple of large government contracts. He'd asked his son Mo, Shahnaz's brother, to make discreet enquiries why they had been so fortunate, half expecting that it was their company's good reputation which had swung the projects their way.

Mo had drawn a blank when he first tried to find out why they had won the new work. Then by chance, he was at a government reception for a visiting construction industry delegation from Italy, when he bumped into an acquaintance who worked for a much bigger and hugely profitable development company.

'Hello Mohammed, I'm glad to hear business is good,' the man had said archly, his eyes twinkling in amusement. Mo had thanked him politely for his interest, knowing the man's company was owned ultimately by the Shah's sister. Mo asked him whether he had heard anything on the grapevine about the reasons for his family's unexpected success.

In answer to the man's gentle probing, Mo had confirmed that indeed, Colonel Raman Zaberani, his brother-in-law was a shareholder in his father's company. After all, it was no secret that Raman had been given about ten per cent of the family company as part of the dowry when he had married Shahnaz.

'Mohammed, your family's company is now one of the magic circle,' the man had said, as if he was pointing out the obvious. 'It was your company's turn to be rewarded.'

Mo frowned uneasily: 'What do you mean, turn?'

The man had taken Mo by the arm and checked nobody could overhear them. 'You must know Colonel Zaberani is already an important Savak officer.' The man looked inquisitively at Mohammed's sharp intake of breath. 'Even though he is still very young, it is said the Shah thinks Colonel Zaberani might even one day be a general in Savak,' the man continued, looking intently at Mo's face, 'that's why the Shah himself has made it known that Raman should share some of the fruits of our country's new wealth. Surely you knew this was the reason?'

Mo was flabbergasted by the man's revelation but quickly covered his composure: 'Certainly I knew, but I wanted to see if there were other reasons which might have helped our bids.'

The man had looked shrewdly at Mo and said the Mostashari family was fortunate to now include someone who, despite his comparative youth, was thought of so highly by the Shah.

Mo gave his polite thanks to the host and slipped away from the reception shortly afterwards, disappointing several Italian businessmen keen to make contact with an up and coming Iranian company.

He made his way straight to the family company's office based on the top floor of one of Tehran's most modern high-rise buildings. Stepping through chromium-plated doors into the lift, he was whisked upwards.

Waiting in the penthouse office for his father and uncle, he gazed out through the tinted glass over the brown smog of Tehran and the dense traffic. All around he saw the familiar forest of tall cranes signifying the city's non-stop building frenzy.

Not for the first time he wondered when and if the boom would ever end. It seemed so simple: their family company bought an office building, sometimes less than five years old, in down town Tehran; knocked it down; built another one, bigger and better on the same site; and then sold it for a healthy profit.

Borrowing money from the banks to finance the development? No problem! Even foreign banks were now falling over themselves to get in on the act, offering money to companies like theirs with virtually no strings attached. And the money kept rolling in. Recycling petrol-dollars someone had called it.

And now it seemed the family company was destined for even greater things as part of the Shah's magic circle, courtesy of his brother-in-law, who it now turned out was a senior officer in the Shah's hated secret police.

As well as the obvious business opportunities, Raman Zaberani's job in Savak brought with it frightening dangers too. All of Tehran's burgeoning middle class knew of someone, maybe a friend of a friend, or a distant relative who had run foul of Savak. Iranians shared with Sicilians long memories and a strong desire for revenge. The faintest suspicion by a victim's family that Raman had been involved in his or her torture, or worse, murder, meant that Shahnaz, her two boys, and even her father, uncle and brother, might be in danger. Mo knew too that political unrest was increasing. Although the Shah was clamping down, who knew what might happen in the future?

'I wonder if Raman was already a Savak officer when he married Shahnaz?' his Uncle Faris asked. 'Is that how he managed to locate and visit me in prison so easily?'

His father and uncle had listened gravely to Mo's news about Raman as they began rapidly to think through the implications and possible consequences.

Adar Mostashari spoke first: 'We will have to consider carefully the future for our family. Thankfully, we do not have to hurry. We have time. The situation will not change much in the foreseeable future.'

Faris nodded in agreement: 'Our first duty is to our family company. Without money we will never be able to do anything. Second, we must protect Shahnaz. This will be more difficult because she is now married and legally Raman has rights over her enshrined in law.'

They made quick decisions between themselves: they agreed that they would delay telling Shahnaz anything about Raman's job until it became unavoidable. In the meantime Mo would quietly visit London, San Francisco, and Paris to identify possible investments so that the family would have resources abroad if they had to leave the country in a hurry. At home, they would maximise their borrowings to free up money for foreign investment. When Mo returned they would discuss the investment opportunities he'd identified.

They also decided that Adar and Faris should confront Raman. They needed to assess the possible dangers to Shahnaz, her children, and yes, themselves. The two brothers also wanted to clear up whether Raman was already a Savak officer when he married Shahnaz. If he had been, Adar would not have permitted the marriage, he thought angrily to himself. They all knew the meeting would need careful handling because the last thing they wanted was to estrange Raman. A senior Savak officer would make a powerful and dangerous enemy.

'No, I was not a Savak officer when I married Shahnaz,' said Raman truthfully, settling into the deep cushion of his favourite chair. He was perfectly at ease in his own home, sipping espresso coffee and enjoying a strong French cigarette. He had readily agreed to meet the two brothers and had invited them to his home. He'd guessed the reason for the meeting. He was only surprised it had taken Shahnaz's family so long to discover his occupation.

'I had been seconded from the special forces to be part of the detachment of the Imperial Guard in charge of the Shah's security. That's why I found it fairly easy to visit you in prison, Faris.' Raman looked at Faris and Adar with a steady confident gaze. 'There was no deception. I was invited to join Savak about a year later. If you are in the army and invited to join, it is very difficult to refuse, particularly if you are ambitious,' he added, shrugging his shoulders. 'I know that many people don't like Savak but I am proud of the work I do in fighting our country's enemies. If Savak did not do its job, Iran would be a primitive country ruled by those ridiculous men with beards.'

There was a silence as the two brothers absorbed what Raman had said. Faris, for his part, felt Raman had insulted their Shia religion with his derogatory remark about its mullahs.

'Look,' said Raman, a note of impatience creeping into his voice as he looked at their solemn faces, 'the fact that I am doing well in Savak should be good, not bad news for you. I've been told you will win many more government contracts,' he smiled knowingly. 'Yes, I know that there will be some gossip about me. But I don't care what people think. And neither should you, nor Shahnaz,' he said, now with a note of proud defiance in his voice.

'Raman,' Adar chose his words carefully, 'Of course we are very grateful for your help in improving our company's fortunes. But rightly or wrongly, Savak has many enemies. And the political situation is becoming, how shall I say, rather fluid again. You must have heard the stories about riots and bombs in the other cities? As a father and grandfather, you must surely understand why I am worried that Shahnaz and your boys might, in some way, come to harm. Apart from you too,' he added hastily.

'You should have no fears about me, or Shahnaz and the boys' safety. You have my word on that,' replied Raman fiercely, his eyes burning in anger at Adar's ludicrous implication that Savak somehow was not in total control of the country's security situation. 'Savak has already captured, or is watching closely all the Shah's opponents in the country. And the riots and bombs you talk about have been minor incidents, exaggerated by the mullahs in the mosques to stir the uneducated masses up.

'Believe me, as soon as a mullah shits, or molests a little boy, we know about it inside five minutes,' he said, looking deliberately at Faris, knowing the older man's strong Muslim beliefs. Faris bit his tongue as he controlled his anger. 'Truly, nothing happens in Iran without us knowing about it,' Raman added, more calmly. 'If anyone threatens my family, they will be dealt with,' he said contemptuously, waving his hand dismissively as if there could be no doubt.

Both brothers shivered as they saw Raman's curled lip and heard the arrogant, menacing tone of his words. They shivered as they realised in alarm that Raman would be very dangerous, if crossed. They would have to tread very carefully.

Adar could see it would also be a waste of time asking Raman about the growing influence of the mullahs' leader, Ayatollah Khomeini, exiled to Iraq. How much of Raman's obvious confidence was wishful thinking he wondered. Surely he knew that resistance to the Shah was increasing inside and outside Iran? Was Raman merely repeating the government's line because he was too scared not to, or did he genuinely believe the security situation had not deteriorated lately? There was no point in talking further: Adar and Faris stood up and shook Raman's hand. The meeting was over.

Raman saw them to the front door: 'I'm sorry Shahnaz is not here to see you. She's out shopping and then she's collecting our boys from school. You must come to dinner soon - it's been too long.'

The two brothers murmured thanks and polite goodbyes and walked in silence towards Adar's parked car, uncomfortably aware that Raman's heavily-built driver was watching them closely from inside his car. 'That must be his bodyguard, Bahram. I've heard he's a nasty piece of work,' said Faris as Adar drove away.

Chapter 25

Raman watched the old brothers leave and thought how ignorant they were and how ridiculous their fears. Although he worked solely on Savak's overseas operations these days, he knew from his colleagues, busy with Iran's internal security, that they were completely confident the current disturbances would be easily suppressed, just like they had been in the past.

Besides, Raman proudly reassured himself, he had been one of only five senior officers privileged to read a recent top secret CIA report, which had concluded that the Shah 'is expected to remain actively in power over the next ten years'.

The CIA is always right, thought Raman. The Americans would never allow the Shah to fall. And ten years was ample time for him to rise to the top of Savak and use his increasing power and influence to gradually take over the Mostasharis' company, either with or without their cooperation. After all, it would only be fair for him to reap most of the rewards generated by his position, wouldn't it? Raman smiled to himself and repeated: 'Stupid old men.'

Raman sunk back into his chair once more with a satisfied smile, crossed his legs and savoured a rare moment of relaxation with his coffee and cigarette. Seeing the two older men together had reminded him of how far he had come in such a short time. Was it luck? No, he quickly reassured himself, it was his ruthlessness and iron will to succeed.

Watching his cigarette smoke drift gently upwards, his thoughts went back to his tough, exhausting training with the SAS. After Hereford, in England, he'd seen active service in Oman fighting with the British to crush a revolt against the ruling Sultan.

In a fierce shoot-out during a raid on a dissident village in Oman's Dhofar province, he'd 'slotted' a couple of tribesmen, as his new SAS colleagues called it when they shot someone. He was not surprised to find that he enjoyed the thrill of the hunt and the satisfaction of a kill. You're a natural, the tough SAS sergeant told him respectfully as Raman finished off a couple of wounded dissidents. Later, watching through a one-way mirror, he'd been impressed and learnt a lot from the Omani security services' torture methods as they interrogated prisoners in the British-built centre in Oman's capital, Muscat.

He'd returned to Iran's special forces with a glowing report. You can always come and join us, mate, if you get bored back in

Iran, the SAS sergeant had said when he left. Raman had noticed too, with pride, how the sergeant had, for the first time, saluted him as an officer.

Pleased to have someone with the British SAS skills, the Iranian special forces soon tested him after he had returned home. He was given an important mission, sanctioned, he was told, by the Shah himself, to lead an undercover team over the border into Iraq to kill a senior officer in President Saddam Hussein's military intelligence, al-Istikhbarat, whose success in running a network of Iraqi agents in Iran was proving to be a dangerous nuisance.

Iranian agents had been watching the officer for months at his office in the Iraqi port of Basra. Now was the time, his commanding officer told Raman, to strike.

Raman's team had been dropped about thirty miles over the border into Iraq by a low-flying, quiet helicopter, on a dark Thursday night. The dropping zone was within a tough half-a-day's march across rocky, hilly terrain to the target's isolated hunting villa. Once they'd arrived, Raman organised an expertly camouflaged surveillance post overlooking the villa.

As expected, Saddam's man turned up with his small entourage, in a convoy of two Jeeps and a big American saloon, late Friday afternoon. Once afternoon turned to a cooler evening, a poolside party started. Watching through his binoculars, Raman positively identified the target. He was clearly enjoying himself on a sun lounger by the swimming pool, drinking beer with his arms around a scantily clad, pretty young woman, giggling as she bounced on his big hairy belly, one of her hands inside the man's swimming costume.

Raman guessed she was a prostitute from one of Basra's brothels. Even though it was too far for a sniper to be sure of a kill through the still-shimmering heat haze, Raman's team could faintly hear the sound of laughter, music and splashing in the swimming pool and, on the gentle evening breeze, a whiff of sizzling, mint-flavoured lamb kebabs. Raman and his team chewed their hard rations, drank warm water from their metal bottles and settled down patiently to wait.

At about 3am, early Saturday morning, after all signs of activity had ceased for about a couple of hours, Raman and his team hid all signs of their look-out post and crept silently down from their hill into the villa compound. Any slight noise they made was completely covered by the all-pervasive gentle, background hum of the villas air-conditioning units. They found a couple of guards sound asleep in the gatehouse and despatched them quickly and quietly with the thud, thud of their pistols equipped with silencers. The only noise outside in the courtyard was loud snoring coming from the servants' quarters.

Leaving two of his team downstairs to deal with any servant or bodyguard who might appear, Raman and another one of his team moved silently upstairs towards the villa's bedrooms. They gently pushed open a heavy wooden door leading into the master bedroom where they found Saddam's man, lying face down, naked and breathing heavily in a deep sleep, one arm draped carelessly over the young woman's breasts, as she lay next to him.

Definitely a prostitute, Raman thought, quickly taking in her smeared lipstick, tacky underwear scattered over the floor, and the smell of cheap perfume. All around the bed were the signs of drunken festivity: hastily discarded clothes, empty whisky and champagne bottles, and overflowing ashtrays.

Motioning his colleague towards the woman, Raman padded softly towards the man and, with one swift, smooth movement slid his left hand down under the target's face, clamped his mouth and nostrils, and firmly pulled the head upwards, exposing the neck.

Before the man could wake his throat was already slit and blood gushing and bubbling out, staining the dishevelled sheets. Raman held his hand over the mouth and nose for a minute before he was certain the target was dead and then gently replaced the head down onto the blood-sodden bed.

The young woman next to him had stirred uneasily as the men approached the bed but she too was silently killed with one bullet between her eyes. Raman wiped his left hand free of blood on the small area of dry bed sheet and looked up at the smiling, superior picture of Saddam Hussein hanging on the wall.

Taking the Iraqi leader's portrait down he placed it carefully on the target's hairy buttocks. With a powerful downwards stab he plunged his knife, with its clear Iranian Army special forces insignia, through Saddam's mouth and buried it savagely up to the hilt into the dead man's anus.

Raman had been ordered to make sure that Saddam Hussein would feel personally insulted and know, without doubt, the identity of the people who had dared to kill one of his senior men. Raman smiled with quiet satisfaction to himself at mission accomplished.

He turned to his colleague, already waiting and guarding the bedroom door. The only sound which could be heard was the, as gentle as a ticking clock, drip, drip of blood onto the floor.

The two Iranians left the bedroom and, taking turns to swivel round and cover each other, they carefully went downstairs and met up with the rest of the team crouching by the front door. From start to finish they had been in the villa less than five minutes.

Raman and his team left as quietly and swiftly as they came, melting into the dark night surrounding the nearby low hills. By mid-day Saturday they were back at the dropping zone where they concealed themselves between rocks and under brown and grey camouflage netting. Taking turns to be on lookout, they lay down and waited under the hot sun.

Apart from a couple of Iraqi helicopters searching vainly in the distance there had been no sign of any pursuit. Their unmarked Iranian air force helicopter swooped in with its muffled engine at about ten o'clock that night. By eleven they were back, laughing and congratulating themselves, at their home base in Iran.

Raman's commanding officer had been impressed and had filed a highly complimentary report, which gradually went up the command chain until one day, a couple of weeks later, it caught the attention of the general responsible for the Shah's personal security. Raman was summoned to the palace in Tehran to be decorated by the Shah. While he was there, the general watched Raman carefully and made final enquires about his background and training. Once the general was satisfied, Raman was transferred.

Some six months later, something about Raman on parade must have caught the Shah's eye: perhaps his powerful presence, immaculate uniform, or his obvious desire to please? Raman never found out. After the Shah had consulted with the general, Raman was transferred again, this time to the Shah's Special Intelligence Bureau, the unit whose job it was to spy on the Shah's senior army and air force officers, to check on their loyalty and prevent a coup.

At first he was assigned to relatively menial, administrative tasks but his obvious total commitment and ambition was rewarded gradually with more sensitive tasks and regular promotion. He realised he was being closely watched and his progress monitored by both admiring and jealous eyes. After another year he found himself working at the nerve centre of the regime. He was trained to use CIA technology to listen in on the telephone calls and wireless communications of the Shah's top commanders in Savak and the armed forces.

At first he found spying on the country's most senior officers exciting but, after a time, he was smart enough to realise that his new job might eventually put his life at risk from either fearful Savak or army generals: he knew too much.

Giving the plausible excuse that he was a man of action rather than a desk warrior, he applied for a transfer to Savak's special operations: its assassination squad. The Shah, who wanted people whom he could trust at the top of his security apparatus, personally approved the transfer. Raman was by now the army's youngest colonel with unrivalled experience of being at the heart of the Shah's regime. The word was out: Colonel Zaberani was the Shah's up and coming man in Savak.

Raman's reverie was interrupted by a polite cough from his bodyguard.

'Yes, what is it?' asked Raman sharply, irritated to be disturbed.

'If we don't leave now, sir, we will be late for your next meeting.'

Raman stubbed the last of his cigarette out and followed Bahram's burly figure out of the house towards his car. He smiled with satisfaction as the car door opened and closed behind him with a thud. Yes, he had come a long way since stealing sweets off snotty-nosed kids in the bazaar.

Chapter 26

Raman had thought nothing unusual about the telephone call from Major Pete Barbowski until he had hung up. After all the CIA's local station head and he met about every three months to discuss Raman's operations.

'Raman, how about meeting me for a beer at the American Club tomorrow,' Pete had said, breezily. 'Something's come up, which I'd like to discuss with you. Six pm in the lounge bar, OK?'

Raman thoughtfully rubbed his chin as he looked at the telephone. Why the American Club? And there was something else: despite the breeziness, he'd detected just the faintest hint of underlying strain in Pete's voice.

The smartly uniformed US Marine guard at the club entrance the next day had been briefed to expect him. A quick check of his name on a list, a cursory glance at his ID, and Raman's car was waved through. Ordering Bahram to stay near the parked car, Raman made his way into the large, comfortably furnished bar. Peering over the heads of the seated crowd of Americans relaxing after tennis or swimming, Raman made out the figure of Pete talking to someone whose back was to him. Iranians were prohibited from joining the club, so Raman was conscious of a few raised eyebrows and whispered comment as he responded to Pete's wave and made his way between the tables.

Raman could now see that sitting in one of the chairs opposite Pete was Charles Stanley. Raman was only mildly surprised. He knew the CIA and MI6 collaborated closely.

Although far less extensive than before WWII, Raman also knew from his time in the Special Intelligence Bureau that MI6 still ran an effective network of informers in most of Iran's major cities. The Shah had overruled Savak objections to the British activities because he found their reports useful as means of checking the information he received from his compatriots.

'Join me in a beer?' invited Pete after Raman had eased himself into a deeply-cushioned wicker chair.

'No thank you. Just a coffee, please.' Raman had no difficulty in concealing his irritation at the Englishman's presence and Pete's choice of the American Club.

Raman liked Pete. He knew that the tough, nuggety man had seen active service with the US Air Force in Vietnam, before being snapped up by the CIA because of his guided missile knowledge. Raman shared Pete's military taste for straight talking and decisive action. He was not too sure about Charles though. He knew the Englishman had been talent spotted at university and had joined MI6 soon after graduation. Charles spoke fluent Farsi with only a trace of a foreign accent. Despite his reputation for being bright, Raman found the Englishman's air of civilian, almost academic, detachment grated on him. And he was still smarting from Charles's warning not to go ahead with the Paris assassination.

Getting straight to the point, the American looked at Raman and asked: 'Colonel, what's your assessment of the current situation in the country?'

Sipping his hot coffee, Raman eyed both men cagily: 'Why ask me?' he shrugged, 'you both know that I work on overseas missions.'

Raman paused and then looked at Pete: 'Why are we meeting here? And why is Charles here? You didn't mention him.'

Pete replied soothingly but with no embarrassment: 'I suggested the American Club because nobody would know you here. And I asked Charles to join us because I thought his views on the security situation would be of great interest to you.'

Pete stopped and looked briefly at Charles, who was puffing on a cigarette. 'Look Raman, both Charles and I think the security situation in the country is deteriorating more quickly than we expected.'

The American exchanged glances with the Englishman and took a sip from his beer. Pete chose his next words carefully: 'We are becoming increasingly alarmed that there might be a serious threat to the Shah's government.' Pete put the palm of his hand up politely, but firmly, to forestall Raman. 'Please listen first to what Charles has to say.'

Charles stubbed his cigarette out and coughed nervously. 'Colonel Raman,' he began formally, 'the revolutionary movement to overthrow the Shah and install an Islamic republic, headed by Ayatollah Khomeini, has reached a critical mass. Without prompt action there is a high chance that an attempt at armed revolution will take place. Furthermore, I believe a small number of senior officers in the army and air force and, yes, even Savak, are helping the revolutionary movement, if only to cover their backsides.'

Seeing no obvious reaction on Raman's face, Charles continued: 'I suspect, for example, that my intelligence reports are being kept from the Shah. The dossiers which the Shah is reading are too optimistic and incorrectly suggest the situation is under complete control.'

Shocked by the allegation that Savak contained traitors, it took all of Raman's training and experience to keep his face emotionless. To give himself more time to digest Charles's words he repeated to the two foreigners: 'Why are you telling me this? Internal security is not my responsibility.'

Charles coughed nervously again and looked at his American colleague. Pete waited for a few seconds, took another sip from his beer and leaned forward. Staring intently into Raman's eyes Pete spoke softly but clearly: 'That's precisely the point Raman. We want you reassigned to a senior position in internal security. Not a desk job but a hands-on role eliminating the revolutionaries. But before we can propose this to your senior officers and the Shah we wanted to be certain you'd agree.'

There was a hush while Raman considered Pete's proposition.

Charles interrupted: 'Here look at this. It's a summary of American and British intelligence.' He handed Raman a slim black dossier.

Pete gulped a mouthful of beer: 'Take your time. We know what we've said takes some thinking about.'

The American and Englishman studied Raman closely as he lent back in his chair with the dossier on his lap, coolly lit a cigarette and asked for another coffee. 'Espresso this time, please.'

Raman crossed one leg over the other and began to read while Pete and Charles admired his calm under pressure. Charles's forehead by contrast, Raman had noted, had a small bead of sweat, despite the club's air conditioning.

This was the first time Charles had actively meddled in Iran's security affairs without London's prior authorisation. Pete had persuaded the Englishman to meet Raman. 'Charles, your intel matches ours. The Shah risks going down the pan unless he starts to hit back hard. And soon.'

Charles had nodded in agreement.

'If the Shah gets the chop my career will be on the skids. And it won't do yours much good either,' Pete had warned.

'Raman is the best guy they've got,' Pete pressed on. 'He's young and ruthlessly ambitious. Look how he ignored your warning not to bump off the guy in Paris. He knows some of his top brass have grown soft and fat on the Shah's coat tails. Once we get him back here on active duty I'll work on the Shah through the Ambassador to promote Raman even more, perhaps even to take over command of Savak.'

Behind his impassive face, Raman's brain was churning furiously as he read Charles's report and sipped his espresso. Only the other day he'd asked a colleague he knew well, about the riots he heard about in Isfahan. He'd been reassured that everything was 'completely under control'. Was this colleague one of the traitors?

Charles's dossier was convincing, very convincing. Raman knew better than to ask for detailed substantiation of its allegations. The two foreigners would not dare risk compromising their relationship by trying to bluff a senior Iranian security officer.

Raman looked up and, taking a moment of abstract reflection, looked around the lounge at the gathered Americans. Most were casually-dressed, fit-looking officers and their predominately blonde, sun-tanned wives. They oozed self-confidence and a feeling of permanence as they drank, gossiped and flirted.

'Tell me, Pete, it wasn't too long ago that the CIA produced a report which said the Shah was safe for at least another ten years?' Raman asked pointedly. Pete returned Raman's gaze with obvious embarrassment. 'You're right, of course.' The American cleared his throat and said defensively: 'But see here Raman, our HQ decided I was too close to the situation. They wanted fresh eyes to take a look so they flew in some analysts from the States. They were god-damn sharp but new to the country. Well, you read what they wrote. It lulled me too into thinking that the situation wasn't that bad,' he finished red-faced.

Raman grimaced inwardly, remembering a time when he thought America was infallible. He too had taken the CIA report at face value.

The evidence in Charles's file was conclusive: Raman was convinced the worsening situation demanded people like him capable of cracking down hard. His knuckles clenched around the dossier. 'Yes gentlemen, if my superior officers order my transfer, I will obey with pleasure and help crush the Shah's enemies.'

Chapter 27

'I felt ashamed to be an Iranian,' said Major Aryanpur, our landlord, who lived with his family on the ground floor of our apartment block.

Steve, who was shortly leaving the country, had invited the major up one Friday afternoon to our flat on the top floor to meet me and Jilly, and have a chat about Iran. Although I had seen the major coming and going a couple of times, out of a window, we'd never actually been close enough to exchange words.

'Remember James, I told you on the plane coming back from Isfahan that I knew someone who might tell you what was going on in this country?'

I was surprised that the person Steve had in mind was our landlord. Now the major sat opposite me sipping an orange juice. He cut a distinguished looking figure with his swept-back, full head of grey hair, clipped moustache and his erect, military bearing. I thought he looked like a British officer in a war film, acting along with David Niven, or another star from that era. I guessed he was in his early 50s but looked younger.

'When I was studying at the Pakistani Army's staff college, everyone else's country had a proper president or a prime minister. What did we have? A Shah who wore silly costumes and called himself Shah-en-Shah the king of kings! Bah! As if anyone in the West was impressed!'

Major Aryanpur was a conscientious Muslim, which is why he had refused my offer of a glass of Château Sardasht, one of the better Iranian wines. Otherwise he and his family appeared completely Westernised. His wife, who was always dressed well but modestly, worked as a doctor in one of Tehran's hospitals, and his son was studying engineering at an American college.

It was no surprise to learn that Major Aryanpur's views had landed him in trouble. He said someone had reported him to the secret police. 'Have you heard of Savak, James?'

He saw from my face I had.

'Well you know already that they are not very nice people. They have killed and tortured many Iranians.'

After a spell in an army jail, where he made it clear that he would not bend his views to swear absolute allegiance to the Shah, he had been court-martialled.

'Fortunately I had some powerful friends who made sure I wasn't treated too badly by Savak and I was released. Of course I have to be very careful about what I say in public, or I might be arrested again because the government is very frightened at the moment by the people who are opposed to it. But I don't mind telling you English people in my house what I know and believe about my country.'

'I've heard stories about bombs and protests against the government. Particularly from Navid, Steve's dry cleaner. Are they true?' I asked him in a light-hearted way, as if I expected anything Navid said should be taken with a pinch of salt.

'Indeed, James, some are true,' replied the major solemnly. 'There is much bad feeling in the country Of course there are many exaggerated stories because the newspapers cannot print the truth. In several large provincial cities there have been demonstrations. Many people have been killed by the army and police.'

'Why are people against the Shah?' interrupted Jilly, 'He's done so much. He's built roads, bridges, airports and schools.'

'That is right Jilly, but our people are disgusted by how much money his family and friends are stealing from our country. You all remember when the price of oil went up suddenly in 1973?'

'How can we forget? We could only work three days a week in England,' said Jilly with a snort.

The major glanced briefly at her and continued: 'For us it meant our country was suddenly getting a fair price for our oil. And the money poured in as quickly as the oil poured out. But not always into the right pockets.'

The major looked at us in turn: 'Do you know that about a third of our oil income is being spent on weapons and planes? Why? We don't need that many. Meanwhile the poor leave the countryside and move to the cities where they live in slums.' The major's voice turned harsh: 'He is trampling on our culture and history, trying to force us into his dream of becoming like the United States. And we feel ashamed that we are an ally of the main supporter of Israel.'

'I never understand why you people here are so anti-Israel,' said Jilly, blithely oblivious to Steve's eyes rolling upwards at her use of the patronising 'you people'. 'After all it's the only democracy in the Middle East. Well it is, isn't it?' she said defiantly, suddenly noticing Steve's face and the major's sudden look of disapproval.

'Of course it's a democracy, but that doesn't make what it is doing right,' said the major brusquely. 'Would you like it if the Danes suddenly said they had a God-given right to England because the Vikings used to rule it nearly two thousand years ago? And they suddenly started to pour into your country in their hundreds of thousands and squeezed you English out? No, of course you wouldn't.'

'Well if you put it like that, I suppose I wouldn't,' said Jilly, flustered by the major's directness. 'But that doesn't excuse the PLO killing innocent people and blowing up planes.'

'No, nothing can excuse that,' agreed the major. 'But just try and remember what the French felt like when Germany occupied their country. Or the Irish still do.' The major sighed as Jilly obviously didn't agree with his analogy. 'Look, I know it's difficult. Let me give you an example: I have a friend. He's a Palestinian, a Christian, in fact. He works here in Tehran as an accountant. He and his family had to leave their home in Jaffa to get work. You know the Israelis have a law that if a Palestinian leaves Israel, he can't come back? His home has been requisitioned and now an Israeli family live in it. He even knows their names. He still has the key to the front door and dreams of returning.' The major paused: 'Do you know what he's told me what his son has done?'

No one answered.

'His son has joined the PLO because he believes that talking to Israelis is a waste of time. The boy says they only understand force. His father has tried to persuade him to leave the PLO but the boy refuses. Now my friend is terrified that his son will get killed.'

The major addressed them solemnly: 'You must understand that we Muslims regard ourselves as like one family. Yes, we fight with each other, but if an outsider attacks one of us, he attacks all of us. That's why there will never be peace in the Middle East until the Palestinians get their country back.'

'OK, I can understand your feelings about Israel, but I really wanted to know more about the Shah and what's happening here,' I said gently breaking the major's train of thought.

The major nodded: 'Where was I? Ah yes: the Shah wants us to copy the example of Turkey where Attaturk managed to make his country more Western very quickly. But we are not Turkey. It will not be quick here. Thanks be to Allah, our Shia religion is too strong.'

'Who are the Shah's main enemies?' I asked.

'There are many. Liberals, socialists and communists. Some live in exile in London and Paris. Others in Syria and Iraq. But the most powerful are the mullahs.'

'Who do you support, Major?'

There was silence. I realised I had asked a question which might be too dangerous to answer.

'I'm sorry. I shouldn't have asked that,' I said clumsily.

Filling the awkward silence, Jilly asked sulkily: 'How can people support the mullahs? They just want to take your country back to the middle ages.'

'You're right that some mullahs are backward, Jilly,' said the major. 'Many of our young teachers, doctors, and students do not agree with their conservative views. But if you are an engineer or technician and you earn a good salary of, say, £20,000 a year, it doesn't count for much if £19,000 goes on rent in Tehran. And it makes it worse if your landlord is the Shah's sister. Remember all revolutions occur when the middle class feel they have nothing to lose. Another reason why many people support the mullahs is that they offer a vision of Iran which is not corrupt.'

There was a hush as we three tried to digest what the major had said. Was he really implying that there was going to be a revolution here in Iran?

'I can see that I've worried you. Well don't be. Whatever happens here will not be dangerous for foreigners,' he said with a calm certainty.

'What is the Shah doing about the mullahs?' I asked.

'There's not much he can do now, James. He made a silly mistake by kidnapping their leader and dumping him over the Turkish border. Even the Shah was too scared to murder him. But now he's free to say what he wants because the Iraqis like him to make mischief.'

'Oh, what's his name?' Jilly asked.

'He's called Khomeini. More and more people support him because the mullahs repeat his words every Friday in the mosques and also give out tape recordings of his sermons.'

'Don't the army and air force support the Shah?' Steve asked.

'They do at the moment. But I think the younger officers are fed up with him and the older ones, who I know, feel that change is coming.'

There was one more question I wanted to put to the major: 'Is the Shah developing nuclear weapons and is the UK helping him?'

'Why do you ask?' the major said warily.

'Steve and I ran into some Australians near Zahedan, about a month ago, who were prospecting for uranium down there. They reckoned the Shah wants to have an A-bomb.'

'Well, you know you British are helping us build an atomic power station in Bushir, that's a city south of here, near the coast?' asked the major. I nodded. 'We need nuclear power for when our oil eventually runs out,' the major explained. 'But it is also true the Shah and the army want nuclear weapons. Building the power station will help us develop nuclear weapons. And why not?' the major said, shrugging his shoulders. 'Pakistan has them. Israel has them and could destroy us inside ten minutes. Iraq is developing them and Saddam Hussein wants our oil. Whoever rules Iran will want nuclear weapons to guarantee our safety,' he ended defiantly.

'You've heard of the expression Mutually Assured Destruction, MAD, haven't you Major?' I asked alarmed, the frightening image of a puritanical mullah's finger on a nuclear trigger in my mind.

'No, I haven't but I think it's very funny and, how do you say, very apposite.'

Major Aryanpur stood up to go: 'It was nice to meet you. I have said enough. Now I have some other things to do. Thank you for inviting me. It was nice to meet you James. And you too, Jilly. Please don't be alarmed by anything I've said. Whatever happens here you will not come to any harm. You have my word.'

I shook his hand: 'Thank you Major. What you said was very interesting. I think I have a better idea now of what is going in your country. By the way, you're the second Iranian officer who I've met recently.'

'Oh, who was the other one?'

'His name was Zaberani. I thought he seemed very young to be a colonel. He's a tall, tough-looking guy. I met him at a British Embassy party. Do you know him?'

The major breathed deeply inwards and braced his shoulders. His hand involuntarily gripped mine tightly and he looked intensely and suspiciously into my eyes: 'No, I don't know him personally. But I have heard of him. He..um,' but he didn't finish his sentence.

There was another embarrassing silence as we realised the major had become very uncomfortable again.

Jilly came to the rescue: 'James knew his wife in London when he was a student. And I teach his sons,' she said lightly. 'Quite a coincidence, isn't it?'

'Yes, quite a coincidence,' repeated the major in a low voice as I opened the front door for him to leave.

'I don't think he likes Colonel Zaberani,' I said to Steve and Jilly, as I swung the door closed.

Major Aryanpur stood for a few seconds in the hall outside Steve and James's flat worrying that he had said too much. He had been shaken to hear that two of the young English people had met one of Savak's most dangerous and hated officers. But going back over what he had said to them, he couldn't think of anything which was too incriminating, even if by some remote possibility they were to have a political discussion with Raman Zaberani.

Glancing out of the hall window on his way to the stairs, he saw a car parked in the space normally used by one of the neighbours. Weekend visitors, nothing unusual about that, he thought as he walked down the steps to his family's ground floor flat, his fingers drumming on the banisters. But there was something odd about the car which niggled his brain. The major couldn't quite put his finger on what it was.

Jilly left soon after the major. As she stepped gingerly out of the front door onto the pavement's cracked paving slabs, she got a strong feeling she was being watched. She shivered as she got goose bumps down her back, stopped and looked up and down the street, but saw nothing unusual or untoward: just parked cars in the quiet tree-lined, suburban side street.

Sitting in a car, watching Jilly leave the flat, Raman asked the junior Savak officer sitting next to him: 'Who is she?'

'Miss Jilly Martin. A teacher at the International School. Her boyfriend is an engineer, James Harding, designing the new port down in Chahbahar. He rents the flat on the top floor from Aryanpur,' replied his colleague, pleased he could reply promptly to his new boss.

Raman chuckled under his breath at the irony. He had finally seen his sons' teacher. Shahnaz would be pleased.

His team had been watching Major Aryanpur's house for a month now, since one of their double agents had tipped them off that Aryanpur was getting suspicious visitors from Syria. Raman had been surprised because, checking the file, Aryanpur had kept resolutely away from all political activity since his conditional release by Savak more than ten years ago. Why would he risk being arrested again?

Something was clearly afoot, thought Raman. He had joined his team watching Aryanpur's house about an hour ago because Friday afternoon, after prayers at the mosque, seemed to be the most likely time for the major to get visitors. So far today, however, they had only seen the British tenants and their friends come and go.

The two Savak officers were sitting in a nondescript, scruffy Iranian-made Hillman car, just like many of the thousands of others in Tehran. To the casual observer, like Jilly Martin, the car wouldn't have been worth a second glance. Keener eyes, however, would have noticed that the car's windows were tinted, completely shielding its occupants from view, and its wide tyres looked more suited to a high-performance auto, something very odd for such a cheap, basic car.

Looking at the car again through a window in his flat, Major Aryanpur now noticed the unusual windows and tyres and guessed correctly who was watching. He made a couple of carefully-coded, warning telephone calls. He would get no visitors today and, in future, they would have to be more careful. Savak had obviously become suspicious.

But it's too late, you bastards. You can't stop us now, the major thought as he smiled with grim satisfaction.

Chapter 28

'No, don't do that! You must go first, not her. Oh you English! You're always polite to the wrong people,' Jilly's headmistress, Mrs Abid, clucked in mock admonishment as I paused to let her maidservant go first through the garden gate.

'I'm sorry,' I replied, embarrassed.

'Don't worry. It's just that you don't understand our people like we do,' she added. By 'we' Mrs Abid obviously meant wealthy Iranians, just like her.

'You see, James, our people regard politeness like that as a weakness. Our masses are simple and easily swayed. You must have seen those hysterical men, backs and faces covered in blood, whipping themselves half-dead during Ashura (the Shia Muslims' day of mourning for the death of Hussein, their leader who died in 680 trying to seize the leadership of Islam). In my country, the men can be more emotional than the women.'

No, I didn't really see, I thought to myself. To me, this attractive middle-aged woman's views on her compatriots were like those of how I imagined her Russian bourgeois counterpart would have been, just before the communist revolution.

Since our disturbing conversation with Major Aryanpur I had become much more observant of the social undercurrents swirling around me in Tehran. But I kept my thoughts to myself as I followed her and Jilly through the garden gate and up the winding path towards the brightly lit house within a stone's throw of the Shah's palace. I nodded at the maid, in her black uniform and white apron, as she stood aside to let me pass, her eyes obediently downcast.

The maid followed on respectfully behind our small group, keeping a distance between herself and her mistress and foreign guests.

Not long after the embassy party, Jilly had invited me to go with her to her school's headmistress - she also owned the school - annual party for her mainly European staff and class mothers: ladies who represented the parents. The party was held around about every Christmas but was definitely not called a Christmas party, to avoid Muslim sensitivities.

I was in two minds but Jilly had said: 'Mrs Zaberani will probably be there. She's one of my class mums.' Jilly observed with some amusement my mixed emotions. 'Come on James, I can see it on your face. You must have had strong feelings for her

104

when you were a student. And I reckon you still fancy her, don't you?'

'Don't be silly. She's married with kids. I got over her long ago,' I replied in what I hoped was a convincing voice.

'Well anyway, the party's good fun,' Jilly said coaxingly.

So I went with Jilly to her school party even though I had half-expected to be bored. But the fact that Shahnaz might be there changed things. Yes, I did want to see Shahnaz again. Jilly was right.

When we had left the embassy party my thoughts had been in a whirl. Seeing Shahnaz again had sparked off half-forgotten buried feelings and memories of those emotionally-charged few months and climatic parting in London over ten years ago.

Now here I was, a still-young early thirty-something who had drifted from one relationship to another in the intervening years. Sure, all the girls had been nice and we'd enjoyed some fun times, but they all sensed over time, as Jilly was now sensing, that I was emotionally-detached. Was Shahnaz the reason I reflected, or was that just the way I was?

I had been stunned by Shahnaz's appearance at the embassy party. Her sleek, well-coiffured hair, expensive jewellery, and elegant silk dress were at complete odds with my recollection of her in a mini-skirt, beads and kaftan.

I felt confused: I remembered my intense feelings for the old Shahnaz, but I wasn't sure what my feelings for the new model were. But I clearly felt something and it was certainly not emotionally-detached, otherwise I wouldn't be getting so worked up about her, I reasoned.

I wondered whether Shahnaz's emotions were also in turmoil now that we had met again? Highly unlikely, I thought. She probably remembered me as that nice boy from her young, carefree days in London, which she had now consigned to history.

'Yes, James had been sweet, but we were so young then. He was just part of growing up,' I imagined her dismissing me softly to her reflection in her make up mirror. I realised that I needed to know what the family crisis had been which had stopped her coming back to London. I had to know, otherwise I would never be able to put Shahnaz behind me.

'James, hello James, earth to James, come in please!'

'What? Er, sorry, Jilly I was miles away. I don't know why. I was suddenly thinking about a problem at work.'

'Hmm..,' said Jilly looking at me doubtfully. 'Well for God's sake cheer up! You've been weird ever since I took you to that embassy party and you met Mrs Zaberani. I really am beginning to think you're pining for her!'

'Don't be silly, I've told you I was just surprised to see her again. Her brother was a very good friend of mine and seeing her brought back all sorts of memories.'

'Well, take this and come and chat to my friends,' Jilly said, handing me a beer and leading me over to a chatting and laughing group of her fellow teachers.

It was no good: I tried to be sociable and friendly with Jilly's friends and make small talk, laugh at their jokes, and contribute to conversation. But I couldn't stop myself from looking around to check any woman arriving at the party to see if she was Shahnaz.

I drifted in and out of conversations as if I were on autopilot. I found myself talking to an Iranian woman, who had asked me to call her Lila. She was the other mother of Jilly's class. It turned out Lila had been at boarding school in England and had fond memories of her time there.

'There is nothing like a British public school education,' she opined in a cut glass English accent, with only the faintest foreign trace, 'I was miserable at first. Oh God, how I hated my parents for sending me away to this miserable, wet country and its ghastly food - but once I made friends they really were the best years of my life.'

'Oh, I'm so glad,' I replied politely, faintly annoyed that this foreigner's English made me self-conscious of my flat London vowels.

'Yes, my husband went to boarding school in England as well. Our six-year old boy is already down for Eton,' Lila continued casually, blowing cigarette smoke, with well practised ease, away from my face. 'He'll be leaving the International School to go to a prep school in England in another two years.'

Poor little sod, I thought. Being forced into a school at that age in a foreign country is going to be tough. He's bound to be teased about his brown skin and foreign accent. Still, she'd probably survived a similar experience I thought, and now look at her, oozing self-confidence and part of an international elite.

'So, you're Miss Martin's boyfriend, I hear?' she fished.

'Well, we're good friends,' I replied cautiously.

'She's an excellent teacher. My boy loves her. Did you know her before you came to Iran?'

'No, we met here at the British Club.'

'Ah, you English, you always club together. You should get out and experience Iran. Get to know my people with all their faults and good points.'

'I think that's a bit unfair. I've only been here six months and I've already been to Isfahan and taken the bus from Zahedan to Chahbahar. I bet you haven't done that!' I retorted, faintly annoyed that she'd assumed I was just another Brit happy to be cocooned in the company of fellow expats.

'No, you're right. Wild horses couldn't drag me onto the Chahbahar bus!' she chuckled, looking more closely at me, heavy gold bracelets glinting and clinking on her wrist.

'Maybe I have misjudged you. Are you really interested in learning something about Iran?'

I nodded.

'Well then, why don't you learn Farsi?' she asked, cocking her head to one side, as if the thought had suddenly crossed her mind. I didn't know what to reply to this. I had thought of it too but had been put off by the need to learn Arabic script. I also hadn't been able find any public courses. Because expensive private tutoring seemed the only option, I'd dropped the idea.

'I don't suppose you know any German?' she went on.

'As it happens, I do. I used to work in Switzerland and I speak it well. Why do you ask?'

'Well, well, a German-speaking Englishman, that is unusual,' she replied patronisingly. 'You should get in touch with a friend of mine, Mrs Kashani. She teaches Farsi for foreigners at the German embassy. The class is in German, of course. I know her next one starts in a couple of weeks. It's very popular with Germans so you'll need to call their embassy quickly to register.'

Learning Farsi in German? Well why not? I thought.

I then noticed out of the corner of my eye Jilly and her friends make way to allow a late-arriving guest to pass. Although my view was obscured, I could see Jilly saying hello in the way teachers do to parents, half friendly, half professional.

The woman turned to move on and I now could see Shahnaz's profile. As she walked towards the hostess I became aware of a frisson of excitement among the other Iranian women in the room. I'd noticed something similar at the British embassy and had put it down to men's admiration and women's jealousy of a head-turning, beautiful woman.

107

But I was wrong. It must have been something different. It must have been what I was now sensing: an air of fascinated, almost tangible, fear of Shahnaz. Women surreptitiously turned their shoulders and averted their gaze but kept glancing at her sideways. What was going on? I wondered.

'I guess you know my fellow class mother, Mrs Zaberani,?' I was conscious that I had rudely broken off my conversation with Lila and must have been guilty of staring at Shahnaz.

'Yes, vaguely. I was at university with her brother in London. I met her a couple of times. You must be a friend of hers?'

'We've been friends since we were little girls. Even when I was at boarding school we kept up and spent holidays together. When I left school I wanted to join her in London but my father wasn't as liberal as hers. How I envied her freedom and the things she told me she got up to. Are you sure you didn't know her well?'

'Yes,' I lied. 'Why?'

'It's only because when she came back to Tehran and got engaged she asked me to post a letter on my next trip to London. It was to an English boy she was very fond of. She'd told me that he was at university with her brother. I can only remember his first name on the envelope. Now what was it?' she asked, cupping her chin with her hand. I could see she remembered perfectly. 'Ah yes, James, that was it. Your name's James, isn't it?'

I felt my face redden as I admitted awkwardly: 'Yes, er, yes, my name's James. But it's a common name, you know. There were other Jameses in our class. I wonder which one he was?' I finished unconvincingly.

'Yes, I wonder too,' she agreed knowingly.

Oh shit! I swore silently to myself. First Jilly and now this bloody woman suspects that there's something between Shahnaz and me.

By now Shahnaz had excused herself from the circle around the headmistress and was sauntering, drink in hand, towards Lila and me. Again I became aware of the half-concealed hostile looks coming Shahnaz's way from some people.

What was that all about, I thought, as I said to Lila with forced jocularity: 'Well, perhaps we can ask Shahnaz who this James was.'

Chapter 29

Shahnaz had seen James across the room immediately she entered. Like James she'd been in two minds whether or not to come to the party. But in the end, she gave in to her desire to see James again. Nobody will suspect anything if they see us talking, she thought. After all he's the boyfriend of my children's teacher, isn't he? Besides there really wasn't anything to suspect was there, she reassured herself, as she looked across the room.

She'd have a chat with James, explain why she had left London so abruptly and give him an edited version of why she'd married so quickly. And that will be that, won't it? 'Oh why does everything have a question mark at the end?' she muttered miserably to herself as she approached Jilly and her group of friends.

'I'm sorry, Mrs Zaberani, I couldn't quite hear you,' said Jilly cheerfully over the hubbub of conversation.

'Oh, I was just thinking aloud Miss Martin. Nothing important,' replied Shahnaz smiling and shrugging her shoulders.

Shahnaz exchanged brief pleasantries with Jilly and the other young teachers around her before turning away to join the circle of senior teachers and other class mothers chatting to the headmistress.

'How nice to see you, Mrs Abid,' Shahnaz greeted the headmistress in English.

'Thank you for coming, Mrs Zaberani,' replied the headmistress carefully in a neutral voice. Shahnaz joined the group's discussion about school matters for a measured five minutes or so before plausibly excusing herself to go and talk to her fellow class mother, Lila.

Shahnaz took a glass of wine from a passing waiter. She needed another drink to steady her nerves before she spoke to James. What was Lila saying to him? She worried.

She'd long ago confided to Lila, when she returned to Tehran, that she had fallen in love with an English boy. She'd got Lila to post her last letter to James in London - she didn't want her brother to see who it was for - once she realised she had to marry Raman. Now, as she walked over to join James and Lila, she realised there was a lump in her throat and her hand was trembling.

I watched Shahnaz over the rim of my glass as she walked towards Lila and me. I tilted my glass further up to hide any tell-tale expression from Lila and carried on looking at Shahnaz.

Through the bottom of my glass my gaze focussed on Shahnaz like a microscope, to the exclusion of everyone else in the room.

She looked even more like Sophia Loren than I remembered, now that she was a mature woman who knew how to dress and make herself up to accentuate her natural good looks. Motherhood had not damaged her figure. In fact she was slimmer and had that added lustre many women acquire from the feeling of self-fulfilment that bearing children brings.

Suddenly, I realised with a feeling of trepidation, that I was within a hair's breadth of falling in love with her again. And how stupidly futile that would be. She was a mother of two kids and happily married to a high-flying army officer. Reciprocating my feelings would be out of the question.

Lila and Shahnaz kissed each other with genuine affection and spent a few minutes chatting quickly in Farsi, now and then looking sideways at me.

'I'm sorry James, but Shahnaz and I don't see much of each other and have a lot to catch up on.'

'Oh, I'm sorry. Shall I leave you two alone?'

'No, no,' Lila shook her head determinedly. 'I must circulate. I'll be back in a minute or two,' she said looking intently at Shahnaz and leaving an awkward silence behind.

'It's nice to see you again, Shahnaz,' I said, sipping my empty glass desperately trying to plug the gap.

Shahnaz looked at me, her eyes strained. She paused, as if deciding to say something important. 'James, we only have a few moments before people will start to gossip about us. I feel I owe you an explanation.'

She rushed on as if she were worried that if she paused she might never continue: 'When I came back to Tehran, my uncle had been arrested on a political charge by the state security. He was in prison and our family was terrified we might never see him again.'

'You mean he'd been arrested by Savak?' I said anxious to display my knowledge of her country.

'You know about Savak?' she frowned.

'Yes, all us foreigners hear about it sooner or later,' I said matter of factly.

She nodded as she digested my words. I could see she was debating with herself how best to go on.

She took a deep breath: 'We knew my uncle was in great danger but it was impossible to contact him. Luckily the son of one of my father's friends was a junior officer in the Imperial Guard

110

working at the Shah's palace. He intervened, at great risk to himself, on my uncle's behalf and managed to get him released - eventually. My uncle only had to pay a fine. Far worse could have happened.'

'That young officer must have been a brave man. I've heard Savak can be ruthless.'

To my surprise Shahnaz winced at my words but then admitted, with odd reluctance in her voice: 'Yes James, he was brave.'

I nodded, mesmerised by her face, which was now an undulating sea of conflicting emotions. Shahnaz glanced around furtively but could detect no unusual interest in the two of us talking by ourselves.

'After my uncle was released my father was reminded of the great debt he owed to his friend's family.' Shahnaz fell silent.

'Er, yes,' I observed hesitatingly, unsure where this was leading.

Shahnaz lowered her eyes: 'My father's friend proposed a marriage between me and his son.' She paused, giving me a moment to understand what she had said.

'What, and you had no choice in the matter?' I demanded furiously. 'What about that crap you told me about not always doing what your father said,' I hissed, remembering her flashing eyes proudly declaring her independence in London.

'No, of course not James. I *had* a choice! But I could not dishonour my father and our family.'

Her voice faltered and I could see tears beginning to well up in her upturned eyes pleading with me for some compassion.

I immediately felt ashamed at upsetting her: 'Oh Shahnaz. I'm so sorry. It's just that I was so badly hurt by you. I really did love you. I think I still do. Oh shit!' I realised what I had just said. 'Forget that please,' I pleaded shaking my head in exasperation with myself. 'I just couldn't understand why you left me so suddenly.'

'No, of course not. How could you understand?' she said with a suppressed sob, as a tiny tear trickled down her cheek.

Well-manicured nails gripped my elbow tightly before I could reach out and hug her. 'That would be very, very unwise, James,' said Lila, who rattled off something in Farsi as she calmly handed Shahnaz a handkerchief with her free hand. Shahnaz quickly dabbed her eyes and composed herself. She walked slowly off in the direction of the ladies' restroom, her shoulders slumped dejectedly.

111

Lila turned to me: 'So you *were* her James. I knew it. Listen,' she said urgently, 'what happened between you and Shahnaz in London was a long time ago. And it's over now, do you understand?'

'Of course. I had no intention of upsetting her. She's explained what happened and that's an end of the matter. I've met her husband and he came across as a pretty tough guy. I can imagine him standing up to Savak.'

'You've met Shahnaz's husband?' asked Lila, guardedly inspecting my face.

'Yes, at a British embassy party. He's an important colonel now in an organisation like our secret service, I think someone told me,' conscious I was gabbling, as I tried to collect my own thoughts.

My words hung in the air between us. Then the implication of what I'd just said hit me hard.

'Oh my god! He's not just any colonel in the army any more, is he? He's a colonel in Savak now, isn't he?' I pressed Lila, incredulously.

She didn't reply. She didn't have to. I saw scared confirmation in her eyes.

I pushed on recklessly: 'And that's why you don't see Shahnaz very often? Of course: and that's why you Iranians stare at her after she's gone past. You're scared of her husband.'

'James, it's better not to discuss these things, not even among your English friends. Savak has ears and eyes everywhere,' Lila said quietly.

'He's hardly likely to touch me is he? And why would he?' I blustered, ignoring the frisson of fear I felt.

'Look, you bloody, fucking idiot,' she fumed with heavy sarcasm: 'This is not jolly England, old chap! This is Iran. Funny things can happen to people here. I heard what you said to Shahnaz, you fool. If her husband suspects that you love his wife, he might react badly and harm you and Shahnaz. So keep your mouth shut about this.' She motioned with her arm to include the conversation I'd just had with Shahnaz.

Startled at her vehemence, I gabbled: 'Yes, don't worry, I won't say a word,' as I saw Shahnaz walking back towards us.

Shahnaz had repaired her face, which, apart from slightly red eyes, now showed no trace of tears. She exchanged quick anxious words in Farsi with Lila who was clearly dictating strong advice. Shahnaz nodded, head down submissively.

Looking up she swivelled around to me and said stiltingly: 'James I hope you understand now what happened since we last saw each other. I think it might be best if we didn't speak again.'

'Of course, Shahnaz. I'm so sorry if I distressed you.'

'It doesn't matter. It was lovely to see you again. I wish you success with your work in Iran,' she said formally in a distant voice. She kissed Lila and hugged her tightly and then shook my hand.

'Goodbye, Shahnaz. Take care,' I said unhappily.

Our eyes crossed only for the briefest second before she walked away. I watched her thank our hostess and say a few polite words to Jilly on her way out. As Shahnaz moved on, Jilly threw me a meaningful look as if to say: 'Ah ha, I thought so,' but I quickly averted my gaze and pretended I hadn't seen her.

I knew that Shahnaz now realised I was still in love with her. But I had also recognised the look in her eyes when we'd shook hands a moment ago: it was the same mix of longing and the misery of forced separation that I'd seen all those years ago in the London taxi outside the *Windsor Castle* pub. I suddenly knew with wild elation tempered by sad hopelessness: Shahnaz still loved me too.

Chapter 30

'The *Shahnama* - the *Book of Kings* - consists of 62 stories, 990 chapters, and 60,000 rhyming couplets. It is more than seven times the length of Homer's Iliad and was written by our greatest poet, Abu'l Qasim Ferdowsi, over a period of several years. He finished it in the early eleventh century of the Western calendar. It is our national epic and a classic of world literature.' Our Farsi teacher, Mrs Kashani, had started her lessons in the German embassy by proudly placing her language's greatest work in its historical context.

I had decided to follow Lila's advice and throw myself wholeheartedly into studying Farsi as a means of getting Shahnaz out of my mind. Most evenings, when not working late, or learning the Arabic script, I played squash or watched TV. I saw far less of Jilly.

She accused me of becoming like a lovesick teenager: 'It's no use denying it James. I saw the way you and Mrs Zabrani were talking and looking at each other. She looked as though she'd been crying too. You must have upset her,' she said in the accusing tones of that universal union of women united against insensitive men.

'Well, you can moon around pining for her by yourself, you idiot.' With that she had dumped me in a cheerful jolly-hockey-sticks sort of way which fortunately meant we still remained friends. We both knew that acrimony would have been difficult in our small expat community.

'Ferdowsi is more important to us than Goethe to the Germans, or Shakespeare to the English,' Mrs Kashani continued, reading from her notes. 'English has changed a lot since Shakespeare but modern Persian, or Farsi, is more or less the same language that Ferdowsi used nearly a thousand years ago mainly because of the legacy of his *Shahnama*.

'Ach, I don't believe he can be better than Goethe,' whispered Helmut in my ear.

I had been startled to see Helmut again when I had registered for the Farsi classes. Learning Farsi would not have been high on my list of Helmut's things to do, or so I had thought. But, over the coming weeks, Helmut surprised me even more with how quickly he learnt the language. He was far quicker and better than me, I had to admit ruefully.

114

'You want to know why my Farsi's better than yours?' he proudly asked me one evening with a twinkle in his eye. I half guessed the reason but nonetheless accepted his invitation to dinner at his flat after class.

Which is why I was not too surprised to find the door of Helmut's flat flung open dramatically by a woman with out stretched arms. She looked well into her 50s, despite a figure-hugging top and skirt, heavily made up face, and more gold bracelets than her plump arms could bear.

'Mutton dressed up as lamb', unkindly sprang to my mind.

'James, this is Tara. She is my Persian girl,' he exclaimed proudly. 'She is my little secret to learning Farsi so quickly.'

Tara put her arms around me enthusiastically and hugged me to her ample bosom. 'Hello James. Helmut has told me how you first became friends on the plane to Tehran. And how lovely it was to meet again at Farsi lessons.'

With Helmut beaming in the backdground already pouring me a large glass of beer, I nodded uneasily: 'Yes, it's nice to meet up again. We'd lost touch. I've spent a lot of time out of Tehran,' I lied smoothly, I hoped.

After a couple of drinks we sat down to eat the tasty Iranian food on the table. Helmut explained that he had met Tara at work. Although her family had lived in Iran for several generations, she still considered herself Armenian. She was also a Christian and, I was intrigued to find out, there were no restrictions placed on her orthodox religion by the Islamic state, provided no attempts were made to convert other Iranians.

Helmut had met Tara at work where she was a secretary. Her husband had apparantly died in a traffic accident some years ago. She had two grown up children. Tara had been delighted when Helmut had shown an interest in her – the chances of finding another Armenian husband had been next to nothing.

After a whirlwind romance, Tara had readily agreed to move into Helmut's flat, despite scandalising her family and other members of her conservative religion.

'We plan to get married, but there's no hurry. We'll wait until I take Tara with me on my next holiday in Germany,' Helmut said proudly while Tara looked at him adoringly. This was a different Helmut from the one of our first acquaintance. He was clearly a reformed man: he sipped rather than guzzled his beer; talk of brothels in South Tehran was clearly off limits; and the double chin had nearly gone, despite Tara's excellent cooking.

'When will that be?' I asked politely.

'Oh, probably in another six months. We had hoped it would be sooner but there are problems at work which I need to sort out.'

Helmut worked for a company which supplied food processing equipment. They had half a dozen contracts scattered around Iran, installing equipment in cheese and biscuit making plants. But over the last few months Helmut's fellow German technicians had started to resign and not return from their regular holidays.

'Why, what's happened? Why aren't your people coming back?'

'They are scared by the riots and violence they are seeing,' replied Helmut gloomly, squinting and swirling his beer around, as if the solution to his worries might be hiding at the bottom of his glass.

'Whereabouts do you mean?' I asked. Helmut named Shiraz, Isfahan and Arak, the three provincial cities where his company was working. Apparantly there had been disturbances in all of them.

In some cases he'd heard from his colleagues that the police and army had opened fire, killing and wounding people. 'If what I've heard is only half-true, the army has only made it worse,' said Helmut. 'I hear the demonstrations are getting bigger. I'm also getting worried that the trouble will start here in Tehran, as well.'

'What do the demonstraters want?' I asked, knowing the reason but wanting confirmation from the only Iranian present.

'They want the Shah to leave,' Tara said increduously. She shook her head in disbelief: 'All my life the Shah has ruled this country. At school we were taught about how wonderful he was. How Iran owed all its wealth to his great leadership. Only after school I realised that he ruled the country like a dictator: nothing happens here without his permission. And now people are openly demanding that he go?' she almost whispered. 'Forgive me, James, but I find it incredible. And very scary.'

'Why scary?'

'Because, if the Shah goes, who knows what will follow?'

Tara swallowed her drink and Helmut said quietly to no one in particular, 'Didn't de Gaulle say: "Après moi, le déluge"? '

'No, I think it was Louis XV. But who cares,' I grinned, trying not to sound superior.

Tara laughed: 'Yes, who cares? Let's enjoy life and not worry about things we can't change.'

The fact that Helmut's colleagues were refusing to come back to Iran alarmed me. Was the situation in the country outside Tehran really that bad? I was unsettled enough to refuse Tara's offer of coffee and left their flat so deep in thought that I nearly walked into the back of a large truck as I turned a corner. Lined up in front of me, their wheels on the pavement, were about ten large army lorries, their engines growling and exhaust fumes rising gently into the cold night. As I passed them, I glanced inside. I could just make out the pale faces of tense young troops, conscripts judging by their youth and the palpable sense of fear they exuded. The dim light from the street lights glinted off new helmets and rifle barrels and highlighted scared darting eyes.

A hand grabbed my shoulder roughly and shoved me away, shouting something aggressively in Farsi. I caught some of it, ordering me to move on quickly. I turned to the strained face of a young officer, hand on his holster, scarcely older than the boys in the trucks. In my fractured Farsi I apologised.

'You American?' he asked, his face relieved when he realised I was not a threat.

'No, English.'

'No good you here,' he waved his arm around. 'Go home,' he ordered. 'No safe you here.'

'What's happening?'

'Bad people come. Make trouble. You go home now!' he said pushing me again, in case I failed to get the message, his other hand now gripping his pistol butt.

'OK, OK, I'm going,' I said, raising my hands, anxious to pacify him.

I walked briskly on past the trucks, keen to get away from someone who looked as though he might panic at any moment and start wildly shooting around. At the top of the lane I looked back. The trucks were still parked, smoke gently puffing out of their exhausts, while the young officer agitatedly paced up and down, his hot, nervous breath caught in the pale street light.

I shivered apprehensively. Were these 'bad people' the start of the trouble in Tehran, which Helmut had foreshadowed earlier on that evening?

Chapter 31

Helmut put the telephone down with a sigh and rubbed his forehead to ease his headache. His colleague, Gustav, in Arak had joined the other rats leaving the ship and just given in his notice to quit.

'Look Helmut, things down here are getting worse. If you don't believe me come down and see for yourself!'

Gustav would leave in a couple of weeks, barely long enough for Helmut to arrange for some sort of handover to their local partners. God knew what the financial consequences would be of this latest example of his firm breaking its contract, Helmut thought miserably. Even worse, what would their boss back in Frankfurt say? Gustav was their manager and last man in Arak; his departure would cause serious difficulties and might jeopardise their most lucrative operation in Iran.

'OK, I'll drive down as soon as I can and sort out things before you go,' Helmut had agreed reluctantly.

The meeting with their Iranian partners had been tense and bad-tempered. Helmut's company had not yet fully completed installing some food processing equipment and the Iranians had demanded to know when Gustav's replacement would be arriving. Helmut had to admit he had no idea.

'Once the political situation becomes better,' was all he could say, weakly, in the face of fierce threats of legal action by the Iranians against the German firm. The Iranians had dismissed Gustav's fears about security: 'We have had political problems before. The Shah will crack down and arrest the ringleaders and things will get back to normal. The Americans will never let the Shah fall. You'll see,' one of them had said confidently while his colleagues all nodded in agreement.

'That may be but I don't want to hang around waiting for the Shah to sort this mess out,' Gustav had retorted. The meeting had broken up in disarray with no agreement on how to proceed.

'Look at the problems you're causing,' Helmut had said to Gustav afterwards in a vain attempt to change his colleague's mind. The two Germans had driven into the city centre to have lunch at a restaurant, which Gustav knew well.

'Helmut, I'm sorry but I'm getting scared. The other day a group of "Beards",' - as Gustav called the Muslim protesters - 'spat at me and shouted, "death to America" as I was shopping.'

118

'Are we safe here then?' Helmut asked nervously, about to pop a forkful of lamb kebab in his mouth, as he looked around the restaurant. All seemed calm and the other diners seemed prosperous and respectable Iranian businessmen.

'Yes, we're in the city centre,' replied Gustav calmly. 'All the trouble's been around the governor's office and police HQ on the edge of town.' The two Germans munched quietly on their rice and kebabs. And then, as if on cue, they began to hear a background murmur, like a faulty air conditioning unit at first, which slowly grew into a sound more like a football crowd in the distance.

'I thought you said it was safe here, Gustav?'

'Well it has been so far,' replied Gustav apologetically.

The restaurant fell quiet: the waiters stopped and joined all the diners in listening intently, ears cocked and eyes exchanging worried looks. Suddenly everyone jumped, startled by the piercing ring of a telephone on the head waiter's desk. The head waiter exchanged quick anxious words with the caller and fumbled as he over-hastily replaced the receiver. He barked out orders to the waiters and tried to answer the anxious Iranian diners' questions, which they were firing at him. The restaurant's waiters moved quickly. Windows were closed and all beer and wine disappeared from the tables into cupboards. Some diners left hurriedly and those who stayed now spoke in subdued tones, some of them clearly worried by Helmut and Gustav's presence.

'Please you go, sir. Now.' The head waiter had come up to their table. It was not a request, rather an instruction.

'But why?' asked Helmut. 'What have we done?'

'Go, sir. Bad if you stay here,' the man gabbled, his brow perspiring in fear.

'But we haven't paid,' protested Gustav, standing up.

'Does not matter. Go, sir. Now,' the waiter repeated, tugging on their arms, gently at first, then more urgently.

'Come on Gustav, let's go,' Helmut said, picking up his jacket and headed for the front door.

The two men left reluctantly. Behind them the restaurant's door was slammed shut and bolted.

Arak's main street seemed deserted. In the direction of their parked car, the sound of a large chanting crowd in the distance was becoming louder by the minute. By now they could hear distinctly slogans orchestrated by loud speakers and repeated in a roar from thousands of men's throats: 'Bad, bad America!'; 'Death to the Shah!'; and above all in Arabic, the Latin of Islam: *'Allah o akbar'*

119

Two police cars came suddenly into view around the bend, veering wildly, seemingly in a panic retreat from the demonstration.

'Sheise, it's too risky to head for the car,' said Helmut, stating the obvious.

The two men turned to head off, away from the threat of the approaching noise but their progress along the pavement was halted as a long line of soldiers, stretched from side to side of the road, marched slowly towards them, rifles and fixed bayonets at the ready. They were trapped. Officers shouted orders to the troops above the noise of the approaching crowd. A helicopter swept low above the soldiers and arced away around the corner in the direction of the demonstration; both Germans shivered as an enormous roar of hate and defiance greeted it and reverberated around them down the street.

Helmut and Gustav looked around for shelter from the inevitable and imminent clash. Noticing a small gap between buildings they scurried down a narrow alley but ran up against a mud brick wall topped by barbed wire; they were trapped in a dead-end.

The two men crouched behind some bags of rubbish, shaking in fear as the crowd's noise rose to a crescendo echoing off the buildings and rattling windows. The demonstration had now reached as far as the entrance of the alley and had stopped in the road. Peeping around the rubbish bags, Helmut could see a loud hailer-carrying Beard, framed by the alley walls to look like a Che Guevara poster, at the front of the crowd, shouting in the direction of the troops, his magnified words drowned out by the whirling blades of the helicopter, now hovering about a hundred feet directly above. It seemed to be a stand off between the army and protesters.

In the helicopter above Helmut and Gustav, Raman sat next to the pilot directing the army and police below. As he had planned, a rapid retreat by the police had enticed the demonstrators into marching along the wide main avenue in the misplaced confidence that the army would not shoot such a large number of people. Raman spoke on the radio to the army commander on the ground. Looking down carefully at the leader of the demonstration, he gave precise instructions.

The Beard leading the protest march turned to his followers, shouted into his loud hailer and waved his arm forwards. The demonstration obeyed his direction and started surging slowly towards the troops. Helmut trembled, sensing what was coming next. Tapping Gustav on the shoulder to follow, they crept under a large steel refuse cart parked next to the alley wall and dragged some rubbish bags and cardboard around them, so they were completely concealed.

Like firecrackers, volleys of rifle fire echoed off the alley walls followed shortly by the screams and groans of the wounded and dying. The demonstration stopped in its tracks and people fled away from the soldiers who began to chase after their leaders. The Beard with the loud hailer strapped across his chest sprinted into the alley and stopped, breathing heavily, as he saw the dead end. He turned quickly around but it was too late. Two soldiers and a civilian, who had been chasing the man now appeared, walking calmly towards him as they realised they had their prey trapped. The man stepped sideways, his back firmly pressed against the side of the rubbish cart and his dirty, threadbare shoes within a foot of Helmut's face.

Helmut heard the man plead for mercy but the civilian cut him short, laughing cruelly. The man began to pray, his voice quivering in fear. Helmut involuntarily wrinkled his nose as he smelt urine trickling down inside the man's trouser legs onto his shoes a few inches from Helmut's face. Two pistol shots echoed around the alley walls and the man slammed against the rubbish cart and slid down its side to the ground. Satisfied their quarry was dead, the three men walked out of the alley, chuckling with satisfaction of a job well done. Helmut thought he heard the soldiers call the civilian by a name: Bahram.

Helmut and Gustav lay there for at least another hour under the cart behind the rubbish bags, now sticky with half-congealed blood, which had seeped out from the victim. After the firing had ceased and the helicopter had disappeared, they could hear the noise of what they thought were ambulances arriving and people being carried away on stretchers. But no one appeared down the alley to recover the corpse next to the cart.

Once Helmut decided it was quiet and safe to move, the two men slid out from under the cart and stood up. Helmut had long composed himself but Gustav, a much younger man with no experience of violence, was still shaking.

'Come on Gustav, pull yourself together. There's no danger now,' Helmut said soothingly, putting an arm around Gustav and preventing him from looking at the fractured skull and debris of brains, which had slid down the side of the cart onto the puppet-like corpse lying on alley floor. Gustav's reaction reminded

Helmut of some of his long-ago World War II comrades after their first experience of enemy fire.

The two men walked slowly out of the alley and onto the pavement next to the road. Strewn in front of them was the detritus of a crowd of people, which has fled in panic from a perilous threat. Caps, shoes, and banners were scattered at random between dried pools of blood. Bloody footprints and marks, where bodies had been dragged away, provided ample evidence of the massacre which had taken place. But no bodies were to be seen. All had been removed while Helmut and Gustav had hidden in the alley.

The two men walked carefully along the road in the direction of Gustav's car. They took in the smashed shop windows, broken furniture and burnt out police cars, still smouldering. Everything was eerily quiet. 'I told you that it was dangerous here,' whispered Gustav exhaustedly.

'Come with me back to Germany, Helmut,' Gustav had urged afterwards. 'There's nothing here to keep you. The project's finished. Things can only get worse.'

Helmut had shaken his head and waved Gustav goodbye at Tehran airport: 'No, there's too much to do first. I'll have to negotiate a financial settlement with our partners; close the office; and pay off my flat's landlord. That sort of thing.'

Helmut didn't mention Tara to Gustav. The younger German would have been surprised. Helmut was well known for his drunken visits to Tehran's fleshpots. Gustav would also have been more than surprised to discover that Helmut was in love for the first time in his life.

On the drive back from Arak with Gustav, Helmut had been chewing the matter over in his logical mind. He loved Tara. That was for sure. They should get married and live in Germany. As a boy he'd seen the same fanatical determination on Nazi brown shirts as he'd glimpsed on some of the faces of the demonstrators. He was now convinced the Shah would fall. Iran was finished for foreigners like him, at least for a long time. So why not leave now? Tara had already agreed to come to Germany on a holiday. If they were married it would make it easier with the Iranian and German authorities, he reasoned to himself.

Tara had been overjoyed at Helmut's proposal but was dismayed at the prospect of leaving her family so soon to live in Germany. She was sceptical that the Shah's regime was really threatened. Despite his vivid description of what he'd seen in Arak she tried to reassure him: 'Helmut, we've seen this before. Riots

122

and demonstrations and killings. The Shah always wins. The Americans won't let him lose.'

Tara's family were adamant that the riots were only a temporary phenomenon. 'The Shah is impregnable,' Tara's father added.

'Anyway, I don't have a passport Tara had added. 'I will need one to get married and leave the country. It will take at least six months before I can get one.'

Helmut had to agree she needed a passport. And Tara promised once she had one, they'd get married and go on a holiday to Germany. Helmut was satisfied for now. Once in Germany he was confident he would be able to persuade her to stay. As his wife, it should be easy to get German citizenship for her.

Chapter 32

Raman was not surprised when he was called to a meeting with the head of Savak at the Shah's palace. The general operated out of an office situated close to the Shah. Raman was ushered swiftly to a large heavily oak-panelled boardroom, and gasped inwardly as he recognised the two men sitting at the head of the table. The general, of course, but next to him, the Shah en Shah, the King of Kings, self-styled saviour of Iran.

Raman saluted formally and stood to attention. He was not, however, unduly nervous. On the contrary, he assumed that the reason for the Shah's attendance would be favourable for him. After all, the only other times he'd met the Shah had been for promotion, or the award of a medal.

The Shah motioned for Raman to sit alongside him. As Raman pulled out a chair he was able to see the Shah's face close up. He was shocked. Since Raman had last seen him, about a year ago, the absolute monarch and dictator had aged ten years. Worry lines creased his forehead and heavy bags hung under his eyes. His hair was a dank grey and so was his pallor. Raman knew instantly that the rumours of the Shah's ill health were well founded.

The general cleared his throat and began hesitantly: 'Thank you for coming, Colonel Raman. We want to discuss your next assignment.'

There was a poignant silence as the general stopped. Raman looked awkwardly at his superior officer. What was he supposed to say? The general coughed again. 'You did well in Paris and your excellent work in Arak has not gone unnoticed.'

Again there was silence. Raman was aware that the Shah was watching him closely, scrutinising his face as the general expressed his compliments.

'I have tried to do my duty, Sir,' Raman responded steadily, looking at his superior officer straight in the eye.

Raman was surprised to see that the general could not hold his gaze. He noticed that the general's body language was wrong. Gone was the arrogant bravado, the puffed-out chest and the expansive arm movements. The man was nervous, even a bit scared, Raman realised.

The Shah now interrupted. 'Colonel Raman, what is your opinion of the current situation here in our country?'

'Your Majesty, we are facing major political disturbances stirred up by your enemies abroad,' started Raman slowly and guardedly, parroting what the Shah himself said in his public speeches.

The Shah shook his head impatiently: 'Colonel Raman, you may speak freely. I am your commanding officer. With immediate effect I am taking personal control of state security.'

Raman could not prevent himself; he drew a sharp intake of breath and looked at the general again, but the man once again could not look him in the eye as his shoulders slumped in tired resignation.

'Colonel Raman, nobody outside this room is to know of this change in command. The general will continue to attend his office but will, in fact, act only as an adviser to me. Is that clear?'

'Yes, your Majesty.'

'As your direct superior officer, I command you to answer my question properly. What is your opinion of the situation in my country?'

Raman cleared his throat. 'Your Majesty, over the last six months your enemies abroad have become more directly and openly involved in the detailed planning and organisation of demonstrations and the open resistance we are now seeing here in the country. They started operations in our major regional cities and became emboldened by their success. They are now planning demonstrations in Tehran.

But what is unusual in the current situation is that increasingly most of your 'liberal' enemies are cooperating with the religious opposition. To judge by what I have seen, I suspect also that former army officers are involved in the organisation.'

'Who are the dissidents?'

'As I'm sure your Majesty knows,' said Raman before he reeled off the names of well-known dissident liberals and religious leaders.

'And your assessment of the threat to my leadership?'

'Your Majesty, it is difficult for me to reply. I do not have enough detailed knowledge of the overall situation in the whole country.'

'Nonetheless, from what you know, what would you do?' asked the Shah, staring intently at Raman.

'Your Majesty, I suspect we have given your enemies enough rope. I would start eliminating them in much the same way we eliminated your enemy in Paris.'

The Shah glanced at the general. 'You see, General, Colonel Raman agrees with me. We have been too soft. We need to strike, and strike hard.'

The Shah waited for the general to reply. The now former head of Savak said: 'Colonel Raman, your analysis is correct. We are confronted by a coalition of enemies and old rivals who are collaborating for the first time. Which is why the situation poses a greater threat to his Majesty than ever before.'

This time Raman interrupted, 'So why do we not strike? Eliminate the leaders one by one. We can make them talk and the movement will be broken.'

The general looked at Raman and then at the Shah, who nodded.

'Colonel Raman, what I am to say must go no further.'

'Of course, sir.'

The general sighed, 'President Carter has gone soft on us. Yes, he supports his Majesty in public, but the CIA has placed limits. They have ordered us not to eliminate the opposition, particularly Ayatollah Khomeini, their figurehead.'

'Surely we can find ways of making accidents happen,' said Raman softly.

'Yes, we know you did well in Paris, but it might be difficult to explain if another six leaders were to fall under a train,' the general added patiently with gentle irony.

Raman had to acknowledge this, but asked, 'Why are the Americans stopping us?'

'We think they are trying to hedge their bets, just in case Khomeini and his rabble succeed.'

'But that's crazy!' Raman burst out. 'The mullahs hate the Americans. They might take any help they can, but return favours? Pah! Never!'

The Shah and the general nodded together in agreement with Raman.

Raman asked the general, 'Why don't you instruct Savak to start a discreet round-up of the second tier of leadership?'

The general looked at the Shah who slowly nodded his head again, to allow the general to say: 'Colonel Raman, I am ashamed to admit that Savak has been penetrated by the Shah's enemies. Even up to the level of Colonel and maybe even some of my personal guards.'

Raman pretended to look aghast. The general had merely confirmed what he already knew from Pete Barbowski and Charles Stanley.

The Shah broke in again. 'Colonel Raman, I have invited you here today to appoint you in charge of Iran's internal security. You will have the honorary rank of full general and report directly to me. As I said, the general here,' the Shah gestured dismissively towards the other officer, 'will continue to act merely as an advisor. But it is to me you report. Do you understand?'

There was dead silence. Raman could see the general was a broken man. The Shah had clearly lost confidence in his ability. Raman took a few more seconds to digest the Shah's words. In effect, Raman was now in charge of the Savak. And he was only thirty-five. He looked straight at the Shah, and didn't hesitate.

'Yes, your Majesty. It will be an honour to serve you and defeat your enemies.'

Raman had quickly weighed up the pros and cons of his new role: promotion and power against increased personal danger to him and his family. And what if the Shah fell? Unlikely, reasoned Raman. He considered himself ruthless and clever enough to crush any opposition, despite any constraints placed by the Americans. Yes, it would be a calculated gamble, but one he was prepared to take.

Chapter 33

Shahnaz was becoming increasingly worried. At first she had noticed a trickle of children leaving the twins' class. But then the trickle turned to a steady stream of one or two departures a week. Knowing she was unlikely to get a straight answer from her fellow Iranian mothers, she turned to the teacher instead: 'Miss Martin, why are so many children leaving the school?'

Miss Martin had frowned in surprised at her question, as if Shahnaz ought to know the answer. 'Their parents are worried about the political situation, Mrs Zaberani. Many of the children who have gone have English mothers. Their husbands want to send them away to England, because it's safer.'

'But we've had political problems before in Iran. Are you sure that's the real reason?'

'Well, that's what they tell me, Mrs Zaberani,' Miss Martin had said cautiously.

Shahnaz had shaken her head doubtfully as she politely said goodbye to Jilly. On the spur of the moment, she surprised herself by asking: 'Miss Martin, do you know if James Harding is still in Tehran?'

Startled, Jilly replied: 'Yes, he is,' Jilly paused and, looking inquisitively at Shahnaz, said, 'I think he's staying on because his company is owed money by the government.'

Shahnaz thought for a second. 'Please tell him I said hello.'

'I will, Mrs Zaberani.'

An awkward silence now hung heavy between the women. Both knew that Shahnaz's request was unusual. In essence she had declared an interest in James, which was extra-marital.

Shahnaz turned away but not without Jilly catching a glimmer in the other woman's eye of happiness, swiftly clouded by sorrow.

Poor woman, thought Jilly. Poor James too, she added quietly to herself.

In the car home Shahnaz's thoughts returned uneasily to the unsatisfactory conversation she'd had with Raman a couple of months previously. Raman had reassured her vehemently, when she'd said she was worried about the big anti-Shah protest demonstrations in Tehran.

'Look Shahnaz, I've already told your father and uncle there's nothing to worry about,' he'd said impatiently.

'My father and uncle asked you about this? When?' Shahnaz had asked, surprised to hear for the first time that her father and uncle had visited her home, something which they rarely did, especially together, except for special occasions like the twins' birthday, or the end of Ramadan.

'Yes. About six months ago. They're both a couple of old fools! I sent them packing. I told them that the Shah and America would never, in a thousand years, hand this country over to some silly old men with beards and turbans!'

Shahnaz had thought for some time afterwards about the conversation. Perhaps Raman was right: her father and uncle, now well into their sixties, were a bit too old now and prone to anxiety? After all, Raman worked for Savak and ought to know the real situation in Iran.

But she had, come to mention it, detected a faint undercurrent of uncertainty in Raman's cutting words, something which she'd dismissed at the time. Nervously tapping her fingers on the armrest, she caught the driver's eye in his mirror.

Swallowing her dislike of the man, she tried to be pleasant as she asked: 'Bahram, a lot of parents are taking their children out of the school. Have you heard anything about this?'

'What do you mean, Madam?' the driver replied guardedly.

Shahnaz sighed wearily to herself and raised her eyes upwards, recognising the familiar, centuries-old tone of the Iranian servant, wary of giving an answer disagreeable to his or her master. 'Haven't you talked to the other drivers about the school parents who are leaving our country?'

'No Madam,' he replied, hastily looking away as Shahnaz stared at him in the mirror.

Shahnaz snorted in disbelief. She knew he was lying.

'Take me to my parents' house,' she directed sharply to the back of Bahram's head, not bothering to hide her annoyance, irritably adjusting her skirt and drumming her finger nails on her handbag.

'Yes, Madam,' the driver nodded, his voice carefully flat and devoid of emotion, but his eyes, now out of Shahnaz's sight, flashed in alarm and his chunky fingers clenched the steering wheel tightly.

The big car purred through the gate in the old brown brick wall around the Mostashari family's villa and came to a stop in front of the house. Shahnaz waited until Bahram opened the door for her and then got out and looked around at the familiar old house with its rose garden and ornamental fountain to one side.

Whenever she returned home her memories of a happy childhood playing in the house and sunny garden would flood back. She savoured the moment briefly and then walked up the steps into the house, curtly ordering Bahram to wait.

The driver watched the curve of her bottom swaying unselfconsciously in its tight, fashionable skirt, up the steps and disappear into the house.

'You bitch,' he thought. 'One day; yes, one day soon, I'll teach you not to look down on me.'

Not for the first time he fantasised what it would be like to take Shahnaz. His fingers clenched his worry beads as he tried to dismiss unclean thoughts from his mind of Shahnaz enticingly in bed stripped down to her expensive French underwear. Oh how he hated her and her godless Western ways, which tempted good Muslims like him. He turned away in self-disgust as his genitals stirred involuntarily, his resolve to punish Shahnaz in the name of Allah only strengthened.

Unaware of the sexual turmoil behind her, Shahnaz entered her parents' house where Aled promptly apologised that he had not had time enough to greet her at the door.

'Don't worry, Aled. Where are my father and mother?' The servant hesitated a fraction. 'Your mother is in the living room reading, Miss. I'll show you in.'

Shahnaz noticed he had unusually not mentioned where his master was. Frowning slightly she followed the old servant as he opened the door into the living room and announced Shahnaz's arrival to her mother.

'Shahnaz, my darling. What a lovely surprise. Why didn't you tell me you were coming? I would have arranged for some lunch for us,' said her mother with arms spread wide open in welcome.

Something was not quite right, thought Shahnaz. Her mother was more demonstrative than usual; her greeting failed to disguise the hint of concern in her voice; and her hug was just a bit tighter than normal.

'I'm sorry to surprise you, mother. I wanted a word with Baba. Where is he?'

Shahnaz looked around the room, furnished with restrained good taste, so unlike the homes of Tehran's nouveaux riches and their ostentatious luxury, which she dutifully visited as Raman's wife.

'At work I suppose,' said Shahnaz answering her own question. 'I'm sorry. Perhaps I should have rung first. No matter, I'll stay for

130

lunch, if I may,' said Shahnaz, knowing her father invariably had lunch at home, followed by a nap before returning to his office.

'He won't be coming, Shahnaz,' her mother said nervously, wringing a small handkerchief she often carried stuffed up her sleeve – her propensity to sniffles was a standing joke in the family.

'He's all right?' gasped Shahnaz, suddenly worried that her father was ill or in danger.

'Oh yes, he's fine,' her mother clucked reassuringly as she patted the sofa next to her: 'Sit down, my dear. I need to tell you where he is.'

The two women sat facing each other silently. Shahnaz realised that her mother was struggling to say something important and was finding it difficult to find the right words.

'Mother what is it? You say Baba is safe but now can't tell me?' she chided gently.

The older woman looked at her daughter: 'Shahnaz, Baba has left the country. He may not return for a long while.'

'But why, mother? He is in no danger, you say?'

'Yes, that's right. But your father, Uncle Faris and Mohammed are busy investing our family money in London and Los Angeles. You know that Mohammed has already been there for months?'

Shahnaz nodded and her mother continued: 'Well, he has been busy looking for opportunities. Now your father has gone to join him and taken most of our money out of the country.'

Shahnaz sat quietly trying to absorb what her mother had just told her. 'But why didn't you tell me that Baba was going away? I don't understand.'

Her mother chose her words carefully and replied slowly: 'Shahnaz, your father's business has done very well over the last couple of years.'

'Yes, I know. Everyone knows that,' Shahnaz shrugged. 'But why didn't you tell me Baba was going abroad?'

'Do you know why the business has been so successful recently?'

Shahnaz thought for a moment. She knew that her father had always had a reputation as an honest man who did good work. She'd always assumed that this was the reason why his business had done so well.

Looking at Shahnaz's puzzled face, her mother went on: 'It was your brother who first noticed it. We were invited to bid for projects bigger than we had ever done before. And then we started

131

to win them, too many of them. At first Mohammed thought it was luck, or just because of the building boom. Then Mohammed was told the reason.'

Shahnaz sat silently looking nonplussed at her mother. She'd had no idea that her mother had such an interest and grasp of her father's commercial life. Her mother smiled, enjoying her daughter's surprise despite the gravity of what she now had to say: 'Mohammed was told it was because of Raman's position that we were getting these contracts.'

'I don't understand, Mother. How? Why?'

'You know Raman is in Savak,' her mother said looking sharply at her daughter.

There was a silence. Shahnaz had never discussed Raman's job with her mother before. She nodded and asked haltingly: 'Yes; you mean that's why Baba's company is doing so well?'

Shahnaz's mother looked steadily at her daughter and took her hand: 'It's common knowledge that your father gave Raman ten percent of our company as part of your dowry.'

'Yes, I know,' replied Shahnaz, 'but he's not that high up in Savak, is he? I mean, he's only a junior colonel, isn't he? There must be many other colonels in Savak?'

'Shahnaz, my dear, you really don't know that Raman is being spoken openly of as the next head of Savak? In fact he might already be in command. No one knows what his real rank is. There are rumours that the Shah himself has given him a special secret rank, perhaps as high as a general.'

'Oh,' said Shahnaz weakly, gathering her thoughts miserably.

Her mother continued: 'There is even talk that he was personally responsible for the assassination of a man in Paris. If the Shah is overthrown it could be very dangerous for anyone connected to Raman. That's why your father is trying to get as much of our money out of Iran now. We could not tell you because you might let something slip to Raman.'

There was hushed silence in the room as Shahnaz stared miserably at her mother. 'Does Baba really believe the Shah will fall?'

'Yes, my darling daughter, he really does.'

'But mother, what about me and my boys?'

'Mohammed is returning soon to watch out for you in case the situation becomes really bad. He'll look after you if you need help.'

Shahnaz sat with her head bowed. She was too proud to let her mother see how upset she was and scared of what the future might bring.

Chapter 34

'James, I'm really scared,' said Jilly in a shaking voice, standing miserably in front of me. 'Could I spend the night here, please?'

Tehran had witnessed some of the biggest peaceful demonstrations the world had seen since Ghandi's India. Over a million people had been at today's march along one of the main city thoroughfares, all chanting for the Shah to leave the country.

And once again there was another power cut by the city's striking electricity workers which would pitch the big city into complete darkness, come nightfall. The smutty joke among British expats confined by curfew to their homes in the dark was that there was: 'Fuck all to do'.

Every evening there were sounds of chanting from rooftops and random gunfire. The security situation was deteriorating by the day. And yet, away from the demonstrations, by day life continued normally among expats. I went to work and Jilly taught at her school.

'Of course you can,' I replied giving Jilly a hug.

'It's the power cuts. I get scared in the dark by myself.'

Jilly's flatmate had not returned from holiday in England and Jilly was now convinced she would never be coming back.

'Nearly half my class has disappeared, you know, James. Nearly all my mums who are married to Iranians have flown to London.' Jilly seemed less scared now that I had sat her down and handed her a stiff gin and tonic and a bowl of her favourite pistachio nuts. 'Even my Iranian mothers are looking very apprehensive. I spoke to your Mrs Zaberani the other day. She looked incredibly stressed as though the poor dear hadn't slept for days.'

I let Jilly's remark about 'your Mrs Zaberani' pass with only a fleeting look of exasperation on my face.

'You know, she asked about you, James.'

'Oh yes?' I responded as casually as I could.

'Yes, I was surprised too,' Jilly said sarcastically, disbelievingly dismissing my lack of interest by raising her eyebrows and tucking her feet comfortably underneath her on the sofa. 'She's never acknowledged to me before that she knew you.'

'Well what did she say, Jilly?' This time I couldn't keep a note of impatience out of my voice.

'Hang on, hang on, lover boy,' said Jilly, teasingly sipping her drink, splitting a pistachio shell, and accurately flicking the nut into her mouth. 'Gosh, that's a good gin and tonic, James. You do have your uses!'

'Come on, Jilly, what did she say?' I prodded.

'Well, it's no big deal, James. She just wanted to know if you were still in Tehran.'

'And what did you say?'

'I just said you were still here because your firm wanted you to stay as long as possible. To make sure they still got paid the money owed to them by the government.'

Yes, that was certainly true. I had floated the idea to my boss, Tim, of my return to London once the trouble had started in Tehran. However, in answer to his concern about my safety, I had confirmed that I felt safe, explaining that, like the troubles in Belfast, Northern Ireland, provided you kept out of certain parts of the city there seemed to be no danger.

Many other expatriates took the same view as me. Jilly was a good example and there were several other teachers, accountants and nurses who I knew were also staying. I had even heard about a couple of ski-crazy Scots, who swore the slopes in the Alborz mountains were the best in the world, and were determined to stay as long as the pistes remained open.

Perhaps we Brits were more sanguine about civil disturbances having long been targets of the IRA. I could tell Tim was relieved that I would stay by the way he had asked me to try as strongly as possible to get the government to pay their outstanding invoices.

'And she didn't say any more?' I pressed Jilly.

'Funnily enough, she did. She asked me to say hello. Strange isn't it,' Jilly mused, 'After my headmistress's party, she pretended she didn't know you. And now suddenly she's acting as if she's known you all along.'

Yes, it was a bit odd, I admitted. I didn't tell Jilly that Shahnaz's husband worked for Savak and that might mean Shahnaz was more worried than most about the political situation. I had taken Lila's warning seriously not to talk about Savak to anyone.

'Are you going to tell me now what happened between you?' asked Jilly, clearly in the mood for gossip.

It was nearly seven o'clock and night had fallen. We were sitting by candlelight, listening to music on the BBC as we enjoyed our drinks. Anywhere else and it might have been romantic.

135

I was saved from answering Jilly's question by the noise of chanting women on the rooftop opposite my flat. Far off in the distance, Jilly and I heard the pop-pop of some gunshots.

'Come on,' I said, ignoring her question, 'Let's go and listen to the BBC News on the rooftop and see what's going on.'

Our courage fortified by alcohol, we climbed the stairs in the hallway and went out onto the flat, black roof, carefully avoiding the air conditioning units looming out of the darkness.

'*Allah o akbar,*' chanted three women in unison, swaying like ghoulish bats, shrouded in their chadors, on the edge of the flat roof of their apartment block on the other side of the road from us. I recognised their voices as those of the mother and her two teenage daughters who lived in the block of flats opposite mine.

Women who would normally dress in smart Western fashions, but had now clearly decided to cover themselves with Islamic dress as a sign of their support of the uprising. It seemed all of Tehran was on their roofs praising Allah as an act of defiance to the Shah. '*Allah o akbar*' , was being chanted on rooftops from all directions.

An army patrol passing in a Jeep below suddenly let loose some warning shots in the vague direction of my opposite neighbours who screamed in fear and pulled back hastily from the parapet, their chadors flapping and slapping against each other. The troops in the Jeep shouted a warning towards the women and sped off, as, appropriately, the BBC News's very martial-sounding signature blared from my radio.

'Allah is great' was screamed even louder from roofs in the next street, taunting and daring the troops to come down their street. The noise was deafening.

No sooner had the shots rung out, then the well-articulated vowels of the BBC newsreader calmly announced: 'Our Middle East correspondent in Beirut reports all is calm in Tehran. Recent demonstrations have passed off quietly.'

Jilly and I chuckled as we could see towards the south of the city some machine gun tracer bullets arcing through the sky like some celebratory fireworks. From every quarter we could hear the gunshots of army and police patrols warning people to stop chanting on their roofs and to go inside. 'Well, it might be peaceful in some bar in Beirut, but it's not quiet here,' Jilly observed.

'Christ, what was that,' I gasped crouching down as a fireball exploded with window-rattling force vertically into the air about a mile away on one of the main roads.

136

Machine guns rattled; tracer zoomed into the air; and a small low flying helicopter with a searchlight whooshed by overhead towards the flames. The female choir facing us screamed again and this time scuttled like cockroaches into the darkness of the stairwell leading down towards their flat.

'I think we should go inside, Jilly. It's getting too dangerous here.'

'No, let's hang on a bit,' said Jilly excitedly, shrugging my arm off her shoulder. Jilly stared towards where the fireball had exploded, her eyes popping out of her head. I was more scared than her but turned reluctantly to look as well.

Flames were still shooting up higher than the surrounding roofs and suddenly there was the staccato crackle of a machine gun from the roof of a flat less than half a mile away from us. Tracer bullets from the machine gun zipped towards the fire but their target was obscured from our view by buildings.

Through the flickering light from the flames, I could see three men crouched around a large machine gun, its barrel mounted on a tripod supported on the parapet. One was firing and the other two feeding bullets into the gun and pointing out targets.

Suddenly the machine gunners' roof was lit up even more by a bright searchlight from the helicopter, first flicking stroboscopically left and right across the machine gunners before holding them in a steady beam.

I could see the men hastily struggling to point the heavy gun barrel at the helicopter but it looked too heavy for them. There was something familiar about the one of the men but before I could think what, we heard the grinding sound of caterpillar tracks on tarmac. 'Tanks?' said Jilly.

I didn't have time to answer: there was an almighty boom and a blinding flash, followed by a whoosh, and then an ear-splitting explosion.

The helicopter's searchlight could now merely illuminate, but not penetrate, a thick, dense cloud of rising smoke and dust, which slowly lifted to reveal a spaghetti-like, twisted mess of steel roof girders, burning timber and smouldering shards of bricks. Of the three machine gunners there was no sign.

A tank now lurched around the corner into our view, smoke gently wafting from its barrel like a gigantic cigar and the head of its commander sticking out from the turret, twisting his head around this way and that, looking for other targets.

This time Jilly didn't resist when I grabbed her arm and we both scampered, crouching low with our heads below the parapet, across the roof and then down the stairs into my flat.

'My God! Did you see that, James? One moment those three guys were there. And then, bang. Nothing.'

'I know.' My voice shook as I sat down trembling next to Jilly. 'I think I knew one of them.'

Jilly turned and looked oddly me.

I cleared my suddenly dry throat: 'Yes, I think one of them was Navid, my dry cleaner. His laundry shop is on the way to my office. He was the first person in Tehran I heard tell me that things might get dangerous here.'

Raman knew that news of his promotion would soon leak out. But he was surprised when only the week after his meeting with the Shah someone tried to kill him.

The long haired young man longed to stretch his arms and legs, but he remained motionless kneeling behind a bush, peering at the large house. From a distance of about 50 yards, watching keenly over the green lawns, he could clearly see into the glass conservatory. He tensed as he saw someone enter and sit down with a cup of coffee and a cigarette.

He sighed with relief and satisfaction that his wait was now over. He could recognise the face. The information his group had received came, he had been told, from a reliable source close to the target.

The would-be assassin adjusted the focus of the telescopic lens and zoomed in, the cross hairs of his sniper's rifle firmly placed on his target's head. He fired once and the target fell. The shooter cheered inwardly in exaltation, swiftly turned and, crouching low, ran the few yards to the perimeter wall where his comrades were already waiting to help him scramble over.

'Did you kill him?' they asked as soon as they had bundled him and his rifle into the waiting car.

'Yes, I'm sure I did,' he replied triumphantly. The Party would be pleased, he thought.

'Amateurs,' Raman thought as he dived onto the conservatory floor.

They should have fired two rapid shots at him: one to break the glass, and the other to hit him. He realised almost immediately that the bullet intended for his head had been deflected by the conservatory glass.

Even so, the bullet had only just missed him: he had felt the wind as it flew past within an inch of his face. As he fell he heard the crack of a sniper's rifle followed by the noise of glass shards and splinters falling around him, and at the other end of the conservatory as the bullet exited the glass-enclosed space.

Raman knew instantly that someone had betrayed him, someone who knew that he regularly took a morning cup of coffee and a cigarette in the conservatory by himself after breakfast. His rapid suspicions were interrupted by Bahram crouching by the entrance door.

'Sir, are you all right? Did they hit you?'

'No, I'm fine. The bullet missed. What did you see?'

'Nothing, sir. I will check the garden, the bullet must have come from down near the wall.'

Raman's bodyguard scuttled off. Watching Bahram running low over the lawn towards the garden wall, Raman's eyes narrowed. Yes, Bahram was a prime suspect, he thought.

Bahram bent down by the bush and picked up a single spent cartridge. He noticed scuff marks on the nearby wall.

'Amateurs,' he thought. Perhaps he should never have passed on the information about Raman's early morning coffee. 'As regular as clockwork,' he'd assured the man, a distinguished-looking middle-aged man who looked as though he had spent time in the military.

Bahram was no fool. His lack of formal education was more than compensated for by a streetwise cunning. He sensed the time had come to hedge his bets when he had been approached.

'The Shah is doomed,' the man had said as Bahram came out of the mosque on Friday. 'We know you are in Savak and that you work for Zaberani. Tell us what we want to know about him and after the Shah has gone you will be rewarded. After all, you are a Muslim and it is your duty to fight Allah's enemies.'

So Bahram had cooperated, but he knew that Raman would now suspect him of betrayal and he would have to be very careful. Fleeing was not an option. Raman would quickly have him hunted down and tortured to find out what he knew about the people whom he had informed. Bahram turned and walked, with as much confidence as he could muster, back towards the house. He felt Raman's eyes watching him and shivered.

Major Aryanpur heard the news of the supposedly successful attempt on Raman's life with quiet satisfaction at first, but then followed by dismay as further news confirmed that Raman was unhurt.

'Amateurs,' he thought. 'We should not have passed the information on to those young hot-headed communists.'

'But if the attempt fails suspicion will not fall on us,' had been the reasoning of his colleagues. 'Let the godless communists try and kill him. In any case, after we get rid of the Shah, we will have to stamp them out too.'

The major sighed: the road to his ideal of a liberal, tolerant Islamic republic was not going to be easy, but with Allah's goodwill it would eventually be realised.

140

Shocked by the sound of the rifle shot, Shahnaz's first thoughts were for her twins' safety. It was Friday, so Fayed and Tourak were at home. She rushed into their playroom and was relieved to find them watching cartoons on the TV, oblivious to any danger.

'What is it, Mama? Why are you frightened?' the boys asked, puzzled and with some apprehension.

'It's nothing,' she lied. 'Just stay here until I tell you.'

Shahnaz waited, her arms protectively around the twins, trying to stay as calm as possible so as not to frighten them. She heard the sound of Raman and Bahram talking and Bahram going outside through the front door. After a couple of minutes she judged it safe enough to go downstairs.

Shahnaz knew it was now or never to confront Raman and demand to know the truth about his role in Savak. She found him sitting in the living room with the inevitable cigarette and sipping another cup of coffee. He looked calm and incredibly at ease, one elegant blue silk-suited leg crossed over the other.

'Raman, what happened? Are you all right?'

Raman looked at the beautiful woman asking him the questions that a dutiful wife should. He felt a momentary pang of regret that any affection they once had for each other had long gone. Nonetheless, he was grateful that she expressed concern, albeit if only out of duty.

'Thank you, I am fine. No harm was done,' he replied matter-of-factly.

'What happened, Raman?'

'Some idiots tried to kill me,' he replied, his voice dripping with contempt. 'Don't worry, I will catch them and they will regret attacking me at home and placing my family in danger.'

Shahnaz saw her opportunity: 'Raman, I wanted to speak to you about Savak and the danger to us. I want to take the boys to England until things get better here.'

Raman's face clouded. 'Out of the question,' he replied curtly.

'But why?' pleaded Shahnaz. 'Many people are leaving to stay in America or England. I am terrified that something will happen which we will regret forever. Surely you must agree that it would be safer?'

Raman drew on his cigarette. How much should he tell Shahnaz about his recent promotion? Well, she would find out soon enough, so it may as well be from him.

'Listen, Shahnaz, I have been promoted by the Shah himself,' he said with pride. 'I am now a general and in charge of Savak.'

Shahnaz's nails gripped her armchair as her worst suspicions were confirmed. 'Surely all the more reason to move the boys to safety?' she pleaded. 'You are a big target now,' she added, pointing in the direction of the conservatory.

'No, if you leave it would be taken as a sign of weakness and an admission that the Shah is not in control. In any case, with me in charge of Savak, you can be certain that the Shah will not be defeated.'

Shahnaz started to cry: not highly-charged torrents of terror, but a gentle trickle of resignation as it dawned on her that she and her boys were destined to remain in Tehran. Once again Raman felt a nostalgic twinge of affection for his distraught wife. But it was too late now.

Banishing any vestige of emotion for her out of his thoughts, he said sharply: 'Pull yourself together. As my wife you cannot afford to look afraid.'

He wheeled around and left the room without a second glance.

Shahnaz heard his car leave and slowly recovered her composure and wiped her eyes dry. She began to think. Clearly Raman truly believed the Shah would not be defeated, despite the opinion of the now fast-fleeing middle class to the contrary. What could she do? What should she do to protect her children if they remained in Tehran? Where was her brother Mo, whom her mother had promised would help her? There seemed to be no answers to her fears.

Chapter 36

Raman looked around the heavy table in the smoke-filled room, at the most senior officers of Iran's air force, police and army. They had all been summoned to an emergency cabinet meeting.

The Shah entered with his prime minister and all stood. Without any preliminaries, the Shah began: 'Gentlemen, I would welcome situation reports from you all, one by one.'

All the reports agreed that the situation was getting worse. Demonstrations were getting bigger with millions out on the streets. Soldiers and air force technicians were refusing to accept orders and were beginning to desert. Only the loyalty of the Shah's Imperial Guard could be counted on.

It was Raman's turn.

'The situation is critical,' he began. 'But Savak has started to eliminate successfully traitors within its own ranks and arrest senior army and air force officers who refuse to obey orders.'

At least the assembled generals and air force marshals had the grace to look ashamed as they heard his words, thought Raman.

'But the process has only just begun. I estimate that it will be another six months before I can neutralise or arrest all the Shah's enemies in our country. I am confident of success but I require assurances from the army, police and air force that they will hold steady and fight to retain some order on the streets.'

Raman looked at the other senior officers present. Most looked away from him, too scared to antagonise the leader of the Shah's secret police.

'Thank you, gentlemen,' replied the Shah, his voice cracking with strain. 'I have to make an important decision today. First I would like you to hear what my prime minister has to say.' The Shah motioned the head of his government to speak.

The prime minister looked at the assembled meeting and announced, so softly that everyone had to lean forward to catch his words, 'Earlier today, the American Ambassador informed me formally that because of the popular support for Khomeini, the US government can no longer support the Shah.'

The prime minister paused to allow the aghast officers to recover from the shock and his momentous words to sink in. The atmosphere became tense as the implications were digested. Some showed incipient signs of panic as foreheads began to sweat and fingers gripped pens tightly.

'The Shah would like all present to advise him whether he should stay and fight, go into temporary exile, or abdicate,' continued the prime minister, more loudly this time.

The Shah's face was impassive as all looked for signs of how they should respond. Years of acquiescence had bred a senior officer class too apprehensive to voice independent, frank opinion. With the exception of newly-promoted Raman, that was.

'Of course the Shah-en-shah should remain on the throne, with or without American support. The Yanks will return once we have re-established control and vanquished his enemies!'

Again all looked at the Shah to see how he would react to Raman's words and indicate what they, in turn, should advise. There was silence as most drew on their cigarettes and sipped tea. Finally the head of the army spoke.

'I agree with General Raman that the Shah should fight. But his Majesty should consider whether this could be best done from abroad. This would diffuse the situation and allow General Raman time to implement his plan.'

So the army thinks the Shah should go, thought Raman. He looked at the army Chief of Staff with hatred and suspicion. The man would go to the top of his list to be interrogated, he vowed.

One by one the other officers professed to agree with Raman but in reality advised the Shah to leave the country and go into 'temporary exile'.

It dawned on Raman that the most senior officers present must have got wind beforehand of the Americans' policy shift and had met amongst themselves and agreed what to say.

'Traitors,' he fumed silently.

The prime minister turned to the Shah.

'Your Majesty, the majority of advice is that you should go into temporary exile until such time as the situation recovers enough for you to return.'

The Shah swallowed. Looking straight at Raman, he said, 'General Raman, it is a pity I did not promote you earlier. If I had I would not be saying these words.'

'No, your Majesty. Do not say them! Listen to me. Let me replace these useless cowards with younger, braver men who will not hesitate to take action,' Raman shouted desperately, leaning forwards and staring straight into the Shah's eyes. Behind him Raman heard the other officers hiss their disapproval.

The police chief broke the silence: 'Your Majesty, do not heed General Raman. Neither the police, the army, nor the air force would accept new commanders at the present time. It would make the situation worse.'

The Shah looked sadly at Raman. 'General, it is a pity your courage is not shared by others.'

He looked contemptuously at the remainder of his senior officers and said haltingly: 'As of this moment I will resign the throne of Iran. I will go into temporary exile. The prime minister will also resign and hand over to his successor, whom he has already approached. General Raman will make arrangements for my safe departure along with my family. May Allah save Iran.'

Raman was shattered. His hopes and dreams of power, prestige and money were destroyed. Along with the others, he filed out silently.

'You will regret your words, young man,' said the police chief softly into Raman's ear as he passed.

Chapter 37

Bahram looked anxiously at Raman as he strode angrily out of the Shah's palace after the meeting. He knew Raman must suspect him of betrayal and with every day, following the botched assassination, his anxiety grew.

But what was the meeting, which had just taken place, about? He'd speculated with the other drivers, all of whom drove for the highest officers in the Shah's armed forces. Something very important was afoot, they'd all agreed.

Raman crisply ordered Bahram to drive him home. He glared at the back of the driver's head with the aggression of a coiled snake. He was almost certain Bahram had betrayed him but his investigating agent could not find the last piece in the jigsaw puzzle: how had Bahram actually made contact with the opposition? Raman had decided that Bahram would have to be brought in for torture and interrogation. But now events had overtaken the matter. Yes, Bahram was very lucky indeed, reflected Raman ruefully.

In the meeting Raman knew immediately he heard the name of the new prime minister that his short term future was perilous; the politician had been a friend of the man he had assassinated in Paris.

Now he would have to break the news to Shahnaz that her fears for the family's safety had been proved well-founded. He expected that he would be arrested soon after the Shah had gone but hoped that he would have enough time to organise the flight of his two boys – Shahnaz's security would have been incidental to his primary concern for his sons except, of course, she was now required as a guard for them.

'The Shah is really leaving?' gasped Shahnaz, her hand involuntarily grasping the necklace around her throat. The event which had been demanded by so many over the last year still seemed incredible to most Iranians raised on the propaganda that the Shah was an invincible father of the nation.

'Yes, he will go into exile. I am to arrange his departure for tomorrow.' Raman paused to look at Shahnaz's face and then said slowly, 'I believe I will be arrested by the new regime.'

Ignoring the look of strained amazement on Shahnaz's face, Raman continued, 'In my career at Savak I have made many enemies who will want revenge for some of the things I have had to do for the Shah. Do you understand what I am saying, Shahnaz?'

'Yes, I do, you fool!' she snapped back. 'The families of people you have tortured and killed will now want to kill you. And they will want to harm me and our sons!'

'Precisely,' conceded Raman, ignoring her taunting words. 'We must now put aside our differences and think about how you and the boys can get out of Iran.'

He stopped and suddenly opened the door. Ali was standing there with fresh coffee on a tray. His incredulous and frightened face told all: he had heard everything.

'I am sorry, Madam. You and the master were speaking so loudly. I could not help listening.'

'Don't worry, Ali,' said Shahnaz soothingly to her old servant. 'Maybe, just maybe Ali, you can be of help. Do you think my sons and I could pass as your wife and sons?' she asked on the spur of the moment. It was not uncommon for older men, particularly among the lower classes, to take much younger wives, especially those who had been left on the shelf.

Ali rubbed his chin and chewed his lip, mulling over Shahnaz's idea.

'Yes madam, it would be possible provided you wear a full chador to cover you and the boys wear much cheaper clothes. They will also need to have their hair cut off and have shaven heads, like most poor boys.'

'Thank you, Ali. Madam may be forced to pose as your wife. Please leave us now for a few minutes to discuss some other matters,' requested Raman politely.

Ali didn't know what shocked him most: the idea of his mistress acting as his wife, or Raman, for the first time, speaking politely to him. He bowed and shuffled backwards out of the room.

As soon as Ali left the room, Raman turned and took a large painting of the Shah off the living room wall. Behind it was the door of his safe, for which only he knew the combination. Quickly tapping in the code, he swung the heavy door open on its well-oiled hinges. Reaching in, he grabbed a large bulky envelope and a small wooden box.

'Shahnaz, there is $100,000 in here,' he said, placing the envelope on a coffee table near her. 'This,' he said gravely, holding the box, 'is an automatic pistol and twenty bullets.'

Raman raised a hand to cut off Shahnaz's words of refusal as she shook her head.

'Listen, Shahnaz. You might need it. Not just to protect the boys, but also for yourself. You are a beautiful woman, you understand?'

Shahnaz nodded dumbly; she understood.

Raman spent the next ten minutes teaching Shahnaz to use the empty gun. It was easy to use with the safety catch off, Shahnaz discovered, but not so easy to load. Firing it also took some practice.

'Unless your target is very close to you, aim low holding it with both hands and squeeze the trigger gently,' demonstrated Raman. Shahnaz tried and gradually got the hang of firing the empty pistol. Eventually Raman was satisfied.

'Perhaps I should have recruited you for Savak,' he said with gallows-humour.

Shahnaz glared at him. 'How can you joke at a time like this?'

Raman shrugged his shoulders. 'I have never been scared of anything in my life. For me it has always been kill or be killed. Even now, I feel no fear for myself. My only wish is for my sons to get to safety.' He paused for a moment. 'We must be prepared for when they come to take me away. Pretending to be Ali's wife is a good idea. I will simply say that you have fled to where I don't know. After that I am not sure what to do. You can't stay here as Ali's wife for more than a couple of days, without attracting attention.'

'My brother Mohammed is meant to be returning to help me,' began Shahnaz desperately. 'He's in England at the moment. I will call my mother and get him to come back quickly.'

Raman looked at her. 'So you have talked about fleeing already?'

'Yes, of course. And thank Allah I have,' she retorted.

'Shahnaz, I am not angry. In fact I'm pleased. You must have some plan?'

'Yes, I have. Or rather my brother Mohammed has.'

'Well what is it?' he asked impatiently.

'No. I am not going to tell you,' said Shahnaz defiantly. There was a pause. 'What if you are tortured?'

Raman chuckled, his gallows-humour tickled again by the ultimate irony: the torturer becomes the tortured.

'You are right,' he admitted with grudging admiration. 'But will you promise me that you will find a way of getting a message to me that you and the boys are safe?'

'Of course,' Shahnaz agreed readily.

148

'Oh, and one more thing, Shahnaz.'

'Yes?'

'Beware Bahram. I believe he betrayed me. And I have seen the way he looks at you out of the corner of his eyes. He desires you and hates you at the same time.'

Chapter 38

Tehran had held its breath as the tension mounted with daily demonstrations and defections of the Shah's supporters. Rumours swirled around the city that the Shah had abdicated. Counter rumours spread that the Americans were invading. The Israelis had taken control of the airport. The British were guarding the Shah's palace. And then the biggest, most astounding rumour of them all. The Shah had gone! 'Impossible', the city said to itself. But then it realised it was true.

State TV excitedly and disbelievingly showed pictures of the Shah and his family saying goodbye to a small retinue of officials at the airport, desperately trying to maintain some decorum to mask what they were doing: fleeing their country.

For a brief few seconds Tehran held its breath and then slowly exhaled in amazement. And then bedlam broke out. The main streets exploded with crowds of celebrating people spontaneously dancing, weeping and screaming themselves hoarse: 'Shah rafteh' '*The Shah's gone!*'

Cars crawled along gently nudging through the swirling throng, their drivers pressing their horns and shaking hands through their windows with the crowd, which was waving and throwing flowers, hundreds of flowers as symbols of peace and friendship.

I was driving one of the cars. At first I was scared, not knowing why all these people were suddenly singing, dancing and throwing flowers at me, worried that I might be attacked as soon as someone spotted a European or, worse, an American.

But there was no room for violence on that deliriously happy day. People just wanted to throw flowers, not stones at my windscreen. I saw troops and police hugging and exchanging greetings with the crowd and then joining in the dancing and chanting with flowers sticking out of their rifle barrels.

I smiled back as people waved at me and hugged each other as they weaved through the jammed traffic. Here and there I glimpsed the occasional face, which was not laughing. It invariably belonged to a bearded man who was holding up a poster of a grim-faced Ayatollah Khomeini, while he shook his fists instead of flowers. Otherwise a total feeling of unbridled joy and relief pervaded everywhere. The Shah had gone. Everything would be fine now. Wouldn't it?

Chapter 39

They came for Raman at his home a couple of hours after he had seen the Shah off at the airport. Raman had felt moved as he witnessed the quiet, dignified parting of the Shah and his family. The Shah had made a short speech and then he was gone, his plane heading west, speeded on its way by a hot easterly wind.

Afterwards Raman had washed and changed into his new General's uniform. He considered praying to Allah but dismissed the urge as ridiculous. He believed Islam had only retarded his country. Raman looked at his reflection in the changing room mirror and saw a young, tough-looking army officer. He briefly reflected on what might have been. Had he made a mistake in accepting the promotion to run Savak? With hindsight, yes. But did he regret his decision? No, for a brief moment he had enjoyed the prestige of the second most powerful man in the kingdom. And he was still only thirty-five.

Raman half-remembered a book of Greek fables he'd read as a boy, and how Icarus, in escaping, had flown too close to the sun so that his wax wings had melted. He also remembered the motto of the SAS with whom he'd trained only ten years ago: 'Who dares wins'. He still had time. Whoever ruled Iran would find his knowledge immeasurably useful, he reassured himself.

The police chief was first out of the car and hammered on the door violently, ignoring the bell button.

'Open up immediately,' he shouted.

Ali opened the door slowly.

Followed by four armed policemen, the chief pushed the servant aside and yelled: 'General Raman: I have a warrant for your arrest. Come out immediately.'

'There's no need to shout, General. You'll only unnecessarily alarm your men,' Raman said softly, as he appeared suddenly behind the police chief.

Startled, the man jumped and spun around, his plump belly wobbling under the tight buttons of his uniform, to confront Raman who saluted him smartly. By contrast, the police chief returned the salute sloppily, barely concealing the triumphant grin on his face.

'General Raman, I have a warrant for your arrest,' he barked.

'On what charge?' Raman enquired nonchalantly.

'On two counts: murder and crimes against the state of Iran.'

The armed men stood nervously fingering the triggers on their rifles, wondering if Raman would resist and whether, even worse, other Savak agents were watching them from the other doors into the entrance hall.

Raman looked at the police chief and said, 'General, enjoy your moment. But you and your friends have taken the lid off the kettle. The Beards have won and there will be no stopping them now. This government will be gone as quickly as snow in the spring. We will have a backward-looking Islamic regime under that medieval peasant, Khomeini. And then your turn will come.'

The police chief gulped and wiped the sweat from his brow, 'What nonsense you talk.' He looked around. 'Where is your family?'

'Why, are they charged too?'

'No, but they may be needed as witnesses in your trial.'

More likely to identify my body, you mean, thought Raman grimly.

'They have gone to my wife's family home. There is only my servant, Ali, and his family here.'

'Yes, I saw the woman and her two brats outside the servants' quarters as we arrived,' the police chief said rudely.

Two policemen held Raman by his arms and marched him out of the house and shoved him into a car. Ali politely closed the front door as the two police cars sped off.

The police hadn't given the chador-clad woman a second glance, nor her two boys playing football next to the small servants' annexe.

Shahnaz had warned the boys not to say anything if they saw their father. 'It's all part of a game your father is playing with the police. You mustn't spoil it by talking to him.'

The warning proved superfluous. The police and Raman did not come close enough to exchange words with Shahnaz and the boys.

'It's OK now,' Shahnaz said as the cars drove through the gates. 'Baba's gone now.'

'Will he come back?'

'Of course, but I'm not sure when. They've gone to play their game in another house,' replied Shahnaz.

Chapter 40

Bahram had been lucky to get away with his life after his arrest at the government drivers' depot. One of his interrogators had been all for executing him on the spot because he had worked for Savak, but his colleagues had been swayed by Bahram's argument that he had already proved himself by betraying Raman. Besides Bahram could be useful again in identifying other suspected Savak members who had been caught trying to flee the country.

Once released, Bahram was in no mood to hurry off without catching up on what was going on. He had cadged a cigarette off one of the police drivers he vaguely knew from the several long meetings to which he had driven Raman; the men would hang around for hours alleviating their boredom by smoking and sipping tea, talking disconsolately about everything from football to the price of bread.

Leaning now against a police car they chatted about the momentous events of the past few days, the other driver mentioned proudly how he had been one of the team who had arrested the infamous Colonel Raman Zaberani.

'You used to be his driver, didn't you?' the man had suddenly asked suspiciously looking sideways at Bahram.

'Yes, that's right. I'd been spying for the Beards though, so I have nothing to worry about.'

Satisfied, the man had nodded his head and grunted: 'You mean just like the Head of Police. He's still in charge because he was also working for the Beards.'

Bahram sighed in relief as he realised that there must have been hundreds of the Shah's men who, just like him, had decided to hedge their bets and cooperate with the Beards.

Puffing away on his cigarette Bahram had asked the man to tell him more about Raman's arrest. The man required little prompting and had described how Raman Zaberani had been defiant and scornful of the police chief, right up to the end.

'And what about the Zaberani's wife and children?' Bahram asked the driver casually.

'They weren't there. Left the country long ago, I expect.'

Bahram knew the man must be wrong. He was certain Shahnaz and her two boys were still in Tehran. And the last time he'd seen her, only a couple of days ago, was at her home with Raman. In fact she'd been ensconced with her servant, Ali, and Raman talking about something important, to judge by Ali's worried face when he'd returned to the kitchen. Bahram had tried to wheedle out of the old fool what they'd been talking about but Ali had resolutely refused to be drawn.

The police driver drew heavily on his cigarette and blew smoke out reflectively: 'No, the only woman there was the old servant's young wife,' he grinned slyly and winked at Bahram, as a fellow man of the world. 'That sly old goat has certainly got his paws on a nice young peach,' he chuckled, 'I caught a glimpse of her figure under her chador as she stood there with her arms around her two brats.'

Bahram wasn't the brightest thug in Tehran so it took a few seconds before he realised the implication of what he'd just heard. Ah, so that's what's happened to Shahnaz, he thought with reluctant admiration at the ease with which the young woman had hoodwinked the police.

'You left the servant and his "family" at the house?' he asked softly.

'Yes,' the other man nodded and shrugged his shoulders clearly not interested in the fate of just another family of servants among the millions in Tehran.

Bahram finished smoking his cigarette, using the smoke to conceal the thoughts running through his brain. He was certain that if he captured Shahnaz and her children he would curry more favour with the Beards.

And nobody would notice or care if he captured Shahnaz and held her prisoner for a couple of days beforehand. The thought of Shahnaz being in his power and what he could force her to do by threatening her children made him smile in anticipation.

Uttering a few brief words of thanks for the cigarette, Bahram left the police station and hailed a passing cab towards North Tehran. He got dropped off about a half a mile from the Zaberani mansion so he could approach unobserved. Nearing the house on foot, he was relieved to see that it was unguarded. He still had his car keys and electric gate controller in his pocket. He slipped through the gate and shut it softly after him.

Bahram trotted swiftly into the foliage near the large garden wall and began cautiously to walk towards the house, using the trees and bushes to conceal his approach. He stated to perspire freely as he got closer to the house and the prospect of getting his hands on Shahnaz became intense.

Bahram had scouted around the house and saw no sign of life except the family servant, Ali, sitting in the kitchen smoking and reading a newspaper. He slipped through the door stealthily and crept quietly up to the old man. Bending down he whispered in Ali's ear, 'So, Ali, where are your wife and children?'

Bahram chuckled as the old man choked on his cigarette.

Ali looked up at Bahram terrified: 'What do you mean?'

'Come on, old man,' Bahram snorted, picking up a long kitchen knife and feeling its edge menacingly. 'I've heard all about how you tricked the stupid police. Where are Shahnaz Zaberani and her brats? I don't want to hurt you, but you know I will if I have to!'

Ali stared at Bahram in disgust and fear as the younger man came closer and seized one of his gnarled hands.

'Ah, you still have fingernails, I see. Where is Mrs Zaberani, you old fool?' he shouted, his face so close to Ali's that spittle flecked the old man's face.

Ali shook his head in refusal and then suddenly screamed in pain as Bahram expertly clamped a thumb down on the kitchen table and stabbed the knife's point under the nail and twisted viciously.

'Where is Shahnaz Zaberani,' repeated Bahram. 'Tell me and the pain will stop. No one can hear you scream here,' he warned.

Ali groaned and passed out for a few seconds. Bahram waited patiently for him to revive and started again on another fingernail. It took a couple more nails before Ali sobbed, 'Her brother has taken her to her parents' home!' Bahram let Ali's hand go. 'May Allah forgive me,' the old man added, weeping, the tears running down his pale wrinkled face racked with anguish and shame.

'I'm sure he will,' Bahram whispered sarcastically as he sidestepped around Ali and placed his big hands on the old man's thin and bony shoulders. In one swift movement he snapped Ali's head back over an arm, breaking the servant's neck. Not for the first time, Bahram felt gratitude for the Savak training he'd received.

Ali lolled dead in his chair. Perhaps it hadn't been necessary to kill the old fool, mused Bahram as he softly padded out of the servants' annexe and flitted from bush to bush down to the entrance gate. But it was best that as few people as possible knew he had worked for Savak. Besides, he enjoyed killing, even though this had been too easy: Ali's neck had snapped like an old dry chicken bone, he chortled to himself.

On the road again, there were plenty of taxis plying for trade and Bahram swiftly jumped into one, giving the Mostashari home address to the driver. After a few minutes, the road ahead became thick with people. The cab driver swore and slowed to a crawl as his cab nosed into a mob of gun-carrying men, excited teenagers and the odd mullah.

'What's going on?' Bahram asked a young mullah, leaning out of his window. Fanatical eyes stared back at him.

'We are going to take over Envin prison. There are Savak people in there who will receive Allah's vengeance!'

'Allah is great!' screamed the mullah, who seemed to be in charge, and his cry was repeated by the mob.

Bahram thought swiftly. Raman Zaberani was inside the jail: was this an opportunity to get rid of someone who might be dangerous to him in the future? He hastily threw some notes at the driver and clambered out.

'I'm coming, too,' he said to the mullah, and shouted out, 'Allah is great!'

Nearing the prison, the few guards at the entrance threw down their rifles and shouted that they supported the revolution. Passing by, now at the front of the mob, Bahram picked up one of the discarded weapons and surged on. He noticed running next to him a man carrying a camera and a bag with the name of one of Tehran's newspapers.

Inside his cell, Raman heard the noise and knew what was coming. He stood up and fastened his tunic, determined to meet his fate like a soldier. A warden unlocked the heavy door hastily and shoved it open.

'There he is,' shouted the man to the rabble behind him. 'Savak's Raman Zaberani.'

The mob, led by the mullah, surged in, pushing the warden aside and started to punch, kick and beat Raman, who fell to his knees and then prone onto the floor. Half conscious, Raman dimly heard a familiar voice: 'Wait, let's take him outside and shoot him. There are photographers here. That way we can show the world how we treat Savak murderers.'

The mullah looked at Raman for a second and roared approval. Raman was half dragged, half carried outside to a dark, shady courtyard where he was roughly propped up against a brown brick dusty wall. The melee formed itself into a semblance of order as half a dozen men formed a line in front of him.

Through the slits of his blood-caked eyes Raman recognised Bahram, grinning at him as his driver aimed a rifle at his former boss's head. Raman stiffened to attention and his eyes glared hatred as he pursed his dry lips, as if to spit at Bahram. A camera

156

flashed. Raman's last thought was of Shahnaz and his boys as the bullets slammed into him and the wall behind him. 'Allah is great!' screamed the crowd, as Raman's lifeless body crumpled onto the ground.

Got you, you bastard, thought Bahram with deadly satisfaction. He joined the others from the firing squad posing proudly over Raman's corpse, riddled with bullet holes, blood seeping into an ever-widening pool. Photographs were taken by the newspaper of the group with rifles in the air and fists clenched as they roared, 'Allah is great!'

After the photographer had taken his last shot of Raman's executioners, looking like proud Maharajahs posing over a dead tiger, Bahram turned to go.

'Now for your wife,' he said half aloud to Raman's bullet-ridden corpse, as he spat accurately at his former boss's face. Bahram turned to leave as the turmoil quietened down but was stopped by a firm hand on his shoulder.

'Your suggestion to photograph the evil Zaberani's execution was clever,' said the mullah. 'What is your name?'

'Bahram.'

'Where are you going?'

Bahram hesitated: 'I, er, have a personal matter to attend to.'

'I could use someone like you, Bahram. I am in charge of the local revolutionary committee and need good men who can get the people to carry out Allah's will. Stay and come to our meeting in a couple of hours,' the mullah said. It was not a request. Not to attend would arouse suspicion. Shahnaz would have to wait, Bahram realised.

That evening the mullah gave a fiery speech denouncing the Shah and all his supporters. He thanked Allah for choosing him to be part of the group which had killed Savak's Raman Zaberani. His tub-thumping rhetoric was greeted with raised clenched fists and reverberating cries of 'Allah is great!' by everyone in the requisitioned local police station.

After the meeting had finished and the crowd had dispersed, Bahram was introduced, over tea and cigarettes, by the young mullah to the other commanders.

'This man, Bahram, served us well. He led us quickly to Zaberani in the prison. And it was he who suggested that we kill him outside so the newspapers would witness the execution.'

The other commanders voiced their thanks, knowing public knowledge of their part in Zaberani's death would be appreciated by other zealots higher up the still evolving revolutionary chain of command.

'We need people too who can control our supporters and channel their enthusiasm in ways of which Allah would approve,' added the mullah meaningfully.

Bahram looked at the other committee members. In addition to the mullah, they were a motley group of five men. A couple of religious fanatics; a couple of small shopkeepers, perhaps a baker or a dry cleaner, he thought; and a policeman. The last, Bahram recognised immediately as a kindred spirit, someone who was an opportunist and would bend with the wind.

'So what is your occupation?' asked the policeman.

Bahram gulped inwardly. How should he reply? To lie about his past would mean years of hiding following the inevitable discovery of the truth. But to reveal his immediate past might put his life in jeopardy. His cunning nature meant he knew he had to give a plausible lie.

'I worked for the revolution by spying on Colonel Zaberani as his driver,' he said, conscious of the beads of sweat forming on his forehead.

The mullah recoiled in disapproval, 'You drove Zaberani? You were a member of Savak then?'

Bahram knew his life hung by a thread.

'No, I was not in Savak,' he lied. 'I was,' he paused for emphasis, 'a government driver assigned to Savak. Before working for Zaberani, I drove army officers, generals and air force commanders.' That much was true, he thought to himself. He pressed on. 'A few months ago I helped the Revolution to try and kill Zaberani after he had been promoted to head of Savak. I told our brothers where and when it was best to kill him,' he added, telling the truth.

'So it was you,' said the policeman. 'I heard that someone close to Zaberani had helped us. It was a pity that the attempt failed.'

'Yes, it was,' agreed Bahram. 'But it seems Allah wanted him killed today.'

They all nodded, the mullah still looking suspiciously at Bahram.

The policeman spoke. 'I think Bahram could be of great use to us. He can help us identify other people who we suspect as Savak officers, can't you Bahram?'

Bahram nodded. 'Yes, I would be honoured to go on helping the revolution,' he said as convincingly as possible.

The policeman turned to his colleagues, but not before Bahram noticed a veiled glimmer of amusement in his eyes. 'Well then, are we agreed? Bahram should be welcomed to our branch?' The others nodded again.

The mullah still stared at Bahram, and asked, 'At the prison you said you had a personal matter to attend to. What was it?'

Thanking Allah for the opportunity to display his credentials, Bahram replied, 'It was not really personal. You see, I think I know where Mrs Zaberani is hiding. I wanted to capture her and turn her over to you,' he said, looking directly at the mullah.

The revolutionaries glanced at each other. Capturing Zaberani's wife could only be another feather in their caps.

'You need help?' asked the mullah eagerly.

'Yes, but only a couple of armed men and a car,' replied Bahram.

'You will have them in the morning. Be here early,' said the policeman flatly. 'You have somewhere to sleep tonight?'

Bahram nodded in assent.

Raman's former driver had plenty of time to think as he walked the two or three miles back to the Zaberani house. By the time he arrived Bahram was confident that, provided he played his cards carefully, there was no reason why he shouldn't succeed under the new regime. There was bound to be another Savak, he reasoned. The new government would have opponents, particularly if it were to become a strict Islamic republic. They would need people like him, he reckoned. And this time he wouldn't be content with just being a driver and someone who was a hired thug, happy to beat people up. Why couldn't he, Bahram, rise up and become an officer? Perhaps he would become the new Raman Zaberani, he chuckled to himself exultantly.

Ali was still where he had left him that morning. Rigor mortis had set in so Bahram had to force the old man's corpse into the shallow grave he dug in the garden next to the servants' quarters. As he shovelled dirt over Ali's body, Bahram grunted with satisfaction. Burying Ali seemed to symbolise to him the closing of a chapter in his life. He looked forward to the next one.

Chapter 41

Unable to control the streets, the new government didn't last long. From my flat the ear-deafening sound of fighting and shooting seemed to come haphazardly from a different part of the city every day. I later worked out that once the main target in one area had been seized, the focal point shifted to the next important objective, be it police station, army barracks or prison in another part.

Many years later I was chatting to an old American who had also been in Tehran during the revolution. As a young man he had seen heavy action in WWII under General Patton but he swore that he had never experienced such loud gunfire as during that time in Tehran. He had shaken his head ruefully: 'Hell, boy, those Iranians fight the way they drive – just plumb crazy!'

Stiff resistance came from the Shah's Imperial Guard but not much from any one else. After about a week's fighting in the major cities, the government fell. Most of the army and air force went over and joined the revolutionaries.

An uneasy calm settled on Tehran as the noise of gunfire receded and the smell of burning tyres blew away on an unusually gentle winter wind. The city's stillness was punctured only by the shrill calls of mullahs summoning the faithful to submit before Allah. Their voices were now redolent with triumph and pride. They did not need to say it: Allah had won and not even evil America could help the Shah.

Tehran held its breath and waited. It was no longer a case of 'Would he come?' but 'When will he come?'

Watching on the TV, I saw a vast crowd of people at Tehran airport. My Farsi was just about good enough to understand the words: two million people! Who knows, perhaps there really were that many, densely packed around the terminal and lining the route back into the city?

The front door of the white Air France jet opened and the crowd roared to greet and acclaim Iran's saviour.

To Western eyes Ayatollah Khomeini appeared medieval in his turban and flowing robes. To most Iranians, he appeared a sincere, simple and, above all, honest cleric. The TV zoomed in on Khomeini's face to reveal a tough old man with flashing eyes.

He was greeted by an entourage of close supporters who had lined up to shake hands with Iran's new absolute ruler. The camera slowly panned down the line as Khomeini shook hands with them one by one, thanking them for their loyalty. One of the men in the line caught my attention: although only in profile and half-obscured by others in the line, there was no doubt. The distinguished crop of grey hair, bowing to honour Khomeini could only belong to one person: my landlord, Major Aryanpur.

Chapter 42

The morning after Bahram had been accepted by the committee, the two men the young mullah had ordered to help Bahram, led him swiftly to an open army Jeep parked about half a mile away from the prison. Bahram jumped into the front passenger seat noticing that it was smeared with dried blood and foam rubber was spilling out of several bullet holes. The driver grinned at him.

'We ambushed a patrol; the officer never knew what happened to him.'

The other beard took up position behind a near-mounted machine gun, glowering fiercely at anything which looked even remotely hostile.

Bahram gave the address and general directions as the Jeep sped off, other traffic swerving to avoid it, alarmed by the sight of the other beard standing up in the back, a menacing presence behind the machine gun with his chest criss-crossed by bandoliers.

'So who are we chasing?' asked the driver, looking at Bahram, one eye on the road ahead.

'The wife of Savak's Colonel Zaberani.'

The driver whistled under his breath. 'You mean the woman of the bastard we killed yesterday?'

'Yes,' replied Bahram brusquely, not wishing to indulge in too much conversation in case it raked over his past again. 'Hurry, we've no time to lose. She may be getting ready to escape right now.'

Despite the fact there was a revolution going on, Tehran's traffic was still bad in places. The Jeep had to slow down and the driver sounded his horn furiously to get through two or three jams in the city centre before Bahram saw the Mostashari villa in the distance. The traffic had thinned out now as the Jeep roared along the North Tehran suburban street bounded by old-style brown brick walls, with the tops of cherry and pomegranate trees hinting at pleasant orchards and shady arbours around the villas of prosperous merchants.

The heavy metal and slightly rusty gate guarding the entrance to the Mostashari villa was secured by a heavy padlock and chain. Swearing in annoyance, Bahram jumped out of the Jeep and pressed the wall-mounted buzzer rapidly, two or three times.

The voice of Aled, the Mostasharis' servant, crackled apprehensively through the grill: 'Who is it?'

'Bahram. I have come to collect Mrs Zaberani. The police want to question her.'

There was a silence and Bahram felt sure Aled was conferring with someone, most likely Shahnaz, he believed.

'She is not here, Bahram,' answered Aled after a minute or so, his voice quivering.

'Listen, you stupid old man,' screamed Bahram. 'Ali told me at the Zaberanis' house that she had come here. Now come down here and unlock the gate immediately or you will be in serious trouble with the new authorities!'

There were a couple of minutes of silence followed by a whisper from Aled, 'Wait there. I will come.'

Mo and Shahnaz had hoped to have at least a day to plan another escape route. The lorry driver who had previously agreed to drive him and his sister to the Turkish border had disappeared, along with the big advance payment Mo had given him.

'There must be someone who has got a car we can borrow,' said Mo desperately, looking at his distraught mother who sat rocking to and fro, her arms wrapped protectively around Shahnaz and her grandchildren.

Mo furiously racked his brains, going through all his friends one by one and dismissing them. Either they had already fled the country or they would be too scared to help.

Looking up at Mo, Shahnaz said softly, 'There is someone. A foreigner. An Englishman. I'm sure he would let us have his car, if he is still here.'

'Who? How do you know him?' asked Mo incredulously.

'It's James Harding. You remember him, don't you?' Shahnaz said quietly.

'James? Here in Tehran?' gasped Mo in disbelief.

'Yes, I met him at a British Embassy party. His girlfriend is my boys' teacher. Incredible, isn't it?' Shahnaz gabbled, looking fearfully at Mo's astonished face.

Mo forced himself to collect his thoughts. 'James's car might be better. It would be registered in a foreigner's name so might not arouse so much suspicion at the checkpoint.' He made a snap decision. 'OK. Where does he live?'

Shahnaz retrieved her address book from her handbag and, suddenly ignoring her mother's look of consternation and without offering any explanation, read out James's address.

From the entrance hall they heard faintly the main gate buzzer followed by Aled's enquiry as to who was there. Then silence, as the servant scuttled into the living room.

'Madam, madam, Bahram is at the front gate demanding to be let in. He says that the new authorities want to question you, Miss,' whispered Aled urgently, looking at Shahnaz as if his words could be overheard by Bahram at the front gate.

'Oh, Allah, have mercy,' prayed Shahnaz's mother aloud.

'Praying won't help us, mother,' said Mo impatiently. He gestured Aled to follow him back to the speaker phone next to the front door. 'Tell Bahram Shahnaz is not here.'

Both men jumped back at the ferocity of Bahram's bellow of rage ordering Aled to open the gate. Mo looked around anxiously at his mother and sister: both women were trembling with fear and over their shoulders he could see the two boys close to tears, lips quivering in terror. There was no time to lose.

'Aled, is the key to the small door from the rose garden into the back alley still in its normal place?' he asked.

The old servant nodded.

'Good,' said Mo as calmly as possible, trying to soothe the old man's clearly jangled nerves. 'Now listen. Tell Bahram you will let him in. Take as long as possible. Make every second count!' Mo turned to the two women. 'Shahnaz, we'll get a taxi to James's and beg him for his car.' He paused for an instant. 'Does he still have feelings for you?' he demanded.

Shahnaz nodded dumbly. 'Yes, I believe he will help us.'

Mo hugged his mother goodbye and shook Aled's hand.

'Oh, my children! May Allah protect you from evil,' cried their mother as she kissed her son, daughter and grandchildren goodbye.

Grabbing the hands of the two boys, Mo and Shahnaz ran out the back door and through the rose garden to a small, thick wooden gate in the garden wall. Mo felt under a brick hidden under a rosebush and grunted in satisfaction as he held up the rusty key. Partly gummed up through lack of use, the lock at first refused to turn. Mo started to sweat as he began to panic and hastily twist the key to and fro.

'It's no use,' he panted.

'Here, let me,' said Shahnaz.

Pulling the key out, Shahnaz bent down and blew into the keyhole, dislodging bits of rust and rose thorns. She re-inserted the key and slowly and strongly twisted it. The lock gave with a squeak of protest just as they heard the noise of a Jeep roar up the drive to the front of the house on the other side. Shahnaz shivered in fear as she recognised Bahram's voice shouting in rage as he pounded the front door.

'Quick, Shahnaz. Our only hope is to catch a cab as quickly as possible to James's place.'

Pulling her chador around her as if to protect her from danger, Shahnaz pushed her two boys gently after Mo and silently closed the gate. A few brown rose leaves rustled in the wind as the door swung behind her and an uneasy calm returned to the rose garden, punctured by shouting in the house.

In the cab, Mo sighed with relief. 'We should have a bit of time to think what next to do when we get to James's.'

He wondered idly what his former friend's reaction would be when he opened his door and saw someone he hadn't seen since university. And a strange chador-clad woman with her two children. Extreme shock, he reckoned. He glanced at Shahnaz and saw she had reacted with alarm to his words.

'What is it?' he whispered fiercely so the driver couldn't hear.

'It's only,' Shahnaz hesitated. 'It's only that Raman once shouted at me when I had complained that he never talked to the boys' teacher.'

She swallowed and whispered, 'He laughed and said he had actually seen her because he had once been watching the block of flats where her boyfriend lived.' She stopped and looked at the cab's floor, arms wrapped around the boys. 'Bahram would almost certainly have been driving him,' she finished despairingly.

The cab drove on swirling through traffic, avoiding other cars, burnt out trucks and, here and there, the odd blackened carcass of a tank. The Shah's Iran was really finished, thought Mo as he looked out through the window. But would the new one be any better, he wondered.

At about the same time, Mo's thoughts were shared less than a mile away where Helmut had finally persuaded Tara and her family that she should leave with him. Now the revolution had succeeded in driving the Shah out and Khomeini had arrived, Helmut had met little resistance from Tara and her shell-shocked family.

'Tara, passport or no passport I'm going to drive you to Turkey. Khomeini has said no harm will come to foreigners.'

'But how will you get me through the border without a passport?' a worried Tara asked.

'I'll bribe the guards. I have $10,000 in cash. That's enough?'

Tara's family agreed: that was more than enough. If necessary, on the way to the border, Tara would hide in the back under Helmut's collection of Persian blankets. At the border, where they all expected the car to be searched thoroughly, Tara would not attempt to hide but would help Helmut negotiate with the guards.

They agreed that driving at night might raise suspicion so they would set off at first light the following day.

Chapter 44

Once Aled had unlocked the front gate, Bahram and the two Beards had burst into house and demanded from Shahnaz's mother to know where her daughter and children were hiding. A quick search revealed nothing. He turned to the middle-aged woman and her servant.

'Tell me, if you wish to live, what has happened to Shahnaz. I know she was here. Answer me, now,' he shrieked in fury.

Turning to Shahnaz's mother he threatened, his eyes blazing in fury: 'Do you wish me to torture Aled until he screams?'

'No, please don't harm him. I will tell you what I know. Shahnaz has gone to someone called James. In Allah's name that is all I know,' Shahnaz's mother sobbed miserably.

Who was James? Bahram racked his brains desperately going back over all he knew about Shahnaz. Cursing silently to himself, he glared once more at Shahnaz's mother.

'Come on, Madam. Who is this James? A foreigner, clearly. American, or British?'

'I only know that Shahnaz knew him when he was a student with my son in London,' she stammered miserably.

'There must be more!' shouted Bahram, signalling to his two comrades to point their guns at Aled again.

'Wait, wait! Please let me think!' the old woman sobbed. 'Yes, like my son, he was an engineer.'

Bahram grimaced impatiently. 'There are hundreds of foreign engineers here. I need more!' He screamed this time, his patience on the point of snapping.

But, cursing inwardly, Bahram and his two new colleagues had had to admit defeat. Shahnaz's mother and the old servant, Aled, were clearly been telling the truth when they said Shahnaz had fled to an English friend called James. He had threatened both of them again but he knew, with the experience of many tortures and interrogations, that there was no point.

If Bahram had been by himself he would probably have killed Shahnaz's mother and Aled. But even in these tumultuous times, he would have difficulty justifying to the new authority the needless killing of two old people.

Who was James? he asked himself repeatedly. There was definitely something about the name. Something half forgotten in his memory, something nagging him.

The two Beards dropped him off near the Zaberani villa to spend the night again. He wandered around looking for clues which might jog his memory. All the while he turned the name James over and over again in his mind. Most of the night he prowled around the big villa, going from room to room looking for something, anything which might jog his memory. Taking a break, he sat down on the bed in Shahnaz's room and glanced at a framed photograph on her dressing table of her two boys and their school teacher.

Bahram frowned: yes, there was something niggling him. He remembered seeing the boys' teacher on several occasions at their school. Ah yes – Martin. Jilly Martin was her name. Wait – he had it! He'd been watching a block of flats in a car with Zaberani when Jilly Martin had come out. He'd overheard Zaberani on the telephone afterwards, checking her out and mentioning that her boyfriend was a James – James Harding! That's it! And he knew where he lived. He smiled at his own cleverness in solving the jigsaw puzzle.

Chapter 45

All expatriates were informed by their embassies that for their own safety they should leave Iran as soon as possible. Arrangements were being made for a mass evacuation of foreigners from Iran by their air forces.

Jilly and I had made our way to the British embassy and boarded the coach laid on by the embassy to take us to the airport. The bus driver inserted a tape cassette of revolutionary Islamic songs and deliberately turned the volume full up so all us Brits could be in no doubt of his political sympathies.

He drove us out of the gates and headed off towards the airport. Traffic flowed freely for the first time in many years, I observed wryly to myself. Suddenly I saw a TV camera crew huddled around a well-known face from the BBC talking into a microphone. The cameraman swivelled around to film us on our way. I wondered in a strangely detached way what the reporter was saying, how would he get his film out, and what our relatives, back in England, would think when they saw his report on tomorrow's news? Did he have inside information that our lives were in danger? Were we being taken to a concentration camp to be held hostage? Would the new regime investigate past corruption, which might implicate me because of the 'commission' I had been paying?

Soon we passed through a cordon of heavily armed revolutionary guards and tanks at the airport entrance. Many of the guards were wearing Arab headdress to show solidarity, I guessed, with the PLO. At the airport we were politely but firmly organised into orderly queues. I saw Americans, Germans and French waiting patiently to check in their luggage - restricted to one bag each - and be processed by immigration officials.

Bizarrely, a three-man team of Jewish money dealers were working the lines of people buying and selling currency. How on earth had they managed to get in to the departure hall? And why were the guards ignoring them?

Suddenly a wave of nervous excitement rippled through the lines of departing expatriates as a group of guards pushed their way quickly through towards the exit. I caught a glimpse of an ugly and hairy face under a black and white chequered headdress, as Yassar Arafat, partially obscured by his bodyguards was ushered swiftly by. A couple of minutes after Arafat's retinue had swept past, the Jewish money traders resumed their trading.

Not for the first time I admired Jewish *chutzpah* and realised that whatever setbacks they suffered, they would always bounce back and prosper.

The young revolutionary at the immigration desk flipped his Arafat look-alike headdress back as he thumbed through my passport. Looking up from my visa, which stated my occupation, he smiled and said proudly: 'I am an engineer too.'

'Oh, what sort?' I asked politely.

'A civil engineer. I work for our government's Ports and Shipping Organisation.'

Oh shit! I thought. Please God, don't let him ask what project I've been working on here. I knew I'd have to lie and my face would surely give me away.

'Why are you leaving?' he asked half-jokingly. 'You can stay and help us build a new Iran.'

'Well, perhaps I will come back sometime,' I said, anxious to placate him. He glanced dubiously at me. 'Where are the RAF taking you?'

'Jordan.'

He mulled over my destination for a few seconds and, just before waving me through, said with real menace in his voice: 'Tell King Hussein, he is next!'

Standing impatiently in the departure lounge, I puzzled over the young revolutionary's words. What did he mean about King Hussein? Of course, it dawned on me, he meant that King Hussein was the next monarch on the list to be toppled by an Islamic revolution. So that's why Yassar Arafat's here, I thought - the hatred between the PLO and the Hashemite kingdom was well known.

I turned and looked out over the parked rows of Iranair passenger planes. Everything was strangely quiet. There was no sound of taking off or landing planes. Or planes with reassuring air force roundels. 'Oh God,' Jilly said nervously. 'Where's the RAF?'

The answer became clear soon enough. The airport had been closed for 'security reasons'. No foreign planes were being allowed into Iran to evacuate their nationals. An announcement over the public address system ordered us to collect our luggage and return to our coaches which would take us back into Tehran.

Utter and complete chaos descended on the departure hall as thousands of expatriates shouted, pushed and shoved around trying to find their bags. Most of the guards seemed to have disappeared, leaving us to sort things out ourselves. Children started crying and men squared up to each other as the shoving became boisterous. But an uneasy calm of sorts descended once the crowd realised there was no baggage in the hall and none seemed to be arriving. Sure, the carousels and conveyor belts were all still spinning and running, but in what was now the wrong direction leading through small openings, shielded by heavy, translucent plastic flaps, in the dividing wall between the departure and baggage handling halls. After about half an hour of fruitless waiting it became obvious that our bags were not going to reappear any time soon on the empty circulating carousals.

I looked around and couldn't see any guards. 'Come on Jilly, I'm fed up with this.' I jumped onto the conveyor belt, pulling a reluctant Jilly behind me, and walked along, ignoring the incredulous looks of the crowd, and ducked down onto our hands and knees as we pushed the plastic flap out of the way, while the belt carried us into the baggage-loading hall.

All the baggage there was piled neatly on small trolleys waiting to be towed towards the non-arriving planes. There were no baggage handlers around but there were a couple of bored-looking guards smoking cigarettes sprawled out, dozing on benches. 'Tough work, revolutions,' said Jilly falteringly, trying to mask her nervousness with a weak grin. The men stiffened when they saw Jilly and me and jumped up, their rifles at the ready. In my broken Farsi I explained and gesticulated that we only wanted to get our bags. A few heated seconds of debate among themselves followed and they said: 'OK. You take bags.'

What followed then will remain with me forever; I still chuckle about it whenever I'm in an airport collecting my luggage. Jilly and I found our bags surprisingly quickly, once we had located the trolleys, which had been loaded for our plane. But now we had to get our suitcases back into the departure hall - against the direction of the conveyor belt. Red-faced with exertion, we repeatedly tried pushing them through the heavy plastic flap but it was no use. The heavy ridged belt just pushed them back at us. Jilly started to giggle: 'Christ, if this weren't so serious, it would be hilarious. Talk about Monty Python!'

Even the guards had found it amusing by now, sitting casually nearby grinning and pointing to each other at our predicament.

'I know,' I panted desperately, 'You crawl through the flap to the other side. Hold the flap up and I'll chuck our bags through for you to grab.' It worked. Jilly grabbed our tumbling bags before they were dragged back by the belt, and I scrambled quickly through after them, ignoring the guards who were by now, hands on hips, roaring with laughter.

Our fellow would-be evacuees, milling around next to the carousel, cheered us as we jumped off the belt with our luggage. Others had noticed our success and started to copy our example. Soon all the conveyor belts were carrying streams of people into the baggage-handling hall, all ludicrously bending low like a flock of synchronised penguins as they went under the plastic flaps.

After about an hour of bags being chucked back one by one into the departure hall, whoever was now in charge of the airport twigged it would take about a two days for everyone to reclaim their baggage this way, so they started herding evacuees in groups out of the terminal to the outside and then back through another entrance directly into the baggage-handling hall.

Gradually everyone was assembled outside the terminal with their luggage and boarded the same buses to take them back to wherever they had started their journey earlier that day.

In our bus we all felt a feeling of depressing déjà vu as we observed the same BBC TV crew filming us leaving the airport, as had previously filmed us travelling in the opposite direction.

'I wonder if that bloke is the same one who had said, "all is calm in Tehran"? You remember, Jilly, when we were standing on my roof?'

'Who cares?' said Jilly drowsily resting her head on my shoulder, trying to ignore the loud music, which our driver was thoughtfully playing for us again, just in case we'd forgotten who'd won the revolution.

We got back to my apartment building via the embassy and a taxi as night fell. Major Aryanpur saw us arriving and asked: 'Why have you come back, James?'

'Foreign planes are not allowed to fly into Iran,' I replied resentfully, conscious that he had a senior role in the new regime. The major frowned and strode off with a determined air into his flat. Jilly and I heard him shouting angrily into the telephone as we wearily climbed the stairs to my flat.

'Gin and tonic?' I asked matter of factly.

'Christ, yes,' said Jilly gratefully, chucking her bag down, kicking up her legs and collapsing onto the sofa.

I popped out to buy a newspaper from a corner shop carrying on business as though life was normal.

The photograph on the front page of the English-language newspaper was brutal and shocking. Taken from the view of someone in a firing squad, the man's face was partially obscured by smoke from the rifles shooting at him. It was still recognisable though.

Behind the man puffs of dust were springing out from the wall as bullets thudded through him into the bricks. He was a very brave man, I thought, as I held the newspaper up, my hands shaking. He was standing erect with military pride as the bullets slammed into him, his torn military tunic still buttoned up to his chin. His eyes were just discernible through the haze, blazing defiance, hatred and contempt. Eyes that had once looked scornfully at me too, on a passenger plane flying to Tehran. It was Colonel Raman Zaberani.

I was transfixed by the screaming headline: 'Savak's chief killed by revolutionaries'. I read on, my hands shaking, how the mob had stormed the prison where senior officers close to the Shah were being held by the new government. The newspaper condemned the lynching – there was no other word for it – saying the eyes of the world were on Iran and even Savak officers deserved a fair trial, not summary execution at the hands of a baying mob.

My first thought was for Shahnaz: Was she safe? Reading over my shoulder, Jilly exclaimed, as only a caring teacher could: 'Oh my God. I hope my boys are safe.'

There was a silence while I tried to visualise where Shahnaz might be: At her home? No, that would be far too dangerous. I guessed there would be a rampaging pack of vengeful people and looters running through her luxurious house. Her parents' home? Yes, that's where she would be, I felt sure.

Back at my flat, Jilly urged me not to worry: 'I'm sure her family are looking after her.'

I ignored Jilly's kind words, too frustrated by my ignorance and inability to help Shahnaz. All I could do was sit around morosely with Jilly until we finally got the call from the embassy telling us to reassemble by 11 am the following morning.

As I put the phone down, the doorbell rang. Expecting it to be the Major Aryanpur coming to confirm that foreign planes were once again allowed into Iran, I opened it without a thought. I was stunned: on the doorstep stood a distraught-looking, trembling Mo Mostashari. And next to him a chador-clad woman, only her wild eyes showing, and two small boys, shivering in fear.

173

I knew instantly it was Shahnaz. Her eyes were impossible to disguise, even sunk within black rings of utter despair. I glanced rapidly at the boys next to her and immediately guessed by their looks that they must be her sons by Colonel Zaberani – the man whose death I had just seen on the front page of the newspaper.

'Hi, James,' said Mohammed quietly, his casual tone belying his face racked with worry.

'Hello Mo,' I replied dumbly, tearing my gaze away from Shahnaz and staring at my erstwhile fellow student and friend.

'It's been a long time, James.'

I nodded in amazement as I stood aside and beckoned them into my living room. I could see the two boys were terrified by the way they clung to their mother's long veil and whose trembling arms indicated she too was close to breaking point. As Shahnaz passed me, her chador veil slipped, revealing a pale face devoid of make up. I shivered: it looked like a death-mask.

Jilly, who had been sipping her gin and tonic and watching from the sofa, gasped as she suddenly recognised Shahnaz. 'Mrs. Zaberani, please come and sit down.'

Shahnaz gave Jilly an exhausted and grateful smile and slumped onto the sofa with her arms around her sons. I fetched the boys some cokes and gave Shahnaz and Mo some water.

Mo began: 'James, I am sorry to shock you like this. Shahnaz is in great danger. You know who her husband is?' I glanced involuntarily at the open newspaper lying on the table and Mo sighed softly.

'Then you know what might happen if Shahnaz is caught by Khomeini's fanatics?'

I nodded cautiously, worried that if I spoke I might further upset Shahnaz.

Mo continued: 'I have to speak quickly. The situation is critical. James, I had a plan, to help Shahnaz to escape, but the organisation with which I had made, er, arrangements is now refusing to help. And some very dangerous people are chasing us not too far behind.'

'What can I do?' I asked apprehensively.

'You have a car?' Shahnaz said suddenly, breaking in, her voice cracking in desperation.

I turned and looked at her, and said soothingly, 'Yes, of course. You're welcome to it. I was going to leave it for Major Aryanpur, but I'm sure he wouldn't mind.'

At the mention of the major's name, Mo's face paled. 'How do you know Major Aryanpur?' he pressed urgently.

'He's my landlord. He lives on the ground floor.'

With impeccable timing my front doorbell buzzed again, smashing into the room's tension. I only caught a half-glimpse of Mo's face, contorted in fear, as I walked over and opened the door.

There stood the major. His eyes swiftly took in the suspicious scene in my living room: Jilly comforting two small, terrified boys who looked as though they might be from Tehran's slums but clearly weren't; a beautiful Iranian woman with a discarded incongruous chador veil; and an expensively-dressed Iranian man who stepped forward as if to defend the woman.

'Hello James, I came up to tell you that your flights had now been rearranged,' he said calmly, speaking as much to the others as to me.

There was a hush as we all digested his words.

'Why don't you introduce me to your friends, James? I don't have much time. My guards are coming to get me soon to escort me to a meeting. I am now on the new government's army command committee.' This time there was no mistake as to whom his words were directed, as he looked at Mo and Shahnaz.

Mo quickly evaluated the major's distinguished appearance and educated English. He decided to gamble. 'Tell Major Aryanpur the truth, James. Tell him everything, please.'

'Ah, ah major,' I stuttered. 'This is Mohammed ... he is a director of his family's building company. We studied engineering together in London. And this is his sister Shahnaz Zaberani who...' I paused awkwardly, '...used to be my girlfriend in London. She is, er, was married to, um, Colonel Zaberani.'

Major Aryanpur recoiled at the sound of Shahnaz's married name.

'You were the wife of Savak's Raman Zaberani?' he asked Shahnaz sharply.

'Yes,' Shahnaz replied resignedly. She hesitated and then bravely looked the major straight in the eye. 'I can tell you are a good man and a gentleman. Please arrest me but, I beg you, promise me that you will let my brother take my sons out of the country without harm.'

175

The major looked intently at Shahnaz and Mo. 'Tell me Madam, were you aware of your husband's work?'

Shahnaz shook her head. 'No, sir. I only know my husband was a monster. My family forced me to marry him to pay back a debt of honour. None of my family knew that he had joined Savak afterwards.'

Mo looked at the major. 'In Allah's name, this is the truth,' he said desperately. 'Our family became aware that Zaberani was in Savak only a few years ago when we began to win unexpected contracts.'

'But you didn't refuse the opportunities?' barked the major.

Mo shrugged his shoulders wearily. 'Yes, that's correct. But we began to plan how to get out of the country without alerting Zaberani for fear of putting my sister in danger.'

Jilly and I sat fascinated, listening to the conversation of the three Iranians. Shahnaz's boys' eyes were wide open and mouths agape too, as they began to comprehend what their mother and uncle were saying about their father.

I was bemused that the conversation was entirely in English. It was as if the major, Mo and Shahnaz wanted us, as English, to witness what was being said at a sort of trial. And to hear the verdict.

The major collected his thoughts and spoke directly to Shahnaz: 'Madam, I believe you. I will not denounce you to the new authorities. But I cannot help you publicly. The revolution has many parts, some more violent and extreme than others. I would put my own family in danger if people saw I was helping Colonel Zaberani's wife to escape.'

The major cleared his throat: 'What will you do now?' he asked Shahnaz more gently.

Mo answered for both of them. 'We will take James's car and drive to the Turkish border pretending to be a man and his family. James's car is not registered in Zaberani's name so he should get through.'

The major looked at them pityingly. 'You will not get far. There are roadblocks everywhere outside the towns and cities. No matter how hard you try to disguise yourselves you are clearly not poor peasants from New Tehran.'

Major Aryanpur swivelled and stared at me: 'However, all the checkpoints have been instructed to allow foreigners through and not to harm them, particularly families with women and children.'

We all grasped the significance of the major's words. A bearded man carrying a Kalashnikov loomed at the still-open door and coughed discreetly to attract the major's attention.

'James, I must go. I will probably not see you again.'

We shook hands and, with a world-weary expression on his face, he added: 'No matter what happens to Iran, James, remember the French revolution took a hundred years. Do not judge us too harshly.'

The major walked in a firm military gait towards the open door, pausing only to half-turn and whisper to Mo and Shahnaz: 'Good luck. May Allah go with you.'

His bodyguard looked inquisitively at our odd group, closed the door firmly behind him, and followed the major swiftly down the stairs, his heavy boots clattering on the marble steps.

Chapter 47

After the major's bodyguard had gone Shahnaz looked down at the tiled floor of my living room, her mind in a whirl. Escape seemed impossible now. The warning words of the major resonated in her brain: 'There's a roadblock outside every town and city.' What could she do? Expecting James to help her get out of the country would be out of the question. She glanced at her boys sitting looking anxiously at her.

'Mama, was Daddy really a monster?'

Overcome with emotion, she choked on her words at first. 'No, no. Of course not. I had to say that because that man didn't like your father,' she lied, knowing full well that sometime the boys would learn the horrific truth – that their father had been instrumental in the torture and murder of many people.

'Shahnaz, you'll have to come with me!' My words pierced her thoughts. 'You heard the major. They are letting foreigners through.'

'Don't be silly. If you're caught, they'll kill you, too,' she replied dismissively, shaking her head miserably.

The boys began to sob at her words. Why would anyone want to kill this nice Englishman? And who would want to hurt their mother?

Shahnaz pulled them closer. 'Hush, hush. You must be brave big boys now. You have to help your mother make sure that some bad people don't catch us.'

'Shahnaz, listen to me. We can do it. We can pretend that you are the wife and children of one of my friends,' I said beseechingly, one of my hands outstretched to include the boys.

'No, it wouldn't work. They would be suspicious of any Iranian-looking woman with a foreigner.' She shook her head determinedly.

'But you might get away with it if they thought you were English, too!' Jilly said suddenly.

We all turned and looked at her as she rummaged in her handbag. After a few moments Jilly produced a British passport and placed it firmly on the dining table.

'This is my expired passport. For some reason,' she glanced at me, 'probably because Charles Stanley renewed it for me, it hasn't had its corners cut,' she said triumphantly.

Mo snatched the dark blue, embossed with gold, document away from her and quickly flipped through the pages to the black and white photograph of Jilly. His shoulders slumped.

'It's obvious you've got blonde hair, Jilly.'

'Yes, it comes out of this bottle,' she said quietly, holding up a large bottle of peroxide. 'It takes ten minutes to work.'

I burst in excitedly. 'We'll dye Shahnaz and the boys blond!' I looked at Shahnaz: 'You can wear a scarf like many European women are doing to respect Islam. We can say the boys are on their father's passport. The chances of them looking closely at you and the passport are pretty slim. Zero, I'd say. Yes, it would work!' I punched one palm with my other fist triumphantly.

Before Shahnaz could pour cold water on the idea, Mo said: 'Yes, Shahnaz and I think it would work. It's our best chance. Even if you're stopped, I don't agree with you. I don't think they'll harm James much.'

Shahnaz looked at me. 'Are you sure?' she said weakly.

'Of course. You know I would do anything to protect you,' I replied, my eyes flashing in grim determination as I bent down and gently clasped both her hands.

'We must hurry. Jilly, can you help Shahnaz do her and the boys' hair, please?' Mo said briskly, taking charge in a business-like voice.

As the boys and the two women left the room to go into the kitchen, I asked Mo: 'Who's after you?'

'Raman's driver. A Savak thug called Bahram. He's persuaded the Beards he's on their side.' Mo paused and dropped his voice. 'I'm sure he wants Shahnaz, too. If he gets her I think he'll force her to let him violate her. Otherwise he'll harm the boys.'

Over my dead body, I thought to myself.

Chapter 48

Jilly sat opposite Shahnaz and slipped on carefully a large pair of dark sunglasses under her headscarf and brushed away a lock of blonde hair.

'There,' she said with satisfaction. 'You look just like that 50s' film star, Grace Kelly.'

Shahnaz looked at her doubtfully. 'You really think I can pass for an Englishwoman?'

'Yes, I most definitely do,' said Jilly with firm reassurance. 'Don't you agree, James?'

'Yes, you can,' I replied. 'What do you think, Mo?'

Mo nodded in assent. 'Yes, provided you keep that scarf on and wear those glasses during the day.'

Bending down he put a firm hand on each of the boys' shoulders.

'You two are going to have to be very brave until James and your mother drive you out of the country. Remember: if anyone speaks to you in Farsi you must pretend you don't understand it, OK?'

'Yes, Uncle Mohammed,' the boys nodded in unison.

Mo tousled their short, newly-blond hair. 'Be good, boys, and do exactly what your mother and James say,' he added.

The boys nodded again, their eyes out on stalks, half scared and half wild with excitement at the imminent adventure.

While Jilly had been dyeing Shahnaz's and the boys' hair and dressing her in some of her clothes, Mo and I had been packing two suitcases with as much food as possible from the tins and cartons in my kitchen and fridge. I guessed we might have to spend a couple of nights hidden off the main road to the Turkish border, perhaps more if we thought someone chasing us was getting too close.

'Mo, this Bahram who is after Shahnaz. What does he look like?'

'I've only seen him once or twice. He's big. He was popping out of his suit when I last saw him. My guess is that Zaberani used him as his personal thug as well as his driver.'

'Oh God, we can't leave now,' I said in alarm as Mo and I started to load my car with our bags. 'My car is almost out of petrol,' I explained despondently, suddenly remembering I had let the tank run down because I thought I would soon be leaving the country.

180

'Shit,' swore Mo in English. 'Why didn't you tell us before?'

'I forgot,' I replied. 'Sorry,' I added plaintively, biting my lip, full of self-guilt. Both of us knew the consequence of needing petrol urgently. For months now, Tehran's petrol stations had run short because of strikes and panic buying. It took about twelve hours slowly inching forward in a queue of cars anything up to half a mile long.

'Right, I'll go and get some petrol,' Mo quickly decided, looking at me in some exasperation.

'You stay here. If anyone sees Shahnaz, just do what we've agreed: pretend she's the wife of one of your friends. And Fayed and Tourak are their children.'

I nodded again, 'I'm sorry.'

'Don't worry,' Mo said quietly, patting me on the shoulder. 'I should be back by early tomorrow morning.'

With my shoulders hunched, I trudged slowly back up the stairs with the bags to my flat. I barely noticed the major's two armed guards who were now stationed outside my apartment building's front door. Shahnaz took the bad news about the petrol without emotion. She was so punch drunk with the turn of events that she seemed to have resigned herself to whatever fate had decided would befall her.

'Well, you'll just have to spend the night here,' said Jilly, as lightly as possible without sounding ridiculous. Shahnaz bowed her head in submission.

'I need to telephone my mother. I promised to call her when I could,' she said softly, looking up.

'The phone's working,' I said, handing her the receiver after checking the dialling tone. Shahnaz dialled the number.

'Hello Mama,' Shahnaz said in Farsi. I could hear her mother reply and watched anxiously as Shahnaz's face showed stark emotion once more, as she gasped and half covered her face with her free hand in shock. She spoke rapidly and looked at me as if I was the subject of the conversation. Then she hung up, gently cushioning the receiver into its cradle with a trembling hand.

Jilly and I looked enquiringly at her. Shahnaz hesitated.

'My mother was forced to tell Bahram, the man who is chasing us, that we have escaped to your flat, James.' She paused, looking at me: 'He knows that we want your car.'

'Well, that's OK, isn't it?' I said. 'He won't know who I am, will he?'

'Oh James, I'm scared, terribly scared, that he might.'

181

I looked at her in astonishment. 'How?' I asked, genuinely puzzled.

'I think Raman must have been watching this building. It must have been because the major was under suspicion,' she said in explanation to my incredulous face, shaking her head. 'One day we had been arguing about the boys. I'd complained he took no interest in their school or meeting their teacher.' Shahnaz continued: 'He let it slip that he had in fact seen you, Jilly. And that you had a boyfriend called James, because he's seen you leaving this James's flat.'

I shivered. The thought of being spied on by Savak was still frightening, even now after Raman had been butchered.

'And I think Bahram would have been with him. He drove him everywhere,' she added, despairingly.

'He hasn't turned up here, has he?' I said, with more confidence than I actually felt. 'Obviously he can't remember me or where I live.'

'Yes, but I'm worried that he might suddenly.'

We settled down for the night, wondering what the next day would bring. Shahnaz was at her wits' end, I could see. I think I successfully masked my fear that another setback, however small, might tip her over the edge. I put Shahnaz and the boys into my bed and Jilly and I lay down together on the bed in the spare room. Jilly puffed on a cigarette and looked at me.

'Sorry, I know you hate me smoking, but I was desperate for one,' she said guiltily.

'Don't worry, I'll let you off this time,' I said wearily, trying to smile. We lay side by side silently for a few minutes.

'James, are you sure you want to do this?' asked Jilly softly, so as not to be overheard by Shahnaz next door. 'I mean, it's dangerous, if you get caught you could be in serious trouble with some of the fanatics.'

'I know, I've thought about it too. But it's something I have to do. I'd never be able to look at myself in a mirror again if I didn't.'

Jilly glanced at me again. 'You still love her, don't you?' It was more of a statement than a question.

I nodded. 'Yes, I do. I've come to realise it over the last couple of months. I thought it was hopeless, but now,' I shrugged my shoulders, 'this revolution has changed everything.'

I paused for an instant and then asked hesitatingly: 'Jilly, do you think she loves me too?'

Jilly thought for a moment and placed a hand on my arm reassuringly. 'Yes, I do. I really do, James. I've watched the way she looks at you sideways when she thinks you won't notice. I can see she's terrified of what might happen to her boys. But I can also see she's crazy about you.'

I lay back, my head settling into the cushion, and fitfully fell asleep while I went over the route from Tehran to the Turkish border. It was straightforward: there was only one major road heading west. The problem was not the road but what, or who, we might meet on it.

Jilly dozed on and off through the night. She would be going back to the British Embassy in the morning to catch the bus back to the airport along with hundreds of other Brits. Would the revolutionary government allow them to fly out this time? She felt for her parents who must be worried sick about her safety. Rolling on her side she looked through half-closed eyes at James – she had to admit that she'd been surprised by the resolve and bravery which James had shown since the revolution had started. She wondered idly whether she had been too hasty in breaking off with him. She could now understand why Shahnaz had fallen for him.

Mo returned in the half-light of early morning. The morning shift of guards at the front door looked suspiciously at him through bleary eyes as he rang James's doorbell. Avoiding their suspicious gaze, Mo spoke quickly into the microphone. 'Open up, James, it's me. I've got the petrol.'

We were all already dressed and it only took about ten minutes to load my car again. Jilly hugged me goodbye.

'James, take care.'

'Don't worry, I will. You take care too. Good luck, and I hope they let you get away with the RAF this time.'

Mo gripped my hand tightly. 'James, may Allah be with you. Please get my sister safely out of my country.'

I punched his shoulder lightly. 'I will, Mo. See you at the Windsor Castle again. You can buy me a pint this time,' I joked. Mo looked blank. 'You know, the pub where you and I had a bit of a punch-up. You remember?'

Mo's face, puzzled at first, frowned as he too remembered. 'James, if I could turn the clock back....,' he began.

'Hey, I'm only joking,' I said as I slid into the car next to Shahnaz. 'OK, boys?' I asked, turning around to the back seat.

'Yes James,' they whispered in unison.

183

Mo headed straight off for the south coast once he had dropped Jilly off at the British Embassy. Unencumbered by Shahnaz and her boys, he made good time. Only a couple of checkpoints questioned him closely. Once they verified that he was not on any wanted lists he was waved through.

He arrived at the port of Bandar Abbas on the Persian Gulf by nightfall. He stayed at the house of one of his business contacts and the next day arranged a passage on a dhow of one the Arab traders who plied their trade between Dubai and Iran. Instead of Persian carpets, the dhows' cargo was now mainly people. It wasn't expensive to arrange for the guards to let him pass through the border security and onto the boat.

Jilly also had an uneventful journey to the airport. Queuing to pass through passport control, she chatted in a desultory fashion to a woman she vaguely knew, her mind really on James and Shahnaz.

The woman suddenly broke off and grabbed Jilly's arm: 'Oh my God, isn't that Charles Stanley from the embassy?'

Jilly stared as Charles was being prodded vigorously along at rifle point by two revolutionaries.

Catching her eye as he was shoved passed, Charles managed to blurt out: 'Don't worry Jilly, I have diplomatic immunity.'

Jilly never saw Charles again. A few weeks later, safely home in the UK, Jilly was staying with her parents while she looked for a job.

'Didn't you know a Charles Stanley, dear?' her mother had said absent-mindedly one morning, reading her *Daily Telegraph* over a cup of tea.

'Oh yes, what's it say about him?' Jilly said, half expecting that Charles had been appointed as an ambassador somewhere.

Silently, with a look of sympathy, her mother handed Jilly the paper and pointed to a short news item.

'Oh no,' Jilly gasped as she read the headline: 'UK diplomat dies in Tehran car crash.'

Reading quickly Jilly saw that an American had also been killed in the same car crash: a Major Pete Barbowski. The new government in Tehran expressed regret at the unfortunate accident. The Foreign Office in London simply expressed condolences to the men's families.

Chapter 50

Bahram had hurried over at dawn to the mullah who once again roused the two revolutionary guards at their homes. Waiting impatiently, Bahram muttered a terse greeting and jumped into the Jeep. He urged the driver impatiently to drive faster through the light early morning traffic. He could sense that he was very close to Shahnaz again.

The driver looked sideways at Bahram and muttered, 'I'm doing my best. We should be there in about twenty minutes.'

'Every minute counts, you idiot,' shouted Bahram.

The driver scowled, not bothering to hide his dislike of Bahram, which had been further fuelled when he learned that the burly man had been a Savak driver. I don't care what they say, he thought to himself. He may have been working for us, but he still looks like a Savak thug to me.

The Jeep sped up the narrow street leading to James's flat, scattering leaves in its wake, and skidded to a halt in front of two guards. Bahram frowned: this was unexpected.

'Salaam alykum,' he said politely as he swivelled out of the Jeep and jumped out in front of the two men.

The guards returned his greeting cautiously and, in answer to Bahram's question, explained that they were Major Aryanpur's guards.

'Of course,' Bahram said to himself. He'd seen the major on the TV as part of the official entourage which had greeted Ayatollah Khomeini and realised that the soldier must have a senior position in the new regime. He would have to tread carefully.

'I am looking for an Iranian woman and two children. She is wanted for questioning by the authorities. Have you seen her entering or leaving this building?' he asked politely.

The guards shook their heads. 'You've come to the wrong place. The only women we've seen here have been foreigners. They were with two men, one of them Iranian. They left this morning very early, a couple of hours ago. I think they've gone to the British Embassy,' one of them said.

Bahram swore under his breath. 'What did they look like?' he asked, already half-guessing what he was about to hear.

'Well, the two women had blonde hair and so did the kids. Two small boys,' he added.

185

She's done it again, thought Bahram in exasperation. This time she's disguised herself as British.

'Are you certain they all went to the British Embassy?'

The guards thought for a few minutes, trying to remember. 'Now you come to mention it, I think the Iranian went off with only one of the women to the British Embassy. They said goodbye to the others so I guess they must have been going somewhere else.'

Bahram thought furiously. Where was Shahnaz heading? She must have persuaded James to drive her out of the country, he reasoned quickly. He turned and looked towards the mountains for inspiration. Driving east towards Pakistan would be at least four times longer than towards Turkey. No, they must be headed west for the Turkish border.

Bahram's two companions protested vigorously. They refused point blank to set off for the Turkish border. First, they didn't have enough petrol and second, who knows what they might run into? It was rumoured that some remnants of the Shah's Imperial Guard had not surrendered; the two men were not about to go off on a wild goose chase. How could Bahram be certain that the blonde foreign woman was actually Colonel Zaberani's wife?

Bahram realised it would be pointless trying to argue further. Also, the young mullah would be hard to convince that he should allow Bahram to chase after the 'foreigners' in one of his group's valuable Jeeps with two of his revolutionary guards. No, he would have to go himself, with or without the mullah's blessing. He had no time to waste.

'All right,' he snapped at the two men. 'Drop me off where I know I can get another car,' he ordered curtly, giving the driver the Zaberanis' home address. He had remembered that there was another car in the garage there. Not the gleaming Mercedes limousine that he had driven, but a smaller Iranian-made car which had been used by Ali for shopping and running errands. With a bit of luck the car would still be there.

'Good riddance,' the driver had spat after Bahram was out of sight, as he sped away leaving Bahram outside the still-unguarded Zaberani luxury villa. The revolution had obeyed Khomeini's orders not to loot or steal, so guarding the homes of the wealthy in North Tehran was not necessary, realised Bahram with relief.

He was lucky too. Ali's car was parked safely in the garage with a full tank of petrol. As he quickly hot wired the engine, he worked out that Shahnaz had about three hours' start: he had no time to lose.

Chapter 51

Driving into the low early morning sun, we hit the first roadblock at the city limits. The usual police checkpoint had been taken over by the local Revolutionary Guard. About twenty or so men, some teenagers, were stopping all cars going in and out of the capital. I noticed as we slowed down that very few cars were leaving; most of the traffic was heading towards Tehran.

'I suppose they are joining in the celebrations that Iran is now an Islamic Republic?' I asked Shahnaz, hoping my question would divert her attention from the fear she must be feeling. Shahnaz nodded briefly and leaned around and said softly to the boys: 'Now remember what Uncle Mohammed and James said. It is very important: you must pretend to be English boys.'

'Yes, mother,' they chimed together.

'Remember boys,' I added, looking at them in my mirror, 'even if they speak to you in Farsi, pretend you don't understand.'

'Yes, James,' they nodded.

Shahnaz squeezed their hands in encouragement and looked at her face in the mirror behind her sun visor. Adjusting her headscarf so that just enough blonde hair showed, she put on her sunglasses.

'How do I look?' she asked.

'Like a million dollars,' I replied, as lightly as possible. 'Yes, you look English,' I added hastily, as she frowned, regretting my English habit of trying to make light of even the most dangerous situations.

Against the rising sun, the men had been dark and indistinguishable. Now that I came to a stop I could see that all of them were wearing scruffy, cheap clothes and shoes. I prayed that none of them would be able to speak good English, let alone read it.

I wound my window down and looked into the suspicious eyes of a young man about my age.

'Salaam alykum,' I began slowly handing him my British passport, handily open on the page with an Iranian work visa stamped inside. Giving him a few seconds to read my visa, I continued in my poor Farsi.

'I am engineer. I take my wife and boys to Turkey. OK?'

The roadblock huddled together, leaning on their rifles, looking at my passport and talking about my request. The man with my passport returned.

188

'Ayatollah Khomeini good?' he said in heavily-accented English.

'Yes, Khomeini good,' I smiled.

'Khomeini say English and American safe,' he nodded and smiled and waved us through.

'Well, he didn't even want to see your passport,' I said in relief to Shahnaz.

'Let's hope they're all like that,' she said softly.

I noticed from the corner of my eye that Shahnaz slowly pulled her hand out from the large bag she had on her lap. What was that lumpy shape sticking into the bag's side, I wondered briefly, too stressed to contemplate what it might be as I forced myself to concentrate on the road ahead.

We made good time. Traffic was light. I drove fast. Every couple of hours we would stop and stretch our legs for five minutes or so. At about noon we pulled over in a deserted lorry park for some lunch. I parked behind some petrol tanks so we would be hidden from the road. The boys ran excitedly around the park kicking a football Shahnaz had taken from my flat.

We chewed on some stale bread, sliced ham, processed cheese, and drank bottled water.

'I've had better picnics,' I observed laconically.

Shahnaz just smiled. 'James,' she said.

'Yes?'

'James, I just wanted to say thank you,' she said, carefully choosing her words.

'For what? We're not out of here yet.'

'Yes, I know. But in case something happens. You know – and I don't get a chance to thank you.' She leant over from the passenger seat and kissed me softly on the cheek.

'Shahnaz,' I began, my voice faint, betraying signs of tiredness. 'I would do anything for you. You know that. I still…'

Shahnaz stopped my words by placing a finger tenderly on my lips. 'Hush, my love. I know. There's no need to say anything.'

It was time to move on. Shahnaz took the wheel for a couple of hours then swapped with me again. We had gone through about two or three checkpoints in the smaller towns, and had encountered no problems. Inquisitiveness, yes. Some of the revolutionaries manning the checkpoints were young peasants who had never seen foreigners before, particularly women. But the Ayatollah had clearly said no harm must come to us, so we were usually waved through after a cursory glance at our passports.

Dusk began to fall on that grey February late afternoon, as we could begin to see in the distance the lights of the large regional city of Tabriz.

'Hang on Shahnaz,' I said, as I made out, dimly through the gloom, a checkpoint manned by a group of about half a dozen figures. 'This must be Tabriz's city limits.'

I slowed down and stopped in front of a white metal barrier.

Shahnaz stiffened as a mullah with a gleaming white turban and swirling expensive-looking, brown cloak strode towards us, followed by four guards. The mullah ignored my greeting and curtly demanded through the open window: 'Passports.'

The mullah flicked through the pages until he came to Jilly's photograph. He glanced at Shahnaz suspiciously, comparing her face with the photograph.

'What your job?' he demanded sternly.

'I am a teacher,' Shahnaz replied politely.

'This man is not your husband?' he said, nodding towards me.

I swore silently under my breath and clenched the wheel; so far nobody on the checkpoints had been able to read English. Clearly this mullah could and had spotted our different surnames.

Shahnaz spoke slowly and carefully, following the script we had agreed in case our different names were noticed.

'My husband is staying behind for his work. He is an engineer and this man is one of his friends. He is driving us to Turkey.'

The mullah sensed there was something that didn't quite add up with this group of foreigners. He knew that everyone was under strict instructions not to harm foreigners and to let them go, but even so he felt there was something amiss so he was reluctant to let us through. He then realised what it was. He looked at the two boys.

'Why they not in your passport?' he asked, his eyes narrowing.

'They are on my husband's passport. We have had no time to put them on mine,' Shahnaz said.

I could see that her lips were quivering and she was about to start crying.

'Please,' I pleaded, on the edge of panic, with the mullah. 'We are very tired and we must find somewhere to sleep for the night.'

The mullah frowned. He realised that he had no good reason to hold them. He relented. After all, it was better that all Westerners were purged from Iran. He spun on his heels and ordered the barrier raised, and waved us through. I let out a sigh of relief and pressed the accelerator. I glanced back at the mullah in my mirror as he receded. He stood staring at us for some time.

'He suspected something,' I said tensely to Shahnaz, my hands still gripping the wheel tightly.

'I know, but he let us through. We must find somewhere to sleep. The boys are exhausted,' she added.

A few miles past the checkpoint on the other side of Tabriz we glimpsed a small, run-down lorry park, bordered by a pair of rest rooms. There was a small light shining in an office. An old man gave me a key and pointed out one of the rooms. Wearily opening the door, we found two beds with thin mattresses. Shahnaz and the boys collapsed on one and I slumped down on the other.

Chapter 52

Bahram had been driving for six hours solid without a break. His foot had been pressed to the floor most of the time. He'd been asked at all the checkpoints where he was going and, in order to avoid lengthy explanations, had said his mother in Tabriz was gravely ill. At one of the larger checkpoints he asked casually if there was much other traffic heading for Tabriz. One peasant boy had chirped up that he'd seen a car full of blond foreigners heading that way about four hours ago.

'A man, his wife and two boys, mister.'

'Did they say where they were going?'

'Yes, for Turkey,' the boy had remembered.

Most of the revolutionary guards had been eager for news of what was happening in the capital now that Khomeini had arrived to 'save the country'. Bahram had disappointed them with his brief descriptions but they quite understood that he desperately wanted to see his mother, who apparently was on her deathbed.

Now Bahram was approaching Tabriz and his cover story would no longer hold water. He slowed down and came to a stop in front of the checkpoint, got out of the car and greeted the group of guards approaching him.

'What is your name and what is your business?' the group's leader asked pompously.

'I am chasing an Iranian woman and her children who are disguised as British. They all have blond hair. Have you seen them?' Bahram asked eagerly.

The leader looked at Bahram, noting his dirty clothes, unshaven face and low-class Tehran accent. This was clearly not a wealthy, corrupt businessman fleeing revolutionary justice. Nonetheless, he grudgingly nodded assent. 'We might have done. Why?'

'They are the family of one of the Shah's generals. She is fleeing the country to avoid justice. Truly, brother, she is a wicked woman.'

The group of guards looked at each other, worried that they might have let an 'enemy of the people' through their grasp.

'How do you know this?' asked the leader weakly.

'I used to be one of the family's drivers. I spied for the revolution,' Bahram said, consciously staring the man down.

'I knew it,' said one of the other guards. 'Our mullah was very suspicious of them. He told me that there was something odd about them. They passed about three hours ago.'

192

'He was right to be suspicious,' said Bahram, pleased to hear that he was gaining on Shahnaz.

'What can we do to help? Do you want some of us to come with you?' the leader bent over backwards now to cooperate.

'No,' Bahram replied, not wishing to be accompanied by a bunch of country bumpkins who would only slow him down. 'I don't need help. There are only two adults and I have a pistol. I need to drive as fast as possible. But I do need petrol, oil and water for the car,' he motioned towards the gently steaming bonnet. 'And I would be grateful for some food and water.'

The guards were only too pleased to help. They had plenty of petrol looted from the local army barracks and they gladly shared their bread and yoghurt with Bahram, who gulped it down voraciously. The leader also gladly complied with Bahram request for a letter declaring that he was acting for the Tabriz revolutionary guards and requesting he be allowed to pass as quickly as possible.

Bahram drove rapidly through a dark and nearly-deserted Tabriz. The few working street lights cast shadows across the streets, revealing here and there a couple of pedestrians scuttling on their way. An occasional Jeep or truck with headlights blazing thundered past him on urgent revolutionary business.

He showed his pass to the checkpoint on the other side of Tabriz and was waved through. The road had even less traffic than before. He was travelling so fast that he barely noticed a small lorry park flash past and certainly saw nothing of a small Renault parked behind one of the cabins.

Chapter 53

There was ice on the windscreen early next morning. I scraped it off with a cap from a water bottle, sucking my fingers to warm them. I started my car's engine and checked the fuel gauge. Fortunately my economical Renault 4 still had enough petrol to reach the Turkish border 200 km away.

Shahnaz and the boys had gulped down a quick breakfast and we sped off at about six in the morning. I reckoned we should make the border in about three and a half hours.

The roads were reasonable and still almost empty of other vehicles. We stopped by the side of the road for a break at about 8 o'clock. The road ran straight towards the border town of Bazargan. Shahnaz and I sat side by side on the bonnet of the car, watching the two boys who were too tired to play but were wandering around investigating the low scrub next to the road.

I felt Shahnaz place her fingers through one of my hands.

'You're cold,' she said, as she started to rub it gently with her other hand.

'I know. I always have cold hands and feet,' I said. I was lying. I was cold because I was scared, very scared of what might happen at the border.

'I wonder what the future holds for those two,' I asked, looking at the boys playing innocently, seemingly oblivious to everything that had happened over the last few weeks.

'Only Allah knows,' whispered Shahnaz.

Unconsciously, I began to slow down as we approached the border. The road narrowed into almost a one-lane carriageway with scarcely enough room for two cars to pass each other. Shahnaz and I saw the border crossing simultaneously. I changed gear and slowed down. In the distance I could see a ridge marking the start of a range of hills. 'Turkey,' Shahnaz said simply and quietly so as not to disturb her sleeping boys.

I drove closer willing our car to shrink and become as unobtrusive as possible. I began to pray under my breath: 'Please God, let me get Shahnaz through to safety.'

We neared the border post where there were two queues of vehicles. On the left a line of about a dozen trucks laden with goods for export. Under their dirty tarpaulins I caught a glimpse of fruit crates and carpets wrapped in plastic. At the head of the queue a group of border guards were poking their rifles into a truck's cargo while the driver stood sullenly watching.

To the right of the trucks was a shorter line of three or four cars. I parked at the end and looked around. The border on both sides was marked by a group of low buildings: offices, toilets and stores. On the Turkish side the country's flag flickered in the puffs of a dusty breeze. On the Iranian side the flagpole carried no national symbol. The Iranian boom gate was down blocking any movement of vehicles.

The Turkish gate seemed permanently open with its counterweight fastened to the ground by a heavy chain. The gate's boom pointed skywards as if to signal that people were free to come and go as they pleased.

A couple of Turkish guards, distinguishable by cleaner and smarter uniforms, were chatting and smoking with their Iranian counterparts, well into the Iran side of the border. Shahnaz muttered: 'They are Kurds, James. Probably all from the same family.' Shahnaz had briefly mentioned before that we were entering the region of Kurdistan, which spanned Iran, Turkey and Iraq.

'You mean like Baluchistan in the south east of the country, which is in Iran and Pakistan?'

She nodded.

'And do the Kurds hate the Persian Iranians as much as the Baluchis do?' I asked, remembering my experience at a tea party near Chahbahar.

'Yes, I think they do,' said Shahnaz.

In front of the main doors to the Iranian border post were two guards, lounging and smoking in cracked weather-beaten plastic chairs. Although they looked bored, I noticed their rifles gleamed with oil and were within easy reach.

About twenty minutes or so passed before the front car was waved through the now open Iranian border gate. By then another two cars had joined the line behind us. We inched slowly forward, the car tyres crunching the gravel stones of the poorly surfaced road. Shahnaz was stroking the heads of her drowsy boys when suddenly she breathed in sharply and put a hand over her mouth in alarm.

Startled I said: 'What is it? What's wrong?'

'That car,' she pointed to a dirty Hillman parked next to the border post. 'I'm not certain, but I think it's Ali's – my servant.'

'Are you sure?' I said doubtfully seeing only just another ordinary car coated with dust.

Shahnaz inspected it carefully. 'No, but look at the number plate. It's a Tehran registration.'

I tried to shrug off her worry: 'But so are probably most of the cars in this line.'

From the back seat one of the boys reached through and clutched her elbow: 'What's the matter, Mama?'

'Oh nothing, my sweet. Mama thought she saw something. She was wrong.'

We resumed our tense wait, our eyes glued to the border, wishing our turn to be searched would hurry up, but dreading what might happen if things turned out badly.

Suddenly there was a commotion. A short and loudly-protesting European was jerked roughly out of the lead car in front of us and shoved, together with a terrified, sobbing Iranian woman, towards the main office. The guards at the front of the door jumped up and pointed their rifles menacingly.

'Oh my God, it's Helmut,' I whispered as I recognised him, and then Tara.

Shahnaz looked at me anxiously.

'I know him. And her,' I said as calmly as I could, as we watched the couple being prodded at rifle point into the border post while Helmut's car was driven by another guard and parked out of the way.

Now it was our turn to be checked. Shahnaz and I couldn't help it: the guilty tension in our car was almost tangible as the guards meticulously thumbed through our passports. By now I was sweating heavily and my hands were clammy on the wheel. I knew, I just knew the guards would suspect something. Shahnaz sat rigid next to me, seemingly too scared to move – to breathe, even.

'You not married?' asked one of the guards, rubbing his moustache and looking quizzically at me.

'No, this is my friend's wife and two children. I am taking them to Turkey,' I said, pointing out the blindingly obvious.

By now the other guard had worked out that the boys weren't on Shahnaz's passport.

I guessed something was wrong as soon as one of the guards held my passport over the car roof so his colleague could get a closer look. I caught my name - 'James' – but everything else was in an unfamiliar language.

'What are they saying?' I asked desperately, twisting to speak to Shahnaz.

'I don't know. I don't speak Kurdish.'

I turned back and jumped in fright as a pistol was shoved into my ear.

'Come. You come please,' was the heavily-accented and incongruously polite command.

Shahnaz, the two boys and I were ordered out and herded through the doors through which Helmut and Tara had been shoved five minutes previously. My shoulders slumped as a feeling of utter defeat overwhelmed me. How could I have been so ridiculously over confident that I would get Shahnaz to safety? I screamed silently to myself. Shahnaz's friend Lila's sarcastic words came back to taunt me: 'This is not England, old chap.'

Chapter 54

Once inside the building our small dejected party was pushed down a dusty corridor into a long, grubby waiting room where the guards motioned us to sit down. As we slumped onto the hard wooden benches, one of the two guards disappeared through an office door at the far end of the waiting room. For an instant I heard Helmut's voice cracked in desperation, and in the background the sound of Tara's sobs, then the door closed.

Looking up from my feet, my head between my hands, I noticed on the wall in front of me, stained with years of tobacco and human sweat, a clean patch where a picture had recently been taken down. A wizened old 'tea boy' was fumbling, trying to hang up a new picture. He finally succeeded and stepped back to admire his handiwork. The fierce, bearded face of Ayatollah Khomeini scowled at him. Unimpressed, the old Kurd grunted dismissively.

As he shuffled off he caught my eye. He winked surreptitiously at me, as if to share his cynicism that the Ayatollah was just another Iranian ruler in the long line that the Kurds had seen come and go.

The door at the end of the room was suddenly flung open. Helmut and Tara stumbled out and were shoved onto the bench opposite us. Helmut gazed at me, through exhausted, unseeing eyes. Suddenly he recognised me: 'James? This is crazy! I've just spent the last ten minutes convincing these people I'm not you. And Tara is not someone called Shahnaz.'

He glanced at the woman who was sitting next to me with her arm around two terrified boys and raised his eyebrows.

'You managed to convince them you weren't me?' I asked superfluously.

'Yes, a man came into the office and said Tara not the woman he was looking for.'

Shahnaz stiffened in fear: 'Bahram,' she whispered helplessly. I realised then that Shahnaz's fears about the car she'd seen parked next to the border post were well-founded.

Helmut looked at her in sympathy.

'Yes, his name was Bahram. He looks a big, nasty brute.'

'So you are free to go?' I asked.

Helmut leant forward and spat out: 'No, the bastards took my $10,000 dollar bribe and laughed. They said it wasn't enough for two Christians. So what happens now I don't know.'

A few minutes passed and the door opened again. Followed by a guard we were pushed into the office accompanied by a quiet 'Good luck' from Helmut.

Sitting behind an imposing desk sat an officer, judging by his smarter uniform. To one side of him, next to the wall, sat a man wearing what I now recognised as a Turkish uniform.

A small kerosene heater had made the room hot compared to the chill outside. We stood sweating in a huddle in front of his desk while the Iranian officer inspected our passports, page by page.

Unprompted, I cleared my throat. 'I am a British citizen and these are the wife and children of a friend. I promised him that I would drive them safely to Turkey.'

There was a silence while my words were digested by the two men.

Suddenly the Turk stood up and grabbed one of Tourak's shoulders. He shook him roughly and demanded in Farsi: 'Who are you?'

The boy cowed back, raising his arm in self-defence . The Turk shook him roughly: 'Who are you? Tell me quick, or I will hurt your mother!'

Tourak began to cry and sobbed in Farsi: 'Please don't hurt my mother.'

'Ah, so you boys do speak Farsi,' said the Turk with satisfaction.

'And do you too, Jilly Martin?' chuckled the officer behind the desk sarcastically, staring at Shahnaz who remained silent.

'Now, who are you really? Answer me!' the man demanded.

Shahnaz took a breath: 'I am Jilly Martin,' she began falteringly, but before she could continue the Iranian Kurd jumped up and shouted at her.

'Don't tell me this nonsense! We know you are the wife of one of the Shah's generals, and these are his two brats. Now tell me, what is your name?'

'James, it's no use. I can't pretend any more,' she said plaintively, her head hanging in shame.

I reached out and held her hand as she looked up and said in a shaking voice.

'I am Mrs Shahnaz Zaberani. My husband was Raman Zaberani. These are my two sons. This man is James Harding and he is helping me to escape. Please, I beg you: do not harm him or my boys, please sir,' she entreated.

The Iranian officer sat down, satisfied, and spoke rapidly in Kurdish to his Turkish colleague. He turned to me. 'You are in big trouble, Mr Harding. This woman's husband was a Savak general. This makes her a criminal because of what she knew. And you are helping her to escape justice.'

'She is innocent, I swear. She knew nothing of her husband's work. She comes from a good family. I was at university with her brother,' I gabbled in panic, stepping forward.

The guard near the door pulled me back roughly. The Iranian officer was relaxed now. He lit a cigarette and drummed his fingers once more. He shouted something in Farsi and a side door into the office opened.

A large, tough-looking man stepped in, looked at Shahnaz, and grinned triumphantly.

Shahnaz's face went pale as she hissed, 'Bahram.'

'You see, Mr Harding', the officer continued, 'I have a problem. This, ahem, gentleman from Tehran,' the Iranian officer gestured with distaste towards Bahram, 'says Mrs Zaberani is wanted for questioning by the new government. What should I do?' he asked me in a more conciliatory tone. 'Is there a good reason why I shouldn't hand you and Mrs Zaberani over to him?' This time he looked at Shahnaz and coughed. 'Perhaps Mrs Zaberani knows of a reason?'

Shahnaz looked at the officer: 'This man, who says he works for the new government, was my husband's driver. He worked for Savak.'

'He has told us that already Mrs Zaberani. He also says he spied on your husband for the revolution. Now, I ask you again, are you sure you don't have another reason for me not to hand you over?'

Shahnaz looked down, rummaged in her bag and quietly handed over a brown envelope.

'I think this is a good enough reason.'

The officer opened the envelope and his eyes opened wide. He passed the envelope to the Turk and they both conferred hurriedly in Kurdish.

The Iranian officer looked at me, avoiding Shahnaz's eyes, and said, 'I think maybe we have found a good reason, Mr Harding.'

He sat back and drummed his fingers on the table. As a Kurd, he felt no affinity with the new government in Tehran. They were Shia and his people were Sunni Muslims. In fact he didn't like Iranian Persians – they had persecuted his people for ages. And the big Savak thug from Tehran had antagonised everyone at the border post with his wild, shouted demands. The officer glanced out of the grimy window towards the hills and remembered his father's words: "The Kurds have no friends but the mountains." He now thought rapidly: his family had done well under the Shah, accepting money to turn a blind eye to all manner of people and goods crossing the border. Now it seemed the good times might be coming to an end under a new puritanical Shia regime in Tehran. Better to make as much money now before times became tougher.

His mind made up, he pursed his lips together in a thin smile: 'I have decided: you are permitted to leave Iran.'

I sighed with relief. Chancing my arm, I pleaded: 'And the two people sitting outside who you mistook for us. Please let them come too.'

The Iranian Kurd shrugged his shoulders. They were going to let the German go anyway. The Armenian woman was a nobody and would just be an unnecessary nuisance until someone came from Tehran to pick her up. They had got $10,000 from the German who didn't have any more. All in all it had been a very lucrative day.

'Why not?' he agreed graciously.

Bahram, who spoke only a couple of words of English, had been following the negotiations slowly without fully comprehending. He suddenly realised that Shahnaz was about to slip through his fingers again.

He bellowed in frustrated rage, jumped forward and grabbed Shahnaz around the neck with one hand, pushing the boys out of the way. His other big fist held a pistol, which he pointed at me as I jerked forward to help her.

Behind me, the guard at the door shouted a warning and raised his rifle but, before he could take aim, Bahram shot him cleanly and expertly through the head. The impetus of the bullet threw the guard back against the door where he started to slither to the floor leaving a trail of smeared blood, hair and brains above his head.

Bahram swivelled round, one hand still choking Shahnaz, pointed his pistol at the two officers and slowly began to drag Shahnaz towards the side door, with Fayed and Tourak futilely tugging her chador. He turned slightly to check that I was not trying to rescue her again. In the split second that Bahram's attention was diverted, Shahnaz had put one hand in her bag and twisted around. I saw her screw her eyes tight and clench her teeth

201

with the effort to lever the bag upwards against the big man's belly.

A pistol shot, muffled by Bahram's fat stomach, rang out. For a moment we all froze and then slowly but surely Bahram, his eyes wide open in disbelief, let his gun slip from his hand. His head lolled sideways and his grasp began to relax around Shahnaz's throat. She ripped his hand away and stood back. Bahram's body fell with a loud thump.

Shahnaz's pistol clattered onto the floor. She stood there shaking as Fayed and Tourak clasped their arms firmly around her legs, crying in bewildered confusion.

The Turk moved quickly and knelt down by the guard slumped by the door. Feeling the man's throat for a pulse, the Turk shook his head sadly and said something in Kurdish to the other officer. Elsewhere there was the sound of voices raised in alarm and the thud of heavy boots running towards us.

Shahnaz, with her arms around the boys, and I stood very still looking at the Iranian Kurd, wondering what he would do.

He stood up slowly, bent over his desk, and stared at Bahram's body. He said with almost English understatement: 'He was a bad man. He deserved to die.'

He raised his head and looked sadly at us. In a voice tinged with fatalism he said softly, almost gently: 'You see that young man,' his eyebrows indicated the dead guard slumped by the door, 'he was our cousin.'

There was silence. The heat in the room became oppressive and I felt a drop of sweat form on the end of my nose. I could see the officer was wrestling with the problem of what he should do with us. He spoke in Kurdish to the Turk, who nodded slowly in agreement.

'You should go now, quickly. Take your friends and leave Iran.'

'How much was in that envelope?' I asked after we had driven across the border into Turkey, followed by Helmut and Tara in their car.

'$100,000,' replied Shahnaz. 'It's all I had. But it was enough 'blood money' for him to share with all his Kurdish brothers.' She was quiet for a moment. 'Raman gave the money and the gun to me just before he was arrested,' she added in explanation.

I stared at her as she fell quiet. Her shoulders slumped with exhaustion and the strain of our escape. I reached out and put an arm around her, while I drove one hand on the wheel. She began to weep silently on my shoulder. Fayed and Tourak in the back were still wide-eyed in shock but, I could see in my mirror, slowly recovering as they realised we had left Iran.

I drove on swiftly up into the Turkish hills for about ten minutes. Looking back over her shoulder, Shahnaz suddenly said: 'Stop the car.' Before I could protest, she ordered: 'Stop the car!'

I gently let the car roll to a halt by the side of the road. Helmut and Tara pulled up behind us and came running, worried at first but then relaxed when they saw that nothing was wrong. Silently Shahnaz took her two boys by the hand and walked them to the top of the ridge we had just passed. We followed.

Looking eastwards towards a pale, ascending crescent in the evening sky above Iran, Shahnaz let slip her chador. A sudden gust of wind caught the sweat-stained, black cloth and started to carry it back towards the border. Shahnaz's stared in hatred at the ugly, shapeless shroud, as it floated down the hill and eventually out of sight.

Shahnaz knelt down; sitting on her heels she drew her sons closer: 'Look boys,' she pointed, 'Under the moon, that's Iran. You must promise me that one day you will go back and help make your country great again.'

She shook their shoulders demanding a reply: 'Yes Mama, we promise,' they replied puzzled by their mother's urgent insistence.

Shahnaz stood up and turned to me. I held her close while the Fayed and Tourak pulled miserably at her chador.

'James, what will happen to us?'

'Don't worry, we'll sort something out,' I said as reassuringly as I could, determined that she would never, ever come to harm.

We both turned at the sound of Tara who had started to wail in panic: 'Oh my family. Oh God, when will I see them again?'

Helmut tugged Tara gently towards him and wiped away the weeping woman's tears. 'Shh, I've told you before. I will always look after you. You are my girl.' Turning so that he was directly in front of Tara, Helmut lifted his arms and placed them on Tara's shoulders. Looking straight into her eyes he was silent for a few seconds. Then, tenderly shaking Tara's shoulders, the German said slowly: 'My Persian girl.'

Shahnaz and I looked at each other in mutual understanding and exchanged exhausted smiles. There was no need for me to repeat Helmut's words.

Far down in the valley, well away from the border post, the tea boy was digging a shallow trench in the hard, stony ground. Giving his back a break, the old man straightened wearily, looked up, and wiped his brow. Squinting through dust and sweat, he fancied he saw a small group of people silhouetted against the sun setting over the Turkish hills. He rubbed his eyes free from grime and looked again. But there was no one there. Grunting irritably, the tea boy wiped his wrinkled, brown forehead once more, spat on his hands, and bent down to finish his work. It took the elderly Kurd a good half an hour to finish shovelling dirt over the blood-stained corpse of the big, fat man from Tehran.

Epilogue

I picked my brother-in-law up at Perth airport late one night. Mo looked tired after the long trip from LA. He was greyer but still instantly recognisable from the last time we'd seen each other, four, no, five years ago. He'd apologised profusely for the length of time since he'd last visited. He'd heard good things and was looking forward to seeing how the family's investment was doing.

I drove us south towards Margaret River through the dark West Australian night. We stopped once for fuel. When I came out from paying the bill, I caught him standing next to the car, gazing up at the night sky, fascinated by the brilliant stars. He explained that he hadn't seen stars that bright since he was a small boy and the family had gone for a picnic, staying late in the mountains north of their Tehran home.

Back on the road, I said how proud his sister was of him and how her two boys, teenagers now, were looking forward to seeing him again, especially since they'd read about him in *Time* magazine which had named him as one of America's rising property stars.

No, we hadn't told the boys yet anything about their father. Shahnaz wanted to do it when the time was right; trouble was we didn't know when that would be. I'd adopted them now so they shared my family's name – a good English name – so there was no urgency.

Mo had seen the photographs but hadn't met our daughter yet. In contrast to her dark step-brothers, she'd inherited my blonde hair, but her mother's personality. Yes, a handful, I laughed.

Shahnaz and I had married soon after our escape to London. Her grateful family had offered me a job in their property development business. Money was no problem; they had managed to get most of their fortune out.

I turned their offer down. I was tired of engineering, keen to do something else, be my own boss. I'd also got a taste for living somewhere warm. Shahnaz was also keen to live far away where nobody would recognise her and the boys.

I baffled her family, and surprised even myself, when I announced that I wished to turn a hobby into a profession by training as a wine grower in Australia. Once I qualified, I worked for a couple of years getting experience, then bought, using her family's money, a vineyard in Margaret River.

205

We lived a quiet life. The business prospered. I produced increasingly better quality wine and began to win awards.

Later the next day after I'd shown Mo around the vineyards, we were sitting around the large table in the kitchen, chatting over some of our wines. Shahnaz took a break from cooking and joined us.

Mo picked up a bottle of red wine to pour her a glass, read the label, and smiled at the irony of Iran bequeathing to the world the name of one of its most widely drunk grapes: Shiraz.

'I've been back to Tehran a couple of times,' Mo said. 'We still have business there. Despite the politics, everyday life is getting back to what it was before: the traffic and pollution, and many of the old families are doing well, particularly in the bazaar.'

I reached out and held Shahnaz's hand. Yes, even Raman's family is prospering again, Mo confirmed quietly so the kids couldn't hear. 'It's still much too dangerous for Shahnaz and the boys to visit though,' he warned.

Our thoughts were interrupted by our daughter who was shouting at her brothers to stop punching each other. Her blond locks shook and her bottom lip trembled as she stamped her foot.

Around the table we sipped our wine and looked at each other, gently smiling as our sombre mood was thankfully broken. None of us needed reminding of a time, it seemed not so long ago, when Shahnaz had tried to separate two young men fighting in a damp, leaf-strewn London street.

Jonathan Rush

The son of a British Army officer, Jonathan Rush grew up in Germany, England, Cyprus, and Australia. In 1978 he took up a job in Tehran where he lived, together with his new wife, through the Iranian revolution. While in Iran he witnessed, at first hand, street and rooftop fighting, bombings, ethnic tension, and demonstrations by over a million people. He travelled widely within the country and his knowledge of Iran, its people and ethnic diversity informs much of his book. He and his teacher wife live near London. They have three grown-up children.

Lightning Source UK Ltd.
Milton Keynes UK
UKOW040859151112

202186UK00001B/8/P